MURDER AT
DOWN STREET STATION

By Jim Eldridge

MURDER AT
DOWN STREET STATION

JIM ELDRIDGE

Allison & Busby Limited
11 Wardour Mews
London W1F 8AN
allisonandbusby.com

First published in Great Britain by Allison & Busby in 2023.
This paperback edition published by Allison & Busby in 2023.

10 9 8 7 6 5 4 3 2 1

ISBN 978-0-7490-2858-9

Typeset in 11/16 pt Sabon LT Pro by Allison & Busby Ltd.

By choosing this product, you help take care of the world's forests.
Learn more: www.fsc.org

Printed and bound by
CPI Group (UK) Ltd, Croydon, CR0 4YY

*To my wife, Lynne, who has been my rock
and my support for so many years.*

CHAPTER ONE

Wednesday 25th December 1940

Detective Chief Inspector the Right Honourable Edgar Saxe-Coburg and his wife, Rosa, known to the public as the jazz singer Rosa Weeks, raised their glasses of red wine and toasted one another across the dining table.

'Happy Christmas,' said Coburg.

'At least for one day,' said Rosa. 'Do you think they might extend the truce?'

A truce for Christmas Day had been agreed between Berlin and London. After three months of constant bombing, mainly at night, the skies above London were clear of enemy planes. Most people had spent Christmas Eve in their deep shelters, which for Coburg and Rosa meant the air raid shelter in the basement of their small block of flats in Piccadilly, while most Londoners had sought refuge on the platforms of the capital's Underground stations. For all of them sleep had been difficult to achieve with the heavy bombing pounding the city, the vibrations felt deep below ground, making everyone worry that at any moment the shelter may collapse and tumble down on them, along with thousands of tons and earth and bricks and rubble from the buildings above them. And then, almost as if someone had thrown a switch, at midnight the pounding ceased. There had been talk of a truce between the two warring nations, Britain and Germany, but most people had been sceptical. 'You can't trust Hitler,' was the phrase on most people's lips, with the word 'Blitzmas' being used to describe this festive season. The year before, 1939, Christmas had been normal, despite war having been declared at the start of September: festivities, parties, presents, carol singers in the streets, Christmas lights, turkey with all the trimmings for Christmas dinner, followed by Christmas pudding. This year there were no Christmas lights, no carol singers, the blackout was strictly enforced and rationing had meant no turkey for Christmas dinner. Instead, it was very small portions of lamb or muttón or – if you knew a butcher who had some – rabbit. With no dried fruit available, Christmas pudding was made from carrots.

Most people had refused to believe there really was a truce and had remained in their Underground station shelters rather than risk coming out. After all, it was now after midnight; the streets were completely dark due to the blackout and torches were forbidden and there was always the risk of someone falling into a bomb crater in the darkness. But as dawn came and still no more bombs fell, gradually people emerged from the shelters and made their way home.

Coburg and Rosa opted to leave their underground shelter at half past midnight and made their way up the stairs to their flat by the light of a torch, deciding to risk it, although it took a while for them both to get to sleep.

When they woke on Christmas morning they listened to the wireless for a while, the news to get confirmation that the Christmas Day truce was still holding, then music, while they made breakfast of toast. They'd decided to leave opening their Christmas presents until they sat down for Christmas dinner, so the morning was spent telephoning Rosa's parents in Edinburgh to wish them happy Christmas, then Edgar's elder brother, Magnus, the Earl of Dawlish at Dawlish Hall, before they settled down to prepare the Christmas dinner together: roast mutton, roast potatoes with cabbage and carrots. The meal eaten, they each handed the other the presents they'd bought, wrapped in thin brown paper because restrictions meant there was no actual Christmas wrapping paper available. Rosa had bought Coburg a diary for 1941, and Coburg had bought Rosa a bath set with special scented soaps.

'This is fantastic!' exclaimed Rosa as she undid the wrapping. 'Exactly what I was hoping for. They said in the papers that soap was in such short supply, anyone hoping to receive it as a present was going to be unlucky. How did you manage to get this?'

'The Eton network.' Coburg smiled. 'An old school chum of mine is married to a woman who's someone important in a big cosmetics company.' He looked down at his empty plate and said, 'I'm feeling guilty. It's Christmas Day. I should have taken you to The Savoy or The Ritz or somewhere for Christmas dinner. Or we should have made the trip to Dawlish Hall. Magnus and Malcolm will be sitting down to roast chicken with all the trimmings with a spread by Mrs Hilton that will have nothing spared. It's one of the advantages of living in the country. Fresh eggs, bacon, vegetables. We could have driven there on Christmas Eve late afternoon after I'd finished work and then come back this afternoon.'

'No,' said Rosa. 'I wanted our first Christmas together to be just us, here at our own home. But, if there really is a truce in place, we can go out for a walk this afternoon.'

'Putney,' proposed Coburg. 'A peaceful stroll along the river before midnight comes and we're once again under the bombers.' He grinned. 'Or, before that, we could return to our bed and take advantage of an absence of air raids to disturb us.'

Rosa got up and took his hand.

'This is what I call a perfect Christmas.' She smiled as she led him towards the bedroom.

* * *

Deep below ground at the Down Street Headquarters of the Railway Executive Committee in the disused Underground station, Edward Pennington walked through the empty offices towards the small section of railway platform that had been added on when the former Underground station had been reallocated. As a senior officer of the REC, Pennington was able to flag down a passing train to get to the next station on the Piccadilly line for onward travel. He was glad to be finishing his twelve-hour shift and get home. Not that Christmas Day held any special meaning for him. He was a bachelor, so there was no young family that needed him at home to entertain them, nor a wife to share the day with, just his very elderly, housebound mother waiting for him so that she could moan to him about their neighbours. Pennington had always found the neighbours on both sides to be amenable, not unduly noisy, polite whenever he passed them in the street, but his mother was convinced they were doing their best to make her life a misery.

'They make faces at me as they pass our window,' she complained to him. 'You ought to report them to the police. They could be German agents.'

In vain he had tried to reason with her that none of their neighbours were Germans, nor were they sympathetic to the Nazi cause, but she resolutely refused to be convinced. *If only I had a sister, or Mother had relatives, who could take her in*, thought Pennington.

He passed through the outer office into the smaller one with the door that would take him out onto the small railway platform. He stopped beside the door marked 'Access To Track' and pressed the red switch on the wall, before opening the door and stepping out onto the platform. The blue light requesting the next train to stop was now alight, and in its blue haze he could see what looked a bundle of rags lying on the platform by the edge.

For Heaven's sake, he thought, outraged. *Who's dumped their rubbish here? One of the train drivers,* he supposed.

He stopped by the pile of rags and prodded it with the toe of his shoe, and was surprised to strike something solid. Curious, he peeled a piece of cloth back, and was shocked to uncover a woman's white face. He saw at once that she was dead; he'd seen enough dead people since this war had started to recognise death.

He turned and ran back to the door and into the office. Once inside he pressed the red switch to turn off the blue light, then hurried to the telephone and dialled 999.

'Police,' he said urgently when the operator answered. 'There's a dead woman here at Down Street.'

CHAPTER TWO

Thursday 26th December 1940

Coburg pulled the police car in to the kerb outside Ted Lampson's terraced house in Somers Town and slid across to the passenger seat to let his detective sergeant get behind the wheel. Lampson loved cars, but couldn't afford one of his own. The journeys he and Coburg made gave him a rare opportunity to drive, sharing driving duties as they did.

'How was your Christmas, guv?' asked Lampson as he put the car in gear and made for Scotland Yard.

'Excellent,' said Coburg. 'How was yours? Did Terry have a good day?'

'He did,' said Lampson. Terry was Lampson's ten-year-old son, who Lampson, a widower, was bringing up on his own with the help of his elderly parents. 'Me and my dad took him to White Hart Lane.' He gave a broad grin. 'We thrashed Everton. Good old Spurs!'

'It's a strange day to have football matches,' mused Coburg. 'Christmas Day.'

'It's traditional,' said Lampson.

'But with so many teams having players away in

13

the services, I don't see how some of them can field a team.'

'Well, that's true,' said Lampson. 'Did you hear about Brighton and Hove Albion?'

'No,' said Coburg.

'They played Norwich, but Brighton only had five players, so they had to cobble together a team from the crowd who were watching.'

'Spectators?'

Lampson nodded. 'It was a brave effort, but hardly worth it.' He chuckled. 'Norwich won eighteen–nil.' Then, thoughtful, he added, 'It seems strange going to work on a Boxing Day. I know we used to do it if we drew that kind of shift, but everyone's going back to work today. It don't seem like Christmas.'

'It isn't,' said Coburg. 'This year was a one-day Christmas. They need to get the munitions factories back to work.'

'Still, at least we were spared the bombing for a day. Pity they can't make it longer.'

'It will be once one side wins the war.'

'You mean when *we* win the war,' Lampson rebuked him.

'Of course,' said Coburg smoothly. 'The alternative is unthinkable.'

When they arrived at Scotland Yard, they found Superintendent Allison in their office, writing a note.

'Ah, good,' he greeted them. 'I was just about to

leave a note for you.' He screwed up the piece of paper and threw it in the wastepaper basket. 'There was a murder yesterday at Down Street Underground station. Or, rather, what used to be the Underground station. It was picked up by Inspector Best, who was on duty on Christmas Day, but unfortunately he was injured last night when a building damaged by bombing collapsed near him.'

'Was he badly hurt?'

'A broken leg, which will put him out of action. He's in hospital and is likely to remain there for a few weeks, at least. It was a bad break. I'd like you to take over the case. You've had recent experience of dealing with a dead body found on the Underground, and, like that one, the victim was found at a Tube station that's been discontinued from active passenger traffic. Although trains still pass through it.'

'Did you say Down Street?' asked Coburg.

'I did,' said Allison.

'That's the one that the Prime Minister's currently using as an underground bunker, I believe.'

'You believe right. Which is another reason I'd like you to take on the case. I understand your elder brother, the Earl of Dawlish, is an old friend of Churchill's.'

'Yes, sir, he is.'

'Which might help if there are complications concerning national security. The former station's been converted into the headquarters of the Railway

Executive Committee, the outfit set up to run the country's railways.'

'Where was the body found?'

'On a stretch of platform there.'

'Does it still have a platform? I thought it had been abandoned as a working station.'

'Inspector Best will have the details. I'm sure he'll be able to answer all your questions.'

'Where is he?'

'At University College Hospital. I've telephoned ahead to alert them that you'll be coming in to see him so you shouldn't meet with any of the usual problems about calling on patients out of visiting hours.' He picked up a cardboard file from the desk. 'I brought this along for you. It's the file Inspector Best opened on the case before he was injured. There's not much there, but I'm sure he'll be able to fill you in.'

As Lampson drove them to University College Hospital, Coburg read through what little information there was in the slim file. The fact there was so little was understandable; Richard Best had only just caught the case and had little time to make any notes from his visit to the scene to look at the body, before he'd been injured.

'The victim was a woman in her twenties called Svetlana Rostova,' Coburg told Lampson. 'She'd been stabbed. She was a fortune-teller, known as Lady Za Za.'

16

'I guess she didn't see this coming,' commented Lampson wryly.

The bed Inspector Richard Best was in at UCH had a canopy erected at the foot of it to protect his broken leg. Best was in his fifties and Coburg and Lampson found him leaning back against his pillows and obviously in pain.

'You'll have to forgive me if I drop off to sleep while we're talking,' he grumbled. 'They've pumped all this morphine into me to ease the pain but it makes me keep nodding off.'

'We won't keep you long,' promised Coburg. 'How are they treating you in here?'

'The same way they treat everyone,' Best said with a scowl. 'They're officious and the ward sister is a right tyrant. And don't get me started on the matron. Awful woman. I'm sure she's got a moustache. It wouldn't surprise me to find she's a draft-dodger posing as a matron.'

Coburg settled himself down on the chair beside the inspector's bed and opened the file.

'I've read your report,' he said.

'That must have taken you all of two minutes,' said Best. 'I'd jotted down a few notes then left the office intending to enlarge on it today. Instead of which, this bloody building came down as I was walking past it.'

'It could have been worse,' said Coburg

sympathetically. 'You could have been killed.'

Best scowled.

'Don't worry, this place'll finish me off,' he grumbled. 'I thought nurses were supposed to be all lovey-dovey and caring.'

'The ones I've experienced have been,' said Coburg.

'You were lucky,' grunted Best. 'I reckon this lot were trained by the Gestapo. So, what can I tell you?'

'The body was found on a platform.'

'That's right,' confirmed Best.

'By a man called Edward Pennington who went out on the platform to catch a train home after his shift had ended.'

Best nodded.

'As I understand it, his shift had ended and another man had arrived to take over.'

'Right again,' said Best.

'Why didn't this other man spot the body when he arrived?'

'Because it was on a different platform,' said Best. 'I'm guessing you haven't been to Down Street since it got rebuilt.'

'No,' said Coburg.

'A platform was added so the senior staff could grab a train to get home, or go somewhere. There are two platforms on opposing sides of the railway tracks: westbound and eastbound. Pennington was leaving on the eastbound platform. The bloke who took over from him arrived on the other platform, the westbound.'

'Have you spoken to the other man?'

'No. I didn't even get a chance to get his name. They're pretty tight-lipped there, think they're some kind of secret service. Bunch of petty bureaucrats.'

'Where was the body taken?'

'Here,' said Best. 'UCH. Dr Welbourne was the attending medic.'

'Yes, we know Dr Welbourne,' said Coburg. 'A good bloke.'

'I don't know him well enough to say,' said Best. 'He seemed alright.'

'Is there anything else you can tell us?' asked Coburg.

'No. Like I say, I was intending to start on it properly today, but that bloody house falling on me put a stop to that.'

'Did she have any next of kin?'

'No idea,' said Best. 'That was another thing I was going to look into. She was Russian.'

'Yes, I gathered that by her name,' said Coburg.

'According to her ID card she came here in 1937. I went to the address on her card, which was a house of rooms for rent, but the landlady said she'd left there two weeks before and left no forwarding address. That was as far as I got before I copped this.'

Coburg and Lampson left Best and made their way down to the mortuary in search of Dr Welbourne.

'Well, there's one bloke whose Christmas was ruined,' sighed Lampson.

'Have you had much to do with Inspector Best before?' asked Coburg.

'No,' said Lampson. 'I've heard about him. People say he's a miserable sod.'

'Yes, I'd agree with that.' Coburg smiled.

'I thought he was in that mood because he broke his leg,' said Lampson.

'No, he's always like that,' said Coburg.

'Has he got family?' asked Lampson.

'He had, but his wife divorced him and took the kids back up north. She said living with him was making her life a misery.'

'Well, he's certainly got a negative view of things. Like nurses, for example. That time I was stabbed and at death's door they were brilliant.'

They found Dr Welbourne just finishing an autopsy on a dead man.

'Just give me a minute or so while I sew this one up,' he said.

'We'll wait outside,' said Coburg, and he and Lampson left Welbourne energetically sewing up a long incision he'd made from the dead man's chest down to his abdomen.

'I don't know how he can do that,' groaned Lampson. 'Every day, blood and guts, taking out brains and examining them.'

'It's not much different to what we do when we examine a murder victim,' said Coburg.

'Yeah, but we only look at their outside. We don't take them to pieces.'

It was another ten minutes before Welbourne came out of the mortuary, wiping his hands on a towel.

'Good morning,' he greeted them cheerfully. 'To what do I owe the pleasure?'

'We've been assigned the murder of Svetlana Rostova,' said Coburg.

'Why, what's happened to Inspector Best?'

'He broke his leg last night. He's currently occupying one of your hospital beds upstairs.'

'Good heavens! What happened to him?'

'A building that had been bombed fell on him.'

'In that case he was lucky to escape with just a broken leg. And he's in here, you say, at UCH?'

'Yes. I'm surprised no one told you.'

'There was no need. He's alive; I only get informed about the dead.'

'So, what can you tell us about Svetlana Rostova, who we're told also worked as a fortune-teller under the name of Lady Za Za?'

Welbourne gestured towards the doors to the mortuary. 'If you come through I can show you her body, and the possessions she was found with.'

Coburg and Lampson followed Welbourne into the mortuary and he took them to a table where a body lay covered with a sheet. He peeled the sheet off, exposing the naked body of a young woman in her twenties. She was thin, and had been attractive with her high Slavic cheekbones and her jet-black hair. Her body was scarred with large stitches where Welbourne had opened her up to take out her internal organs for examination, and then sewn her up again.

Welbourne pointed to the wound just below her left breast. 'Stabbed,' he said. 'A thin, long-bladed weapon, something similar to a stiletto. Very neat. One thrust straight into the heart. Either the killer knew enough anatomy to avoid the ribs, or they were lucky.'

'Time of death?' asked Coburg.

'From the contents of her stomach I'd say some time between four o'clock and six o'clock yesterday.' He looked down at her ruefully. 'Not the best way to spend Christmas Day, getting murdered.'

'Did you talk to anyone at Down Street yesterday?'

'The person who found her body, a man called Edward Pennington. He was supposed to leave as his shift was over, but he felt it his duty to wait until I arrived.'

'Her body was found on a small platform there, we understand.'

'Yes, that's right. Have you been to Down Street?'

'Not yet, we thought we'd come and see you first to get as much information as we could before we talked to them. I got the impression from Inspector

22

Best that the people at Down Street might be difficult. He described them as tight-lipped, petty bureaucrats.'

'I'm afraid Inspector Best can be quite an abrasive person.' Welbourne smiled. 'I think your calmer, friendlier approach might prove more effective in this case.' He replaced the sheet over Svetlana's dead body, then took them to a large open cupboard containing a series of drawers. He pulled one of the drawers out and put it on a table. It contained clothes, a handbag and an official visitor's pass on a lanyard. 'These are what were found on her.'

Coburg opened the handbag and took out the contents. There were cosmetics, lipstick and face powder, and her ID card. It bore the word 'alien' above her name. In the section 'nationality' it said 'Russian', and 'date of arrival' read 'January 1937'.

'Can I take this?' asked Coburg, holding the ID card. 'I'll give you a receipt for it.'

'Of course,' said Welbourne.

'Can you make out a receipt for Dr Welbourne, Sergeant?' asked Coburg.

Lampson nodded and produced a dog-eared receipt book from his inside pocket, and proceeded to fill in one of the slips; while Coburg turned his attention to the visitor's pass, which bore the stamp of the Railway Executive Committee.

'It seems that she was at Down Street officially,' he said.

'Well, this Edward Pennington didn't seem to know her,' said Welbourne. 'Nor did anyone else. Mind, it was a skeleton staff yesterday, being Christmas Day. I assume you want to take that with you as well.'

'Yes please,' said Coburg. 'Hopefully it will help us find out what she was doing at Down Street.' He handed the pass to Lampson. 'And another receipt for this, please, Sergeant.'

CHAPTER THREE

Thursday 26th December 1940

As Rosa and Doris brought their ambulance in through the gates of the Paddington St John Ambulance station, they saw their boss, Chesney Warren, standing by the door to the building, waving to them to hurry.

'Something's happened,' said Doris, concerned.

They'd just returned to the station from delivering a woman with a suspected burst appendix to the nearest hospital. Rosa stopped the ambulance beside Warren and Doris wound her window down.

'What is it and where is it?' she asked, reaching out for the usual piece of paper.

'Neither,' said Warren. 'It's the BBC on the phone for Rosa.'

'For me?' said Rosa in surprise.

'Yes. I saw you coming in as I picked the phone up and this chap said, "Excuse me, would it be possible to speak to Rosa Weeks? I'm calling from the BBC." Very posh-sounding.'

'How did he get this number?' asked Rosa.

'I've no idea,' said Warren, 'but the fact he did

suggests he definitely wants to talk to you.'

Rosa got down from the cab and hurried into the building and Chesney Warren's office, Warren following her. She picked up the receiver and said, 'This is Rosa Weeks.'

'I'm very sorry to trouble you at work, Miss Weeks,' said a cultured but very gentle man's voice. 'My name's John Fawcett and I'm the producer of *Henry Hall's Guest Night* on the BBC Light Programme. I know this is very short notice but I wonder if you might be free next Tuesday, the 31st December, New Year's Eve, and if you might consider appearing on the show.'

Rosa was momentarily stunned into silence, then she said, doing her best to keep her voice controlled, 'Yes, I would. Thank you.'

'It is a live broadcast,' said Fawcett. 'Next Tuesday we'll be at the Finsbury Park Empire. The show is broadcast from 6 p.m., but you'd be needed for rehearsals that afternoon, from one o'clock, if that would be convenient for you.'

'Yes, indeed, that would be convenient.' She looked at the intrigued Chesney Warren and mouthed 'I'll tell you in a moment' as Fawcett said, 'That is absolutely wonderful, Miss Weeks. Can we meet to discuss your slot on the programme?'

'Of course. When do you suggest?'

'Can you be free for lunch tomorrow? The BBC canteen does reasonable fare.'

'Yes.'

'Excellent. It'll have to be at the Maida Vale studios in Delaware Road. We've got a few problems at Broadcasting House. Bomb damage, I'm afraid. Do you know Maida Vale?'

'Yes,' said Rosa.

'Very good. I'll see you there. Will one o'clock suit you?'

'One o'clock will be fine.'

Rosa replaced the receiver and looked at Chesney Warren, stunned.

'That was the BBC,' she said.

'I know,' said Warren. 'I was the one who told you. What did they want?'

'They want me to appear on *Henry Hall's Guest Night* next Tuesday, live from the Finsbury Park Empire.' Apologetically, she added, 'He asked me if I would, and also if I'd meet him for lunch tomorrow to discuss my spot, and I said yes without asking you. I'm very sorry.'

'Nonsense,' said Chesney. 'No apology needed. D'you think you'll be able to get a mention about the St John Ambulance and that you're a volunteer driver?'

'I can certainly ask,' said Rosa. 'With a war on they might be pleased to tell the audience that.'

Or they might get upset with me for daring to ask and drop me, thought Rosa. However, John Fawcett had sounded the sort of kind man you could ask things without him taking offence. And it wasn't as if she was demanding something for herself.

The exterior of Down Street had been kept intact despite its closure as a working Underground station; the three-arched semi-circular window above the entrance, the familiar coloured tiles in general use across the London Underground system were fixed to the walls as décor, and above the arch on the right that led to a rear courtyard a sign still read 'Down Street'. Coburg and Lampson went to the black door to the left and rang the bell. A disembodied voice came from the grille on the right asking what they wanted.

'DCI Coburg and DS Lampson from Scotland Yard,' Coburg said to the speaker. 'We're here to investigate the recent murder here.'

'One moment,' said the voice.

There was a pause, then the door opened and a man in the uniform of London Underground's Transport Police looked out at them. Coburg and Lampson showed him their warrant cards, and were admitted.

'I'll take you down to see Mr Purslake,' said the officer.

They followed the uniformed officer to the head of a circular staircase and then down the winding stairs to deep underground. As they descended, they passed different places where there were exit points from the staircase going off into long corridors. It was at one of these exit points that the uniformed officer stopped. A man in a very smart clerical dark grey suit and bow tie was standing waiting for them.

'The gentlemen from Scotland Yard, Mr Purslake,' said the officer.

'Thank you, Wilkins,' said Purslake. 'I'll take over from here.'

The uniformed officer headed back up the stairs, and Purslake held out his hand in greeting to the two policemen.

'Jeremy Purslake,' he announced, shaking their hands. Coburg and Lampson introduced themselves to Purslake, who led the way further down the winding staircase.

'It's very deep,' he said, 'which is why it was chosen.'

'No lift?' asked Coburg.

'There is a two-person lift, but it's usually kept for senior personnel in case of emergency. I prefer to use the stairs.' He gave them an unhappy look. 'This is all most unpleasant. We've never had anything like that here before.'

'How long have you been here?' asked Coburg.

'Since last year.'

'I thought the station had been closed long before that,' said Coburg.

'It had,' said Purslake. 'Down Street opened as a station in 1907 and closed in 1932.'

'Why did it close?'

'Too few passengers were using it. We believe because, as it was in an affluent area, most of the local residents didn't use public transport but preferred cars and taxis. The other problem was its close proximity to other Tube stations, Green Park, which was originally called Dover Street, and Hyde Park Corner.

'Once it closed as a working station for passengers in 1932, the tracks were altered and the platform tunnels rebuilt to allow a junction to be installed with access from both the eastbound and westbound services to a new siding located between Down Street and Hyde Park Corner. The siding was mainly for westbound trains to reverse into it, but there was enough space for it to be used for servicing the trains. A small foot tunnel was built from the western end of the siding to Hyde Park Corner station. The lifts were taken out and the lift shafts adapted to provide additional ventilation.

'Early in 1939 the station was chosen as an underground bunker for the use of the government in the event of war. The station's great depth means it will be safe against bombing. Brick walls were constructed at the edges of the platforms, and the enclosed platform areas, along with the spaces in the passages, were divided up into offices, meeting rooms and dormitories.

'The small two-person lift I mentioned earlier was

installed in the original emergency stairwell and a telephone exchange and bathrooms were added. It was intended that the Railway Executive Committee would be the sole occupants and from here we'd be able to ensure the trains across the country would keep running. That's why having the switchboard based at the deepest point is so essential: there will always be telephone connections to everywhere on the rail network. Previously the Railway Executive Committee had been based at Fielden House in Westminster, but the basement there was unsuitable. It wouldn't have been able to withstand heavy bombing.'

They had now reached the lowest level and Purslake led them along a short section of tunnel to an office. Inside the office, ten people were hard at work at desks, some on telephones, some typing, some sorting through reports. The workers gave the visitors brief glances, then returned to their tasks.

At that moment there was the loud rush of a train hurtling past and the wall vibrating. Lights from the passing train flickered in a metal grille set high in the wall for ventilation.

'As you see trains still pass along this line, the Piccadilly, and very close to the walls that were put up at the edge of the platforms. It's something we just have to put up with.'

'And this short platform that was added during the rebuilding is where the woman's body was found?'

'Yes. It's a mystery where she came from. There's no evidence that she came from inside the building, so we believe she was thrown from a passing train.'

'But the doors can't open when the train is moving,' said Coburg.

'That's generally true,' agreed Purslake. 'But it is possible. The other option is that her body had been placed on the roof of a carriage and it fell off as it passed here.'

'Can we see where her body was found?'

Purslake took them through the large office, then out of a door at the far wall and into an adjoining one. This one was smaller, and empty of people, with two desks, a telephone and filing cabinets. A door set in the wall that had been built at the platform's edge had a large sign on it that said: 'Caution. Access to track.' There was a large red switch beside the door.

'That red switch operates a blue light in the tunnel,' said Purslake. 'When a driver sees that blue light is on, he pulls up beside the door and whoever is waiting on the platform gets on the train.'

'May we see it in operation?' asked Coburg.

Purslake nodded. He flicked the red switch, then opened the door and stepped out onto a short section of enclosed platform that had been constructed, Coburg and Lampson following. The tunnel was illuminated with the dull glow of overhead lighting, and also by a blue light from a lamp situated near to where they stood. Purslake pulled the door shut behind them. 'We have to keep it shut otherwise it creates a terrible draught inside the offices.'

Directly opposite, on the other side of the railway tracks, was an identical short platform, also with a lamp – currently not glowing – set in the wall.

'This side is the eastbound track. That platform is for the westbound one,' Purslake explained.

They stood there on the short section of platform for about four minutes, and then Coburg heard the sound of a Tube train approaching and saw the glow of its lights as it drew nearer, then heard the sound of its brakes being applied. The train drew to a halt with a screech and a judder, bringing the driver's cab level to where they were standing. The driver opened the door and looked at them questioningly.

'Thank you, driver,' said Purslake. 'But we won't be travelling at this time. This is Detective Chief Inspector Coburg from Scotland Yard, who's making an examination of our systems.'

The driver nodded, pulled his cab door shut, then set the train in motion again. The noise as it raced past them was deafening and the rush of air seemed to suck them forward towards the train lines. Coburg and Lampson noticed that Purslake had stepped back and was by the door, as far away as he could get from the edge of the platform, and they decided to join him.

When the train had disappeared, Purslake opened

the door and they went back into the small room. Purslake flicked the switch and checked that the blue light had vanished before closing the door.

'The door's not locked?' Coburg observed.

'No. If someone arrived on the platform to get to us, they would be able to get in.'

'So there's always access between the railway tracks and these offices?'

'Yes.' Purslake nodded. 'Twenty-four hours a day. These premises have to be operational the whole time. We have a staff of forty working in two twelve-hour shifts.'

'I understand that the Prime Minister is also based here,' said Coburg.

'Temporarily,' said Purslake. 'His office and facilities are on the next level up. He's staying here while the Cabinet War Rooms are being renovated.'

'Renovated?' asked Coburg. 'I thought they were already operational.'

'They were, but they decided the War Rooms needed reinforcing to protect against the heavy bombing, so they began to put in extra layers of concrete. Since late October this has been effectively the Prime Minister's underground bunker.'

'So he's here at the moment?'

'His staff are,' said Purslake. 'A smaller staff than he has at the Cabinet War Rooms, but large enough for his needs. He's mainly here at nights. His sleeping accommodation, dining, bathroom and toilet facilities are in a corridor that had already been converted into rooms. His secretaries and key staff members also have room in the same corridor.'

'Do you often see him?'

'Now and then, if he's bored and feeling trapped in that one corridor, he'll come down here to see how the trains are running.'

'The dead woman was wearing a visitor's pass,' said Coburg. He took the pass from his pocket and handed it to Purslake. 'Do you know who authorised it?'

Purslake took the pass and studied it. 'Svetlana Rostova,' he murmured. He went to one of the desks and took a ledger from the drawer. On the front was label with the words 'Visitor Passes'. He looked at the number on the pass, then opened the ledger and ran his eye down the list until he found the number.

'It was authorised by Grigor Rostov.' He ran his finger along the entry and said, 'He's in the accounts department.'

'Can we see him?'

Purslake picked up the telephone and dialled a number. When it was answered, he said, 'Purslake here. I need to speak to Grigor Rostov. Can you ask him to report to me by the platform office.' He frowned on hearing the reply, then replaced the receiver. 'It seems he's not in today,' he told the detectives. 'He telephoned in ill, saying he suffered food poisoning as a result of something he ate.'

'Whatever he had for Christmas dinner, I presume,' said Coburg. 'Do you have his address?'

'Certainly,' said Purslake, and he took another ledger from the drawer.

'The fact they have the same surname indicates he's related to the dead woman,' said Coburg. 'Russian women's names end in an "a" added to the family name. If she was Rostova, he'd be Rostov. He's Russian, I assume?'

'I assume so also,' said Purslake. 'It's not a common name among our staff. But whatever their relation is, I don't know. Husband and wife, brother and sister. I'm afraid I don't know Grigor Rostov personally.'

CHAPTER FOUR

Thursday 26th December 1940

The address they'd been given for Grigor Rostov was a small terraced house in a back street in Paddington. Coburg was just about to knock at the door, when it opened and a young woman pushing a pram looked at them in surprise.

'Good morning,' said Coburg. 'We're sorry to trouble you.' He produced his warrant card and showed it to her. 'I'm Detective Chief Inspector Coburg from Scotland Yard. This is Detective Sergeant Lampson. We're looking for Grigor Rostov. Does he live here?'

'Yes. I'm his wife,' she said warily. 'What do you want Grigor for?'

'We need to ask him some questions about an incident that occurred yesterday at Down Street.'

'Grigor was here all day yesterday,' she said. 'It was Christmas Day. Whatever it is, he can't have anything to do with it.'

'Nevertheless, we do need to talk to him,' said Coburg.

The woman hesitated, then called, 'Grigor!'

A young man in his twenties appeared from inside the house and walked towards them, but stopped in the passage when he saw the two men standing with his wife on the doorstep.

'They're police,' she said. 'From Scotland Yard.'

Grigor Rostov looked at them even more warily than his wife had done.

'May we come in?' asked Coburg.

Mrs Rostov turned to her husband and said, 'I'm taking Mary for her walk. She needs the fresh air.' Then she turned to the two policemen and asked, 'Or do you want me?'

'No thank you, Mrs Rostov. We just need to talk to your husband.' He stepped aside so she could get out of the house. The young woman hesitated, then, with a last worried look at her husband, pushed the pram out into the street and walked off. Coburg and Lampson entered the house, and Rostov gestured for them to go into the front room. The three sat down, and Rostov looked at Coburg and Lampson with deep unhappiness.

'I know why you are here,' he said. 'I had a telephone call last night.'

'Svetlana Rostova,' said Coburg.

Rostov nodded. 'She was my sister.'

'Who telephoned you?'

'A colleague from work. They were on the late shift and they heard about this woman who'd been discovered dead there. Stabbed. They guessed she was related to me once they found out her name was Svetlana Rostova.'

'Does your wife know?'

'Priscilla?' Rostov shook his head. 'I told her it was someone from work telling me about things I'd need to know when I went to work today.'

'But you didn't go to work.'

'No. I thought I'd be questioned. I couldn't face it.'

'So you phoned in and pretended you had food poisoning.'

'I just said I had an upset stomach.'

'Your wife wasn't suspicious?'

'She knows I suffer with my stomach,' said Rostov. 'I will tell Priscilla about Svetlana being killed. I will tell her that is why you came to see me today.'

'Did you see your sister yesterday?'

'No. I hadn't seen her for more than a week.'

'You authorised a visitor's pass to Down Street for her.'

'Yes. She was desperate for somewhere to be safe at night during the bombing.'

'There are plenty of air raid shelters she could have gone to.'

Rostov gave a sad shake of his head. 'Svetlana wouldn't go down them. She had had this vision of herself dying in one. She wanted somewhere safer, deeper underground.'

'The inspector who was first on the scene went to the address on her identity card and was told she no longer lived there. That she left two weeks previously.'

'She did not leave. She was told to go by the woman who owned the house where she was lodging,' said Rostov bitterly.

'Do you know why?'

'The woman who owned the house had taken against her. She didn't like Svetlana using her room to have customers to tell their fortunes. She said if she'd known she was going to do that, she'd never have let her move in. She said it was against her religion.

'Svetlana had nowhere to stay and she begged me to find her a safe place to spend the nights during the bombing. She'd had a vision that she'd die in an underground air raid shelter, so she was scared to go to the Underground station or the public shelters. I couldn't let her stay with us at home – my wife doesn't like her. Svetlana is – was – odd. She frightened people with her looking into the future.'

'According to her ID card she arrived in England in 1937. I'm guessing you arrived at the same time?'

'Yes. We came here together.'

'Your English is excellent for someone who's only been in England for three years or so,' said Coburg.

'In Russia I worked in the department that monitored British financial transactions.'

'For the Soviet government?'

'Yes.'

'Why did you and your sister leave Russia?'

'To escape the Terror.'

'The Terror?'

'Stalin's Terror. If we'd stayed in Russia we would have been killed.' He saw the enquiring expression on their faces, so he enlarged on what had made them flee their native country.

'Between 1936 and 1938 about three quarters of a million Soviet officials were executed and more than a million sent to the labour camps. Stalin is paranoid, convinced that the people around him are plotting his downfall. Many of them were people who'd been with him during the revolution that had ended the reign of the tsars and brought in a communist government. Nearly all of the old Bolsheviks who'd been with him before 1918 were purged.'

'Purged?'

'Killed. Even Trotsky, who'd been an architect of the revolution, was expelled from Russia in 1929.'

'He was killed a couple of months ago,' said Coburg. 'I saw it in the newspapers. In August, I think.'

Rostov nodded. 'In Mexico. He was killed by one of Stalin's secret assassins. He was just one of Stalin's former comrades who suffered that fate. Zinoviev and Kamenev were others who were accused of plotting to overthrow Stalin. They were tortured to make them confess their alleged crimes, and then executed.

'Several show trials were held in Moscow as an example to local courts throughout the country to show what was expected of them. The Trial of the Sixteen was the first one in December 1936.

'Our father was a general in the Red Army, completely loyal to Russia, and when he realised what was happening, that key figures in the Soviet establishment were being rounded up, tortured to make them confess, then executed, and that their families were also being killed, he ordered Svetlana and me to leave the country in secret. He managed to get us smuggled out through Scandinavia and we made our way to England, which he said was the only place we would be safe. He ordered our mother to accompany us, but she refused to go, saying she agreed Svetlana and I should leave, but she would stay with him.

'We managed to reach England in January 1937. That same month there was the second show trial in Moscow, the Trial of the Seventeen. Then, in June of that year came the Trial of the Red Army Generals, including our father. They were all executed. Our mother was shot as well.

'Following that came the Great Purge of 1937. In this it was ironic that the prosecutors who conducted the cases against the generals were themselves arrested and tried and executed. Stalin got rid of everyone he suspected of plotting against him, which was virtually everyone. In the armed forces alone, thirty-four thousand officers were executed. The entire politburo and most of the central committee were killed. About two million people were killed during the Great Purge.

'In addition to the official show trials, the NKVD, Stalin's secret police, arrested and executed anyone suspected of opposing Stalin's regime, and gossip alone was enough for a death sentence. By the NKVD's own account, seven hundred thousand people were shot during 1937 and 1938 alone.

'With that kind of background, I hope you can understand why Svetlana became, as they say, odd.'

'Who do you think might have a reason to harm your sister?'

'Stalin,' replied Rostov.

'But he's in Russia,' pointed out Coburg.

'Yes, but his assassination squads are everywhere, including here in England. I told you that Stalin is paranoid; he's fearful that the families of his victims might take revenge on him, so he has them killed.'

'But what threat would someone like Svetlana pose to him?' asked Coburg.

'A paranoid person doesn't need a reason to fear people,' said Rostov.

'How did you meet your wife?' asked Coburg.

'At work. At the Railway Executive offices. We went out together, then got married last year when we knew war was coming. It seemed the right time.'

'What about Svetlana? Did she have any romantic attachments?'

Rostov thought it over, then said, 'To be honest, I don't know much about her life. Priscilla didn't like her so she didn't come here.'

'You must have seen her at Down Street? You were working there and you'd got her a visitor's pass.'

'We agreed that it was best if we avoided one another there to stop questions about who she was and if we knew one another. We came up with the idea that she was a cleaner working there at night, if she was asked.'

'What about people she met away from Down Street? Her fortune-telling business?'

'She used to go to hotels in London and leave her card for people to find. If they wanted a consultation, they left a message in a box at the hotel that had her name on it, leaving their name and address. At first she used to take her clients to her room, until she was turned out. Since then I suppose she went to their houses.'

'You're not sure?'

'As I said, I haven't seen much of her since I arranged the visitor's pass for her.'

'Which hotels did she use?'

'I know she went to The Dorchester, but I don't know if she used others.'

'And The Dorchester allowed her to use their place to get customers?'

'I think she paid them for each one she got.'

'Who did she pay?'

'The concierge, I assume.' Then a thought struck him and he said, 'You asked about romantic encounters.'

'Yes,' said Coburg.

'At the same time as she came to ask me to get her a visitor's pass for Down Street, she mentioned that she'd been seeing someone. An RAF pilot.'

'Did she tell you his name?'

'Colin. That's all she told me.' He thought again, then added, 'She said he was based at Biggin Hill.'

As they left the house and made for their car, Lampson shook his head in disbelief and said, 'How many millions did he say Stalin had killed?'

'A lot,' said Coburg.

'And all the people who were close to him!' exploded Lampson indignantly.

'Politics is a tough business,' said Coburg. He looked at his watch. 'I'm heading back to the Yard to update the superintendent on what we've found. Do you want me to drop you off there?'

Lampson shook his head. 'No. I usually end up getting caught for something, and I promised Terry I'd be home on time today.'

'In that case, I'll see you tomorrow morning at the usual time. It looks like we're going to have a busy day. We'll need to talk to the woman who turfed Svetlana out of her lodging house, and The Dorchester, as well as checking out the other hotels. But our first call should be to Biggin Hill to track down this Colin. Fancy driving to Kent?'

Lampson smiled broadly. 'My pleasure, guv!'

Coburg was still thinking about the murder of Svetlana Rostova and what her brother had told him about Stalin's assassination squad when he arrived home that evening, but the expression of joy on Rosa's face drove further thoughts of the murder out of his mind.

'You look like you've had some good news,' he said as he took her in his arms and kissed her.

'I had a telephone call today from the BBC,' she told him excitedly. 'They want me to be on *Henry Hall's Guest Night*.'

'That's wonderful!' he said. 'When?'

'Next Tuesday. It'll be a live broadcast from Finsbury Park Empire.'

He looked at her quizzically and asked, 'Isn't it a bit short notice? I thought the BBC arranged things well in advance.'

'I expect someone's let them down,' said Rosa. 'It happens all the time in our business. Someone's booked to appear then they get laryngitis or something. Anyway, hard luck on them but great news for me.' She gave a frown. 'What puzzles me is how they knew I could be contacted at Paddington St John Ambulance.'

'Ah, that would be me,' said Coburg. 'Someone from the BBC phoned me at Scotland Yard first thing this morning. She said she was the secretary to a producer and he wanted to talk to you. She said they'd tried our home number, but there was no answer. So I told them about the St John Ambulance and gave them the number.'

'And you weren't going to tell me?' demanded Rosa.

'Not if they didn't actually contact you. I didn't want you to get disappointed.' He hugged her again. 'Congratulations, my darling.'

CHAPTER FIVE

Friday 27th December 1940

Bert Marsh sat at his desk in the offices of the *Daily Globe*, going through the list he'd made of potential stories for the next day's edition. Marsh was the human-interest stories correspondent, which meant almost anything. It didn't include politics, nor tales of military victories or losses during the war. Instead it looked into the lives of ordinary people and how the war was affecting them. Someone in a London slum who'd given their small backyard over to chickens to supply eggs to a local orphanage, or a woman who was knitting socks for soldiers. The problem was those sort of stories were now commonplace; every other paper was running them. He needed something *bigger*, something that would stand out. Something that no one else was covering.

A shadow fell over his desk and he looked up to see the grinning features of Wes Morgan, the paper's racing correspondent. Marsh wondered why Morgan was smiling; there wasn't any real racing going on because of the war.

'I picked up a story that might be right up your

street, Bert,' said Morgan, accompanying it with a confidential wink, which had become a habit of his. Picked up from his association with racecourse bookies and tipsters, Marsh assumed.

'Oh?' asked Marsh.

'I got it from this rail transport copper who's at Down Street, the old Tube station.'

'Oh?' said Marsh again, the mention of Churchill's secret underground bunker rousing his interest.

'It seems a dead body was found there on Christmas Day. A woman. She'd been stabbed. And, get this, she was a fortune-teller. Called herself Lady Za Za.'

'Who'd want to murder a fortune-teller?'

'Yeah, well, that's the mystery, isn't it. What's more, she was Russian – Svetlana Rostova. And her brother turns out to work there.'

'What, at Down Street?'

'Yes.'

'That's Churchill's bolt hole at the moment, ain't it?' asked Marsh, checking for confirmation.

'Only while the Cabinet War Rooms are being strengthened.'

'So does this brother work for Churchill, or the railway lot?'

'The railway crowd.' Morgan grinned. 'Bit of a mystery that might grab the readers. A dead Russian fortune-teller found in Churchill's bunker. What d'you think?'

Marsh nodded thoughtfully. 'It sounds promising. What's the brother's name?'

'Grigor Rostov. A good old-fashioned Russkie name.'

Coburg and Lampson's journey took them south of the river, past the ruined suburbs of South London, then through Bromley before they reached Biggin Hill. The airfield itself seemed as busy as it had been during the Battle of Britain. Although the Germans had switched from daylight raids on the airfields to predominantly night raids on London and the cities – the Blitz – young airmen were still busy making sure the Hurricanes and Spitfires and all other aircraft we ready to go into action. The police car they were travelling in gained them immediate access to the airfield and within a short time they were in the office of the airfield's commanding officer, Group Captain Desmond Crombie.

'We're looking for one of your pilots called Colin,' said Coburg.

'We have about a hundred men called Colin.'

'Unfortunately we don't have a second name,' apologised Coburg.

'If you tell me what this is all about, perhaps we can narrow it down,' said Crombie. He gave a worried frown. 'I assume that as you're from Scotland Yard, this Colin of ours is in some sort of serious trouble.'

'No, not at all,' Coburg assured him. 'We're looking into an incident involving a Russian woman called Svetlana Rostova.'

'I assume she was attacked and claims this Colin did it?' said Crombie. 'That's usually why we get the police turning up.'

'Again, that's not the case,' said Coburg. 'We're trying to find out all we can about this woman, who also worked as a fortune-teller called Lady Za Za. The only thing we know about her was that she had been seeing a young pilot based at Biggin Hill called Colin.'

'I assume from what you're saying that she's disappeared.'

'Yes,' said Coburg, deciding that if he told the group captain she'd been murdered he would be even more reluctant to reveal who this mysterious Colin was. From his time in the army he knew that commanders in the services did everything they could to protect their men, even if they were suspected of having committed murder.

'A Russian woman?' mused Crombie thoughtfully.

'Young,' said Coburg. 'Very attractive. Quite thin. Pale features and long black hair.'

'I think I saw her here a week or so ago,' said Crombie. 'Quite noticeable, almost exotic. She was with Colin Upton. He's with B Flight, a Defiant squadron.'

'Defiants?' said Coburg. 'He's lucky to be alive,

from what I hear. I heard they had a bad reputation during the Battle of Britain.'

'That was then,' said Crombie tersely. 'Now, the Defiant is the reason you people in London are surviving. I don't know if you've noticed it, but the past month or so the Blitz on London hasn't been as heavy.'

'That depends where you are in London,' said Coburg. 'The docks are still taking a hammering.' Then, reluctantly, he added, 'But you might be right. The raids at night don't seem as bad as they were. To be honest, I just thought we were getting used to it.'

'Two reasons,' said Crombie. 'It looks like the Germans have switched much of the emphasis of their bombing campaign to the north of England. Just before Christmas the Luftwaffe bombed Liverpool for three nights on the trot. The local wags called it the Christmas Blitz. And then just immediately before Christmas they began bombing Manchester. Six hundred people killed and two thousand injured.'

'Why have they switched their bombing to the north?' asked Coburg.

Crombie shrugged. 'Who knows? But in my opinion it's got something to do with the Defiants. You're right that their performance during the Battle of Britain wasn't up to that of the Spitfires and Hurricanes, but that was because of its design.' He put on his cap. 'If you come with me, I'll show you what I mean, before

I take you to meet Wing Commander Upton.'

'Wing commander? How old is he?'

'Twenty-one,' said Crombie. 'The rate we're losing pilots, it's quicker to rise through the ranks.' He gave a rueful smile as he added, 'At this rate, he could be an air vice-marshal by twenty-five, if he lives that long.'

As Coburg and Lampson followed the group captain out of the office and to the airfield, Lampson whispered to Coburg with a groan, 'We're going to get a lecture on this Defiant, aren't we?'

'It seems we are,' Coburg whispered back. 'But we need the group captain's co-operation if we're going to be able to talk to this Wing Commander Colin Upton.'

'A wing commander at twenty-one years old,' said Lampson, awed.

'Unfortunately, all promotions in times of war are the result of stepping into a dead man's shoes,' said Coburg ruefully. 'That's how I got my promotions during the first lot, all the officers above me dying. If it had gone on any longer, the junior quartermaster would have been in charge.'

They walked to where a row of small planes were parked up. Unlike the Spitfires and Hurricanes, which consisted of a single-seater cockpit for the pilot, this plane had a turret immediately behind the cockpit from which bristled four machine guns poking out aimed, at the rear.

'The Boulton Paul Defiant,' Crombie told them

proudly. He pointed at the machine guns sticking out from slots in the turret. 'Those are the armaments. Four 7.7mm Browning machine guns. The Defiant was intended to fire backwards and upwards. At a pinch the guns can rotate forward and fire on either side of the cockpit, but in practice it's not recommended. Shooting the pilot is always a possibility.'

'What about forward guns?' asked Coburg.

'None,' said Crosbie. 'Which, at first sight, is the disadvantage the Defiant suffers when compared to the Spitfire and Hurricanes. In a dogfight, fighter plane on fighter plane, in the Defiant you have to get behind or below an enemy plane to shoot it down. That rarely happens with Messerschmitts; they come at you head-on at full throttle. So gradually, the Defiants were phased out of the Battle of Britain and the boffins went back to the drawing board. They added in radar.

'Now we have a two-man fighter plane that can fly at night and spot approaching enemy planes by radar. Spitfires and Hurricanes depend on the pilot picking out the enemy with the naked eye, so in the darkness of night-time the pilots are as good as blind.' He patted the fuselage of the Defiant affectionately. 'This beauty spots the enemy coming in using radar and goes out to meet them. It then flies beneath them and either gives them a burst from the machine guns in the turret pointing upwards, or flies past them and then hits them from behind. It may not be as romantic as the

Spitfire or the Hurricane, but my God it's effective!'

He smiled at the plane, then said, 'Anyway, enough of this. You want to meet Colin Upton. He'll be in the mess. A grand chap. The best of the best.' He looked at them, concerned. 'I really hope he isn't in any trouble.'

'He isn't; we just want to pick his brains,' Coburg assured him while at the same time thinking, *I hope not, too. Could it be something as simple as a lovers' quarrel that got out of hand? Or Upton discovered something about Svetlana that posed a threat to him and his position?*

As they entered the mess, the young airmen sitting at the tables with cups of tea in front of them spotted the arrival of the stiff-backed, moustached group captain and immediately sprang to attention.

'At ease!' barked Crombie.

The young men resumed their places on the long wooden benches beside the tables, but kept their eyes alertly on the group captain and the two civilians who were with him. Lampson heard low muttering from some of the airmen – 'It's the police' – and thought to himself, *Are we so obvious? Do we look like coppers, even though we're wearing civilian clothes?*

The group captain stopped by a table where a group of four young men had been chatting, and now looked with deep uncertainty at their commanding officer.

'Wing Commander Upton,' said Crombie.

One of the young men leapt to his feet and stood

to attention. He looked even younger than his twenty-one years, a short, slim, red-headed young man. 'Sir!' he barked.

'These men are from London and need to talk to you,' said Crombie. He looked at the other three young men. 'You may excuse yourselves while the wing commander is in discussion.'

'Yes, sir,' said the three in unison, and picked up their cups and made for another table, but one that appeared to Coburg to be still within earshot.

'I'll leave you to it,' said Crombie. 'If you need me afterwards, I'll be in my office.'

'Thank you, Group Captain,' said Coburg.

He and Lampson sat down on the benches vacated by the young airmen.

'My name's Detective Chief Inspector Coburg from Scotland Yard, and this is my sergeant, Sergeant Lampson,' said Coburg, and he and Lampson produced their warrant cards and showed them to the bewildered Upton.

'Scotland Yard?' said Upton, baffled.

'We'd like to talk to you about someone we understand you'd been seeing recently. Svetlana Rostova. Also known as Lady Za Za.'

'Why? What's she been up to?'

'How well do you know her?' asked Coburg.

'Well, not in depth, I suppose you could say,' said Upton awkwardly. Then he gave a self-conscious grin and added, 'I was in London on leave, and I picked up this card in The Dorchester: *Lady Za Za, fortunes told.*' He chuckled. 'Like many of the chaps, you can't help but wonder how long you've got. So, mainly for a laugh, I decided to have a session with her. I liked her. I expected it to be a bit of a con, these things usually are, but she seemed genuine. So I took to coming to London, and one weekend I borrowed a pal's car and took her out for a drive in the country.'

'Where were you two days ago?' asked Coburg. 'Christmas Day.'

'The same place I've been every day for the past week,' sighed Upton, and he pointed upwards. 'Taking on Jerry.'

'There was a truce on Christmas Day,' said Coburg.

'Yes, so we were told, but very few of us believed it. In any case, we fly at night, so during the day we spend the time making sure our kites are ready for action. I'm due some leave from tomorrow, so I was thinking of getting back to London and seeing Svetlana again. She looks very serious, but actually she's a lot of fun.' He looked at them anxiously as he asked, 'Something's happened to her, hasn't it? And I mean out of the ordinary. You wouldn't be here if she was just another victim of the bombing.'

Coburg nodded. Keeping his voice low, his expression sympathetic, he said, 'I'm sorry to have to tell you that she's dead. Her body was found at Down

Street, the former Underground station. She'd been stabbed.'

'Stabbed? She was murdered?'

'It looks that way. Unfortunately, we know very little about her. We know she had a brother, Grigor, and we've talked to him.'

'His wife didn't like Svetlana,' said Upton. 'She told me.'

'Did you know where she was living?'

'I knew she'd been kicked out of the bedsit where she was staying, some holier-than-thou biddy who disapproved of her telling fortunes. Svetlana said she lived in shelters because she couldn't go and stay with her brother because of his wife.' He looked around at the busy mess. 'I'd have brought her here like a shot, but that was out of the question, of course.' He shook his head. 'How awful!'

Coburg and Lampson left him sitting at the table and staring mournfully at a cup of tea.

'There's something I need to check,' said Coburg. 'On any military base, people leaving or coming in need to check in and out.'

'You think he's lying about being here all day, guv?'

'There's one way to find out,' said Coburg.

They made their way to the main exit and showed their warrant cards to the airman on duty at the guard hut.

'I need to look at the record for Christmas Day,' said Coburg. 'Who left the base and came in, and at what time.'

The airman flicked back through the pages of the record, then showed Coburg the pages for Christmas Day. Coburg ran his finger down the exit entries until he came to one that showed Wing Commander C. Upton leaving the base at 4 p.m. He then checked those entering the base and found Wing Commander C. Upton returning at 7 p.m. He checked the other names and times to see if anyone else had left the base at the same time as Colin Upton, but Upton had left alone. It was the same story for his return to base.

Coburg and Lampson returned to the mess in time to see Upton walking out with his comrades. Coburg summoned Upton over.

'Just one last question,' said Coburg. 'You signed out from 4 p.m. to 7 p.m. on Christmas Day.'

'Did I?' queried Upton. Then he nodded. 'That's right, I did.'

'Where did you go?'

Upton looked momentarily stumped. 'I might have gone out with some of the boys. We often go to the pub.'

'No one else signed out at that time,' said Coburg.

'No?' said Upton. 'No, that's right.'

He fell into a thoughtful silence.

'Maybe you went to see family?' asked Coburg.

'Christmas Day, and all that.'

'No, my family are in Derbyshire. And none of us really believed the Germans would keep the truce.'

'So you stayed local?'

'Yes,' said Upton.

'So I ask again, where did you go?'

Upton shrugged.

'I just drove around,' he said. 'I needed to get away from the base for a bit. Just for a couple of hours. I was near enough if the Germans started bombing after all, but I had a bit of time to myself if they didn't. I needed to be back for seven because if they did start their night bombing, that's when they do it.' He looked at them, a forlorn expression on his face. 'It's not much of an alibi, but it's true. It's pretty intensive here. When we're not up in the air battling with Jerry, we're on edge, preparing.'

'What do you think about what he said?' asked Coburg as they drove away from Biggin Hill.

'It's thin, but it sounds like truth to me,' said Lampson. 'I can understand what he said about it being intense there, day after day, hour after hour. I can imagine he'd want to get away on his own for a bit.'

CHAPTER SIX

Friday 27th December 1940

Rosa arrived at the BBC's Maida Vale Studios at one o'clock, as suggested by John Fawcett. That was a difference from the last time she'd been on Henry Hall's radio show, a year previously. Then the producer had been a martinet, Dennis Main, who insisted on strict regulations and times being observed. There was never any hint of Dennis Main 'suggesting' things; he gave orders to people. This John Fawcett sounded an altogether different type of producer.

Unlike the tall, imposing, white building in Portland Place that was Broadcasting House, the studios in Maida Vale appeared single-storey, although much of it, including the actual studios, was below ground level. She remembered that when she'd been here before she'd been told that the place had been a former ice rink.

She went to the reception desk, where she gave her name and who she was due to meet. The receptionist picked up the phone to someone, and within five minutes the short, elegant figure of John Fawcett appeared, smiling and holding out his hand to her in welcome. He appeared to be in his forties, slight of build, with a neat Van Dyke beard.

'I'm not sure how to address you,' said Fawcett with an apologetic smile. 'As Miss Weeks, or Mrs Saxe-Coburg? I understand you're married now.'

'Rosa will do fine.'

'Rosa. Thank you. I didn't want to appear presumptuous. You've been here before?'

'Yes. I did a broadcast for services radio from here.'

'Then you'll have experienced the canteen,' said Fawcett, steering her towards the stairs. 'Not bad food at all, considering the circumstances. And they do a decent tapioca pudding as dessert.'

They walked down to the basement level where the canteen was based, and Rosa felt a familiar feeling as she walked into it. It may have been called a canteen, but unlike some work canteens where she'd played, this one had crisp white linen tablecloths on each table.

Fawcett ordered a salad starter and main meal of cutlet with vegetables, and Rosa elected to have the same.

'You mentioned bomb damage at Broadcasting House,' said Rosa. 'Was it serious?'

'I'm afraid so,' said Fawcett. 'The first one was in October. Ironically, there'd been complaints from the people who lived around Portland Place about the whiteness of the building standing out like a searchlight during the blackouts because of the white stone used in its constructions, and there were plans to get a team of painters to darken it down. Unfortunately, before that could be organised, during an air raid in the middle of October a five-hundred-pound bomb came through a seventh-floor window. It went through two more floors before it came to rest in the music library on the fifth floor.

'What no one realised was that it was a delayed-action bomb. Staff began to try to drag it towards a window to get it out into the street, but tragically, it went off. Seven people were killed and twenty-three injured.'

'How awful!' said Rosa, horrified.

'Three studios were so badly damaged that it will be at least a year before they can be used. And unfortunately, that wasn't the end of it. Earlier this month a landmine the Germans had dropped using a parachute got caught up with a lamp post right outside Broadcasting House. The blast killed a couple of people, injured many more, and destroyed quite a few of the offices inside the building as well as rupturing water mains and shrapnel from the mine starting electrical fires. What with one thing and another, a lot of the studios and facilities are out of action, which is why we're here at Maida Vale.' He gave her a rueful smile of apology. 'But then, plenty of people have had much worse happen to them.

Someone told me you'd lost your flat in Hampstead.'

'Yes, the block was bombed flat. Luckily for us, we were out at the time, so at least we escaped with our lives. And Edgar, my husband, was able to fix up another flat for us. This one's got a reinforced air raid shelter in the basement.'

Their meals arrived, and they tucked into them while Fawcett talked to her about the forthcoming broadcast.

'I know this is very short notice, for which I can only apologise,' said Fawcett, 'but one of the acts we'd planned to have on the show has got problems, so we wondered if you'd agree to come in. We remember you were on Henry's show before, and he speaks very highly of you.'

'I'd be delighted,' said Rosa. 'I remember when I was on the show before I did two numbers. Would that be the same again?'

'It would, and I'm so pleased you agree to appear.' He looked thoughtful as he continued, 'We thought, to balance the music, if you started with a tuneful but quiet song for your first one, followed by a rousing number, something to lift the audience. The audience both at the theatre and at home do like something jolly at this dreadful time. It gives them a chance to escape from the horrors of the bombing.'

'Of course,' said Rosa. 'How about Hoagy Carmichael's "Stardust" to begin with, followed by

"When the Saints Go Marching In"? People like to sing along with that last one and it gives a real community feeling to the occasion.'

'Excellent!' Fawcett beamed. 'I assume you'd like to get the feel of the piano before the actual broadcast. It is live. This time it's going out from the Finsbury Park Empire. The broadcast begins at six o'clock, so you'll be on at about twenty past. Can I suggest you come to Finsbury Park just after lunch on the day, early afternoon. You can try the piano out while the technicians are setting up the microphones and other equipment. Would one o'clock be suitable for you?'

'One o'clock would be perfect,' said Rosa. 'Who else is on the bill? I only ask to make sure I won't be stepping on anyone's toes. For example, if someone else is already thinking of doing "The Saints", for example.'

'No, no one has said they'd like to do that. Consider it yours.' Fawcett smiled. 'After lunch we can go to my office and I'll let you have a list of the rest of the programme. Now, for your billing. Do you still appear under the name Rosa Weeks?'

'I do. It's less confusing for the audience who know me.'

The landlady of the house where Svetlana Rostova had lived before being asked to leave was a Mrs Agatha Parchment, a tall, thin, austere-looking woman in her fifties. The house was a tall Victorian three-storey building in Lambeth, near the bridge and not far from the Houses of Parliament on the other side of the Thames. Mrs Parchment had a flat on the ground floor, close to the front door so – Coburg and Lampson guessed – that she could keep watch on who came in and who went out. She looked to be that sort of woman. The rest of the house was divided into bed-sitting rooms, with a toilet and bathroom on the first and second floors for her tenants. Mrs Parchment invited the two detectives into the sitting room of her small flat, after first subjecting their warrant cards to close inspection to establish they really were who they claimed to be. The sitting room was small, furnished with dark oak furniture overlaid with pieces of lace embroidery. Nothing was out of place, and Lampson, in particular, felt that his very presence in this room was somehow ruining the decor.

'Miss Rostova was a heathen,' Mrs Parchment informed them. 'She engaged in ungodly practices.'

'Her fortune-telling,' said Coburg.

Mrs Parchment gave a deliberately loud sniff to show her strong disapproval. 'If I'd known she intended to use one of my rooms for such a practice, I would never have let her enter my door.'

'How did you find out about her fortune-telling?' asked Coburg.

'I noticed there were a great many ladies of all sorts

traipsing through my house accompanied by that woman to her room. I became suspicious.'

'No men?' asked Coburg.

'Absolutely not,' said Mrs Parchment firmly. 'This is a house for ladies to lodge. Men are expressly forbidden. My ladies know the rules: no men in their rooms.' She gave a superior look as she added, 'I have had some women try to fool me telling me the man was a relative, a father or a brother. But I told them all the same. A man is a man. Men are not allowed in the rooms.' She gave them an enquiring look. 'But why are you asking questions about Miss Rostova?' She leant forward, an expression of prurient interest on her face as she asked, 'Has she been arrested for something?'

'No. Tragically, she was found stabbed to death two days ago.'

Mrs Parchment looked at them in horror. 'Stabbed to death? Who by?'

'That is what we're trying to find out, so we'd appreciate everything you can tell us about her. The people she knew, for example.'

'I have no knowledge of the people she knew,' said Mrs Parchment primly. 'People who go to a so-called fortune-teller are not the kind of people I wish to associate with.' She thought for a moment, then said, 'Devil-worshippers.'

'Pardon?' asked Coburg, puzzled.

'She was involved in the occult, wasn't she? This

so-called fortune-telling, a black art. The work of the devil. It will have been some of the people she was involved with in the world of the occult that did it. Possibly as some kind of ritual sacrifice. That's what these people use knives for, isn't it?' She shuddered. 'Black magic and devil-worship, here in in this God-fearing house. It's sacrilege, that's what it is.'

'Devil-worshippers?' said Lampson as they left the house.

'I'd hardly put Wing Commander Upton in that category, but you never know,' said Coburg.

'You're not serious, guv?!' said Lampson, incredulous.

'No I'm not, but I always believe in keeping an open mind. In the meantime, I suggest our next port of call is that den of black magic and the dark arts, The Dorchester hotel.'

Bert Marsh stood in the doorway of an empty shop directly opposite the old entrance to the former Down Street Underground station. Wes Morgan's contact had given him a good description of Grigor Rostov, and the time he finished his shift. He watched as the workers came out, some old, who he dismissed, along with the many women. As the result of men enlisting in the services, there seemed to be very few men in their twenties coming out of the building, which made the job of spotting Rostov easier. Rostov was nearly the last to appear. Marsh left the shop doorway and hurried over towards him, catching up with the Russian.

'Mr Rostov!' he called.

Rostov stopped and turned around, a look of surprise on his face.

'Mr Rostov,' said Marsh, putting on his well-practised expression of earnest concern, 'my name's Bert Marsh and I'm a reporter with the *Daily Globe*. Please accept my condolences over the loss of your sister. Our readers are keen to find out more about her. If I could have a moment of your time to talk about your sister, what sort of person she was . . .'

Rostov gave a violent shake of his head. 'No,' he said.

'It may help the police find the person who killed her quicker,' urged Marsh. 'I'm sure you feel the same way, too.'

Again, Rostov shook his head and said, even firmer this time, 'No.'

With that he made off with a burst of speed that took Marsh by surprise. Marsh considered chasing after him, but he stopped. *I know where you live*, he thought. *I'm not giving up that easily*. Then he smiled to himself. No, Rostov's curt refusal and running off like that had given him his story. Rostov would come crawling back to *him*.

* * *

As Coburg and Lampson entered The Dorchester, the face of the royal blue-liveried concierge at the reception desk lit up.

'Mr Coburg!' he exclaimed in delight, giving them a broad, welcoming smile. 'It is a long time since we have had the pleasure of your patronage. Are you here to book a room, I hope?'

'Sadly, no, Alphonse,' said Coburg. 'This is my sergeant, Ted Lampson.'

'Good afternoon to you, Sergeant.' Alphonse smiled.

'We're here to talk to you about Svetlana Rostova, also known as Lady Za Za.'

'Ah, our fortune-teller!' exclaimed Alphonse brightly. 'A lovely and personable young woman. Highly respectable, not like some of these people who claim to be able to read fortunes. She did mine by studying the palm of my hand and I have to tell you, Chief Inspector, it was truly remarkable. If it had not been we would not have accepted her request to put her cards on display.' He pointed across the reception area to a small table, adorned with a flowered tablecloth, on which was a small pile of visiting cards in front of a small placard. Coburg and Lampson wandered over to it and each picked up one of the cards and studied the display. It was all very discreet and tasteful, in keeping with The Dorchester.

Lady Za Za. Fortunes told in complete confidence.
Discretion guaranteed. Take a card and write
your name and where I can contact you on the
reverse side and place it in the box provided.

Next to the placard was a discreet plain wooden box with a slit in the top for the cards to be dropped into it.

Coburg and Lampson returned to the reception desk.

'I'm sorry to tell you, Alphonse, that Lady Za Za has been murdered.'

Alphonse stared at him, horrified. 'Murdered?'

'Her body was found early yesterday morning at Down Street, the former Underground station, now the headquarters of the Railway Executive Committee. She'd been stabbed to death.'

'So that's why she hasn't been in,' said Alphonse. 'Normally she came in every day to see if she had anyone wanting a consultation. I assumed she'd had Christmas Day off and continued the break for Boxing Day.'

'How did it work?' asked Coburg. 'Did she just come in and collect the cards and go?'

'No. She always brought the box to the desk here. Whoever was here would open it and count the number of cards inside, before handing them to her. She would then return to the box to the table.'

'Did you keep a record of who had asked for a consultation?'

Alphonse shook his head. 'It was purely to see the numbers.'

'You had an arrangement for her to pay you so much for each client?'

'Exactly. Although it was just a token payment. A shilling a card.'

'How much did she charge?'

'That depended on the particular client. If she thought they were fairly well off, she'd charge them more than she'd charge, say, someone of limited means. She was very fair.' Firmly, to make sure his point had been made, he added, 'She was not a con artist.'

'No, of course not,' said Coburg appeasingly. He turned to Lampson and asked, 'Can you bring the box over, please, Sergeant.'

When Lampson returned with it, Coburg passed it to Alphonse. 'I notice it has a small lock in the back.'

'Discretion and confidence,' said Alphonse.

'I assume you have the key.'

'I have one key,' admitted Alphonse. 'She had the other. I assume you want me to open it.'

'Please,' said Coburg. 'We need to explore every avenue if we are to find the person who killed her.'

'You think it was one of her clients?' asked Alphonse, opening the box and removing four cards from inside it, which he handed to Coburg.

'At this moment we have an open mind,' said Coburg. He looked at the display. 'I think it's time for it to be taken away.'

'I'll attend to that,' said Alphonse. 'Shall I keep it for her next of kin? She had a brother, I believe.'

'She did, and we'll mention it to him. However, he may not want the items. I get the impression his wife doesn't approve of her fortune-telling activities. One last question, Alphonse. Do you know which other hotels she used to advertise at?'

Alphonse looked affronted at the suggestion. 'Absolutely none,' he said. 'We at The Dorchester pride ourselves on our exclusivity. It was made absolutely clear to Miss Rostova that we would only entertain being part of the project if we were the only such premises engaged in her promotion.'

As they left The Dorchester, Coburg said, 'We need to get hold of the cards with the names of her previous clients. I assume she kept them with her, but there was no sign of them when we examined her possessions.'

'There might have been a lot for her to carry around,' pointed out Lampson.

'In which case we need to find where she kept things.'

'Down Street,' suggested Lampson. 'She spent nights there. She must have had a hidey-hole where she stored things. Spare clothes, that sort of thing.'

Coburg nodded. 'Good thinking. First thing tomorrow, we'll go back there and take a look.'

That evening, over supper, Rosa told Coburg about her meeting with John Fawcett. 'He's so nice, so very different to some producers I've worked with, who act like mini dictators. I'm so excited about the show. It's been a long time since I appeared in front of a large audience, and there'll certainly be one at the Finsbury Park Empire for this. Wherever Henry Hall appears, the crowds pile in.'

'It starts at six, doesn't it,' said Coburg.

'It does.'

'Then I'll be there for it.'

'I'll make sure there's a ticket on the door for you. As I say, there could be crowds and if you're late you may not get in.'

'I won't be late,' promised Coburg. 'Who else is on the bill? He usually has a mixture: comedians, musicians, all sorts.'

Rosa produced the list of performers Fawcett had given her from her bag.

'Here you are,' she said.

Coburg perused it. 'Dickie Henderson,' he said.

'He's a comedian.'

He frowned. 'And who's this one? Peter Brough with Archie Andrews?'

'He's a ventriloquist.'

'A ventriloquist on the wireless?' said Coburg, amused. 'My God, that's scraping the bottom of the barrel.'

'He's said to be very good,' said Rosa. 'He's quite young; he only started appearing in variety halls last year. But he's experienced. He was in a film with Billy Cotton and his band that came out this year. *Cavalcade of Variety*. He was the compère.'

'Yes, but the point of a ventriloquist is you're not supposed to be able to see their lips moving.'

'Well, people won't.'

'Of course people won't; he'll be on the wireless. That's my point.'

'I meant the people in the theatre won't. As I said, I hear he's very good.'

'Which one's the ventriloquist, anyway? Peter Brough or Archie Andrews?'

'Peter Brough. Archie's his dummy.'

Coburg continued studying the list. 'I see whoever you're replacing, their name's been very heavily crossed out so it can't be read. Didn't you ask who it was?'

'No, that's not the done thing. I don't know why he or she dropped out. Problems, the producer said. I didn't like to ask what sort of problems.'

CHAPTER SEVEN

Saturday 28th December 1940

While Rosa made porridge for their breakfast, Coburg went to the nearest newsagent's to get a newspaper. Rosa eyed the tabloid he came back with, alongside *The Times*, with suspicion.

'What's that rag?' she asked.

'The *Daily Globe*,' said Coburg.

'You don't normally get that.'

'I saw it had a bit about the case I'm working on.'

He put the papers down on the table as she served two bowls of porridge. Rosa picked up *The Times* while Coburg read the report of the case he was working on in the *Daily Globe*.

'This is awful,' he said, frowning. 'Tabloid trash. "Stargazer butchered in Churchill's secret bunker".'

'Was she butchered?' asked Rosa.

'Hardly. Stabbed once, and very neatly, direct in the heart. I agree it's not a good way to die, but it hardly merits the description of her being butchered.' He then read the rest of the story aloud to her. '"The murdered woman has been identified as an immigrant

Russian fortune-teller, Svetlana Rostova, who carried on her fortune-telling trade under the stargazer name of Lady Za Za. We tried to talk to the late Lady Za Za's brother, Grigor Rostov, who works at the Railway Executive Committee offices at the former Down Street station, where Lady Za Za's body was found, but he refused to talk to us. Why? What is he hiding? What is the secret of Lady Za Za? Could it be connected to the fact that Down Street Tube station is now operating as Churchill's secret bunker?"'

'Not so secret any more,' said Rosa. 'Are these reporters allowed to print this? Isn't it against the Official Secrets Act?'

'It's an offence against good journalism,' said Coburg grumpily. 'Have *The Times* got anything about it?'

Rosa smiled. 'No, but they've got something about me.'

'About you?'

Rosa read aloud: '"We understand that the BBC have booked the eminent jazz singer and pianist Rosa Weeks for next Tuesday's *Henry Hall's Guest Night*. Rosa Weeks, who has appeared on the show before, will be a warmly welcomed guest to the show, which will be broadcast live from the Finsbury Park Empire at 6 p.m."'

'"Eminent?"' Coburg smiled. '"Warmly welcomed?"'

'It's *The Times*,' she said. 'You won't get alliteration like that in the rag you're reading.'

* * *

Lampson was holding a copy of the *Daily Globe* when Coburg picked him up in Somers Town.

'Have you seen this?' he demanded, obviously put out, as he slid behind the steering wheel and handed the paper to Coburg.

'I have,' said Coburg, dropping the newspaper on the back seat. 'I wonder where this Bert Marsh – the alleged journalist who perpetrated it – got the story from?'

'Someone on the inside earning a few bob by tipping him off,' said Lampson sourly. 'Down Street?'

'Yes, please,' said Coburg.

At Down Street, they made their way down the winding staircase to the lower depths, where they sought out Jeremy Purslake and asked if they could talk to Grigor Rostov.

'Of course,' said Purslake. 'Though I must warn you he's terribly upset. Not just about what happened to his sister, but yesterday he was harassed by a newspaper reporter.'

'Yes,' said Coburg. 'We saw the report in the *Daily Globe*.'

'No respect for people's grief, some of these reporters,' said Purslake in disapproval.

He took them to the empty office with the door to the small platform that they'd visited before. 'If you wait here, I'll bring Grigor to you. I'll be easier for you to talk to him away from the rest of the staff.'

Purslake left and they settled themselves at the desk,

just as an Underground train rattled past at speed on the other side of the brick wall.

'Provided we can hear one another with all that noise,' commented Lampson sourly.

A short time later the door opened and Purslake ushered in Grigor Rostov, who looked at them warily.

'Good morning, Mr Rostov,' said Coburg, gesturing towards the empty chair.

'I am being harassed,' complained Grigor as he sat down.

'Not by us, I assure you,' said Coburg. 'We're just trying to find out who killed your sister.'

'I mean by the press,' said Rostov. 'Yesterday I was chased along the road by a reporter shouting at me.'

'Yes, we saw the item in the paper,' said Coburg. 'We shall be having a word with Mr Marsh and hope he might leave you alone. The reason we've come today is because we understand that your sister left a box for potential clients at The Dorchester to put a card in with their name and contact details.'

'Yes,' said Rostov. 'That is correct.'

'We've looked through her bag and other possessions, which the University College Hospital is still holding for you, but we haven't been able to find the cards. Or anything relating to her activities as a fortune-teller. We wondered if perhaps she had left them here. After all, she was staying here at Down Street at night.'

Rostov nodded. 'Yes,' he said. 'She had nowhere to keep her things, so I let her share my locker here. It's in the locker room.'

'Perhaps you'd show us?' said Coburg gently.

Rostov got up and made for the door, Coburg and Lampson following. They walked down a corridor until they came to a door marked 'Locker room'. Rostov led them in, and to an array of narrow metal cupboards. He went to the one marked 'G. Rostov', took a key from his pocket and unlocked it.

'There,' he said. 'Most of these items are Svetlana's. I keep most of my things at home.'

Coburg and Lampson removed the items from the locker and put them on a table in the locker room. Rostov stepped forward and picked up four books.

'These are mine,' he said. 'Language dictionaries, which I need for work.'

Coburg and Lampson went through the remaining items. There were clothes; a pack of tarot cards; a book on palmistry; another on the signs of the zodiac, both of which were English editions. There were also books in Russian that appeared to be on astrology and other aspects of fortune-telling. There was a bag, shut with a drawstring. Coburg pulled the drawstring and opened the bag to reveal about forty cards, the same as the ones they'd seen on the table at The Dorchester. Each card had a name written on the reverse, with contact details. Each card also had details of money paid written in pencil.

'This is what we're looking for,' said Coburg. 'We're hoping that possibly one of these people may be able to give us information that may lead to your sister's killer. With your permission, we'd like to take them with us.'

'Of course,' said Rostov. He gestured at the other items on the table. 'Do you want these?'

'Not at the moment,' said Coburg. 'Can we ask you to keep them here, in case we might need to look at them in the future.'

Henry Bidlow MP sat at the desk in his office in the Houses of Parliament studying the day's newspapers. Not the riff-raff, of course, only the quality: *The Times* and *The Telegraph*, along with the *Daily Mail*, because the *Daily Mail* also had its ear to the political grapevine, albeit nearer to the voting public than either *The Telegraph* or *The Times*. It was all about reading the runes, looking at who was in favour and who was likely to be removed from the Cabinet, thus leaving a vacancy for the right man. And, in Bidlow's opinion, there was only one right man, if only he could get himself noticed in a favourable way by Churchill. Goddammit, Churchill had appointed those socialist upstarts Bevan and Bevin to the War Cabinet. He could understand Churchill having to appoint Attlee – the man was the leader of the opposition – but Bevan and Bevin for heaven's sake! If he and other like-minded people didn't take action, the Cabinet would be dominated by these lefties, and where would the Tory party stand then?

He was interrupted by a knock at his door and was annoyed to see it open before he'd had a chance to call 'Come in!' The arrival was his junior secretary, Martin Higgins, who should have known better than to enter without being summoned. Higgins had that sly smirk on his face he so often wore, usually when he'd undermined one of Bidlow's political rivals and was keen to report and exult in his success. Higgins laid a newspaper on his desk. Bidlow looked at it in puzzled disdain. The *Daily Globe*. A tittle-tattle gossip sheet. What did Higgins think could possibly be in there that would be of interest to him?

'What are you bringing this rag in here for?' he demanded.

'Page four.' Higgins smirked. 'Your problem is fixed, thanks to me.'

Intrigued, Bidlow turned to page four and scanned it. One headline leapt out at him: *Stargazer butchered in Churchill's secret bunker*. Bidlow read the story with mounting horror:

The murdered woman has been identified as an immigrant Russian fortune-teller, Svetlana Rostova, who carried on her fortune-telling trade under the stargazer name of Lady Za Za. We tried to talk to the late Lady Za Za's brother, Grigor Rostov, who works at the Railway

Executive Committee offices at the former Down Street station, where Lady Za Za's body was found.

Bidlow looked at Higgins, horrified. '*You* did this?'

Higgins smirked again. 'I'm hardly likely to admit any such thing,' he said. He looked around the room. 'The one thing about this place is there are ears listening everywhere. All I'm saying is you asked me to fix a problem, and it's been fixed.'

Bidlow stared at him. 'But . . . but . . . but,' he burbled, then stopped, at a loss for words, a look of horror on his face.

'Following orders is what they call it.' Higgins smiled. He leant over the desk so his mouth was close to Bidlow's ear. 'I believe there was a payment offered for a successful outcome,' he whispered. 'As I recall it was a hundred. But, in view of the awkward nature of the remedy, I think five hundred would be a fairer price, don't you?'

Bidlow stared at him, shocked. 'Five hundred pounds? Are you mad?'

'If it comes to it, I could always plead insanity,' said Higgins with a chuckle. 'Driven mad by my member of parliament employer who insisted I did an unpalatable thing. Not just unpalatable, very definitely illegal and a hanging offence. You'd be in the dock with me. That wouldn't look good, would it. MP on trial for murder.'

'This is lunacy!' burst out Bidlow. 'I never ordered you to kill anyone!'

'You told me to end a serious problem you had,' said Higgins. 'Your wife giving certain secrets of yours away to some Russian fortune-teller. Secrets that could cost you a pretty penny if they came to light, not to mention a big blot on your political career. If you even had a political career if the story came out. So I dealt with it.' He tapped the newspaper and gave Bidlow a smile. 'I'd prefer cash rather than a cheque.'

When she got to the St John depot, Rosa found an envelope marked for her attention.

'It was in the letter box this morning,' Chesney Warren told her.

'Possibly your friend at the BBC,' said Doris with a smile as they walked towards their ambulance.

Rosa opened it, and as she read it her face registered shock.

'What's the matter?' asked Doris. 'Bad news?'

Rosa held out the letter to her. It was unsigned. In block capital letters it said:

IF YOU APPEAR ON THE HENRY HALL SHOW ON TUESDAY YOU'LL DIE. I MEAN THAT LITERALLY. I'LL KILL YOU. I KNOW WHERE YOU LIVE. I KNOW WHERE YOU WORK.

'My God!' said Doris. 'This is some maniac, it must be.'

'But a maniac who knows where I live and work,' said Rosa, obviously concerned.

'You've got to take it to the police,' said Doris.

'Fortunately I've got one at home,' said Rosa.

'You've got to show this to him,' said Doris. 'Get them to test it for fingerprints, or whatever it is they do.' Then she asked, worried, 'What are you going to do about the show on Tuesday? Are you going to cancel being on it?'

'Am I hell!' said Rosa fiercely. 'If this lunatic thinks they're going to stop me being on the show, they've got another think coming.'

Coburg and Lampson stood on the small piece of platform where the body of Svetlana Rostova had been found.

'The logical conclusion is that she was killed inside the building and her body dumped here afterwards,' said Coburg thoughtfully. 'I doubt if she'd been here to flag down a passing train because she wasn't an employee of the REC; she just had a visitor's pass.'

'Makes sense.' Lampson nodded. He gestured along the platform in the direction of Hyde Park. 'Although there's always this foot tunnel from Hyde Park.'

'But anyone using that would take a chance of being hit by a passing train once they'd left the foot tunnel and joined the main line,' said Coburg. 'And if they were carrying a dead body there's always the risk of stumbling on the live electric rail.'

'All too risky,' agreed Lampson. 'So the foot tunnel's out.'

'Jeremy Purslake suggested the body might have been dumped from a train,' mused Coburg.

'I can't see it,' said Lampson. 'If it was from inside a carriage, someone would have seen what was going on. And I can't see it being dumped from the driver's cabin. Any driver would know a dead body being found would bring suspicion on him.'

'I agree,' said Coburg. 'But we can work out when the body was dumped, and talk to the drivers of the trains passing Down Street in that timeframe. See if any of them look shifty.' He gave a sigh as he added, 'But I agree, that's highly unlikely. As is Purslake's suggestion that her dead body had been put on the train roof and fell off as it passed Down Street.'

'He's just trying to divert attention away from the REC offices,' said Lampson. 'He doesn't like to think it was someone who works here who killed her.'

'Even if she was killed here, it doesn't mean it was by someone who works here,' said Coburg. 'Say she had one of her fortune-telling clients here?'

Lampson shook his head. 'They'd never have got past security upstairs.'

'No, you're right,' agreed Coburg. 'We need to talk to everyone who was here on Christmas Day. Security staff, workers, cleaners, everyone. Someone must have seen Svetlana around.'

'It's a big job,' said Lampson. 'The train drivers and people here.'

'It is,' said Coburg. 'So I suggest we split it. You take the train drivers who were on duty that day and I'll talk to the staff who were working here on Christmas Day.' He patted his pocket, where he'd put Svetlana's client cards. 'And along with that, we'll talk to this lot, her clients.'

That evening, Rosa showed Coburg the threatening letter. He read it, then looked at her, his expression troubled.

'It could be a joke,' she said.

'A not very funny one,' he said darkly. 'Have you ever had this sort of thing before?'

'No. You get the occasional person who hangs around wanting to talk to you after a gig, and some of them can be quite oddball. But nothing like this.'

He folded the letter up, replaced it in the envelope and put it in his pocket.

'I'll look into it, check it for fingerprints, that sort of thing. You never know. They might have done it before. But what are you going to do about the show on Tuesday?'

'I'm going to do it, of course.' She smiled. 'After all, I'll have my own police protection with me.'

CHAPTER EIGHT

Sunday 29th December 1940

Coburg and Rosa were settling down to breakfast when the phone rang. Rosa was the one who answered it, and she was surprised and pleased to hear the voice of her brother-in-law, Magnus, the Earl of Dawlish.

'Magnus,' she said. 'How lovely to hear from you.'

'I'm phoning because I read in *The Times* that you're doing a live broadcast the day after tomorrow. The Henry Hall show from the Finsbury Park Empire.'

'Yes,' said Rosa.

'Would it be possible to arrange a couple of tickets for Malcolm and myself? As you know, Malcolm is a huge fan of yours and it would make his year to come to see you in a live broadcast.'

'Leave it to me,' said Rosa. 'All I can do is ask the producer, which I'll do first thing tomorrow, and phone you back.'

'I shall keep my fingers crossed,' said Magnus.

Rosa was just heading back to the table when the phone rang again.

'I expect that's Magnus again with something he'd

'forgotten to say,' said Coburg through a mouthful of sausage and beans.

'Coburgs,' said Rosa.

'Sorry to trouble you at home, Mrs Coburg,' said a man's voice. 'This is Scotland Yard duty office. Is DCI Coburg there, please?'

'One moment,' said Rosa. She held out the phone towards Coburg. 'It's Scotland Yard for you.'

Coburg got up from the table and took the receiver. 'DCI Coburg.'

'It's the duty office, sir. I'm sorry to trouble you at home but we've got a note that if anything happens at Down Street you're to be contacted.'

'That's correct,' said Coburg. 'What's happened?'

'A dead man's been found outside the entrance. He's been identified as a Mr Grigor Rostov.'

'Is anyone from the Yard there?'

'Just a beat constable who was called by someone who works there.'

'Let him know I'm on my way. And put through a call to the medical team for someone to attend. Ideally, Dr Welbourne from UCH, if he's available.'

'Yes, sir.'

Coburg hung up and turned to Rosa. 'I'm afraid I've got to go. Another person's been killed at Down Street. The brother of the previous victim.'

'A family dispute?' asked Rosa.

'I don't think so,' said Coburg. 'I'll call you and let

you know if I'm going to be late.' He sat down again at the table. 'But first, I'm finishing my breakfast.'

Henry Bidlow munched without enthusiasm at the breakfast that had been laid before him by his housekeeper, Mrs Partly. Usually he enjoyed his Sunday breakfast of eggs, sausage and bacon with lashings of butter on his toast. Being a member of parliament for a rural constituency had major advantages; he didn't have to think about rationing. Rationing was for the peasantry, not for people like him. But today the sumptuous feast on his plate turned into ashes in his mouth as he thought about Martin Higgins. The absolute bastard! Even worse, a murdering bastard if he was to be believed. And there was no reason not to believe it.

He recalled his conversation with Higgins after he'd discovered that his wife, Eleanor, had been going to see a fortune-teller. 'You know how these people work, Higgins; they worm information out of the people who come to them so they can pretend they know things about them they could only learn "from the stars". That way lies blackmail.' He'd given a sarcastic laugh. 'It was only when I questioned her properly that Eleanor admitted she'd let slip to this woman about my links with Krupp. For God's sake, it's just business. But if it gets out that'll be the end of my political career. They'll be calling me "the MP for the Nazi Weapons Machine", or something similar. You've got to find this Russian fortune-teller woman, Higgins, and make sure she stays silent. A hundred pounds should do it, and tell her firmly there'll be no more forthcoming. And if she opens her mouth, I'll make sure she's deported back to Russia.'

Instead, according to Higgins, he'd killed her, thus solving 'the problem'. And now he was demanding five hundred pounds for it!

He cursed his wife, who was currently upstairs in bed, nursing one of her headaches. Stupid woman, to gabble that way to that Russian charlatan. What did she expect? A good beating, that's what, and that's what he'd given her.

The question was, what the hell was he going to do about Higgins?

It was raining heavily when Coburg arrived at Down Street. The pavement outside the building's entrance was awash, the rainwater running off the edge of the pavement and filling the already overflowing gutters. A police constable wearing a long waterproof cape was standing beside a man's body lying on the rain-soaked pavement. He saluted as Coburg got out of his car and came towards him.

'Morning, sir,' he said.

'Morning, Constable.' He looked down at the body of Grigor Rostov. 'Do we know how he died?'

'No, sir. I didn't want to disturb the body. And the

medical people haven't arrived yet.'

'Who found him?'

'A woman. She works here and she was leaving the building when she saw him. She thought at first he'd fainted or something. She's done first aid so she could tell he was dead.'

'Where is she?'

The constable gestured towards the black door of the REC. 'In there, sir. I couldn't see there was any reason for her to get soaked.'

'Good thinking, Constable.'

'Chief Inspector!'

Coburg turned and saw Dr Welbourne hurrying towards them, an umbrella held in one hand and his medical bag in the other. Welbourne stopped beside the body on the ground. 'Who is he, anyone know?'

'Grigor Rostov.'

'Any relation to the previous victim, Miss Rostova?'

'Her brother.'

Welbourne frowned. 'Well, we know there's a connection between the victims.'

'Can I leave you to do a quick examination in situ while I talk to the woman who found him?' asked Coburg. 'She's in the building.'

'Lucky her,' said Welbourne. He looked at the puddles of rainwater forming around the body and gave a rueful sigh. 'I'm going to ruin these trousers kneeling down in this.'

'You can use my cape, sir,' offered the constable. 'It's already wet, but the inside is dry.'

'Thank you, Constable,' said Welbourne gratefully. He looked at Coburg and murmured, 'This young man deserves to go far.'

As the constable took off his cape and handed it to Welbourne, Coburg asked him, 'What's the woman's name who found him?'

'Dorothy White, sir.'

'Thank you, Constable. And what's your name? '

'William Bone, sir. PC432.'

'Thank you. I'll remember that. You've done a good job here.' To Welbourne, he said, 'If you finish before I do, you'll find me in the building.'

Coburg was admitted to the building as soon as he rang the bell. Dorothy White, who was waiting for Coburg in a room just inside the entrance, was a woman in her forties. Coburg introduced himself and enquired gently, 'How did you come to be here at this time on a Sunday morning?'

'I work here,' she said. 'At the REC. I was leaving to go home when I saw this man lying on the pavement.'

'Did you recognise him?'

'No. I work on the switchboard. We don't see many of the other people who work here. I'd finished my shift and Betty Smith arrived to take over.' She looked at Coburg and asked warily, 'I got Betty to put through a call to my home to let my husband know I'm going

93

to be late. I hope that's alright?'

'Did you tell him why?'

'Not, just that there'd been an incident at work that meant I had to stay behind for a bit longer. George, that's my husband, is used to this sort of thing happening. Me getting held up cos something's happened. It's the war.'

Coburg nodded, then listened as she described her exit from the building and finding Rostov lying on the pavement by the door.

'What time was this?' he asked.

'About a quarter past eight,' she said. 'My shift finishes at eight in the morning. Most shifts do. It's twelve hours on, twelve hours off. It takes me longer to get up the stairs because the switchboard's right at the very bottom.'

Coburg thanked her and made a note of her address and telephone number, then told her she could go. He then went in search of the team leader in Rostov's department, a short man called Harris.

'Grigor left the office just after eight,' he said. 'He was the last to leave. Most of his colleagues like to make sure they're by the door by eight.'

'So he would have walked out into the street at what time, do you think?' asked Coburg.

'About five past or so,' said Harris.

So everyone else had already gone, thought Coburg as he mounted the stairs and headed upwards to the street level.

Dr Welbourne had finished his examination and was

arranging with an ambulance crew to take the body to University College Hospital.

'He was stabbed in the heart,' Welbourne told Coburg. 'Same as his sister. At first sight it looks like the same kind of weapon, but I'll know more when I've taken a proper look.'

'Thank you, Doctor,' said Coburg. He turned to the constable, who was now wringing wet, having lent his cape to the doctor. 'Well done here, Constable. I think you need to get back to your station and get out of those wet clothes. Tell them that was an order from DCI Coburg.'

'Yes, sir. Thank you, sir.'

Coburg then went to his car and put a radio call through to the duty office.

'I need an experienced WPC to accompany me to the family of a murder victim,' he said. 'I'm coming to Scotland Yard now to pick her up.'

'You seem in a good mood today, Martin,' said Pauline Higgins as she handed her husband his coffee.

Martin Higgins lounged on the settee, Sunday papers around him, and gave her a smile.

'I am, my love.' He beamed.

'Something good happen?' she asked.

'Something good is about to happen,' he told her cheerfully. 'I think I'm about to get a rather good bonus from old Bidlow.'

'If so, it's not before time,' snapped Pauline. 'That man takes advantage of you. You're too amenable for him, Martin. I've said it before.'

'You're right, my darling,' said Higgins. 'So yesterday I took him to task. I asked him – no, I *told* him – that for the work I did for him I deserved a proper reward. And not just tickets to some place he's got an interest in, but real money.'

'What did he say?' asked Pauline, stunned.

'He didn't exactly say yes, but that was the impression I got,' said Higgins confidently. 'I gave him something to think over, with my ultimatum about what I'd have to do if he didn't cough up.' He gave a smirk. 'He was quite taken aback, but I knew I'd hit a nerve. He'll cough up alright.'

'Oh, Martin, you are brave!' said Pauline admiringly. 'To stand up to him that way. Especially when everyone knows what a dreadful bully he is.'

'Yes, well, he ain't gonna bully me no more,' Martin said with smug determination.

Pauline looked at him with new respect.

'You sit there and read the paper,' she said. 'I'll just go and get you some biscuits to have with your coffee.'

With that, she went back to the kitchen.

Higgins looked at the paper. The murder of Lady Za Za was still featuring in the pages of the papers, all of which would make Bidlow sweat when he saw them.

Pauline was right when she described the MP as a

96

bully. When Bidlow had said 'when I questioned her properly', it meant that Bidlow had beaten the admission out of his wife. Not that there was any danger of Bidlow doing the same to Higgins: Bidlow may be a bully, but he was also a coward. Weak women were his favourite targets for physical violence, unless they had a male who would defend them: a brother or a son. With women Bidlow didn't know properly, he'd shout at them, but not physically assault them in case they had male relatives in the background who might come after him. So it was Mrs Bidlow, Eleanor, who was mostly on the receiving end.

Higgins had gone to see Lady Za Za, or Svetlana Rostova as he found out her real name was, and offered her money to promise not to reveal to anyone whatever Mrs Bidlow had told her. But not the hundred pounds – instead he'd offered her twenty pounds, fully intending to tell Bidlow he'd given her the hundred and he'd pocket the balance for himself. But when he saw in the paper that she'd been knifed to death, this new and more lucrative variation had come into his head. Five hundred pounds! And what was even more delicious was that Bidlow would surely be frightened of Higgins now at the thought that he, Higgins, was capable of killing someone. Yes, Bidlow would be in all sorts of panics.

The problem was that Bidlow might not pay up, and what would Higgins do about it? He could hardly go to the police and make a confession; that would end up with him on the gallows. The other option was to send an anonymous letter to this reporter who wrote about Lady Za Za's murder in the *Daily Globe*, Bert Marsh, hinting that Henry Bidlow MP might be involved in the woman's death. As soon as this Marsh character came around asking questions, that would send Bidlow's heart fluttering and the five hundred would be in Higgins's pocket.

Higgins smiled to himself. Justice for the way Bidlow had treated him like some peasant lackey for so long.

A uniformed WPC in her middle thirties was waiting for Coburg in reception area at Scotland Yard.

'WPC Valentine,' she introduced herself with a smart salute.

'Good morning, Valentine. We're going to Paddington to advise a woman her husband's just been murdered. She's quite young with a small baby and when I met her before she seemed quite a stressed person. I'd like you there in case she needs emotional assistance.'

'Yes, sir.'

'Have you had much experience of this sort of thing?'

'Too much, I'm afraid, sir, with all this bombing. Every day I seem to have to tell someone one of their family's been killed.'

When they pulled up outside the small terraced house in Paddington, Coburg noticed Priscilla Rostov peering out at the police car from behind her curtains. She was at the door by the time they arrived at the house.

'If you're looking for Grigor, he isn't home yet,' she said. 'I assume he's working late because he's usually home by now.'

'It's about Grigor I need to talk to you,' said Coburg.

'Why? He's not in any trouble, is he?' she asked in alarm.

'May we come in?' asked Coburg.

Mrs Rostov hesitated, then opened the door wide. 'But don't make any noise,' she whispered urgently. 'I've just put Mary down in her cot.'

They walked past her into the house and she ushered them into the front room.

'What is it?' she asked, puzzled.

'I'm afraid to tell you your husband has been killed, Mrs Rostov.'

She stared at him, shocked. 'Killed?'

She fell back onto a settee, her mouth opening and closing in shocked disbelief. Coburg gestured for the WPC to sit down on the settee next to her, then took a chair opposite them.

'He was stabbed to death as he left his office this morning.'

'Stabbed?' She stared at him, disbelief and incomprehension on her expression. 'He can't be dead.'

'I'm afraid he is.'

Suddenly anger flared up in her face. 'The same as that bloody mad sister of his! This is her fault!'

'At the moment we're trying to establish a motive—' began Coburg, but he was cut short by her leaping to her feet and screaming at him, 'This is your fault! You killed him! He told you about Stalin's assassination squads killing the families of his victims. They killed Svetlana and now they've killed Grigor. He told you but you didn't give him any protection!'

Her voice had risen louder and louder, and now they heard the baby crying, woken by her mother's shouting. Priscilla Rostov suddenly rushed out of the room, calling, 'Mummy's coming!'

Coburg rose to his feet and said to Valentine ruefully, 'I think we'd best leave her. I don't think there's much we can do at the moment. I'll run you back to the Yard.'

'You don't need to do that, sir,' said Valentine. 'I can walk back.'

'I've got something I need to drop off there, anyway,' said Coburg.

He could hear the baby still crying upstairs as they left the house. Both brother and sister dead, he thought. Was Priscilla Rostov right? Had he been at fault in not giving Grigor protection?

After Coburg had returned WPC Valentine to Scotland Yard, he went upstairs to the technical department and handed them the anonymous threatening letter and envelope.

'You'll find my fingerprints on it, and also my wife's,' he said. 'If you can check it over and see anyone's you can find and identify, that would be great.'

'It'll be a good idea to take your prints, Chief Inspector,' said the technician. 'So we can count you out.'

Coburg nodded, and handed the technician a blank sheet of paper. 'I've brought this in. My wife's and my fingerprints are both on it for you to check against the letter.'

Coburg let his fingerprints be taken, then headed home, the accusation that Priscilla Rostov had made against him nagging him all the way.

'The brother of the woman who was killed?' said Rosa when he told her about the murder he'd been called to.

'And it looks as if he was killed the same way. Stabbed in the heart. In this case, as he left work to go home. My worry is for his widow and her baby daughter. I don't know whether she has any family to help her.'

'She lives in Paddington, you say.'

'That's right.' Coburg told her the address.

'My St John station is in Paddington, and my co-driver, Doris, is a nurse at Paddington Hospital. She seems to know everyone around there; she might even know this Priscilla Rostov, if she had her baby at the hospital. Why don't I have a word with her and see if she knows the family, and what help Mrs Rostov might have?'

'That's a lovely idea.' Coburg nodded. 'Anything you can find would be great.'

CHAPTER NINE

Monday 30th December 1940

'Grigor Rostov was killed yesterday,' Coburg told his sergeant as Lampson climbed into the car next morning. 'Stabbed, just like his sister. A long-bladed knife straight into the heart.'

'Bloody hell!' said Lampson as he put the car into gear. 'What's going on? First the sister, then the brother. Why?'

'Priscilla Rostov had a go at me about what Grigor told us,' said Coburg. 'About Stalin's paranoia about the families of the people he executed. Bumping them off to stop any chance of them taking revenge on him, and using his assassination squads to do it.'

'You think this is what happened?'

'I don't know,' admitted Coburg. 'It seems a bit extreme. But then, from what Grigor told us about the Terrors under Stalin, it happens. And both Grigor and Svetlana were stabbed the same way.'

* * *

Bert Marsh sat at his desk looking at his notes and weighing up the merits of competing stories. There was one about a duchess who'd been found having sex with her footman in the Anderson air raid shelter in her garden, and by the footman's wife, who wanted revenge and compensation – but particularly compensation – which is why she'd contacted Bert Marsh about it. The other story was about a bulldog puppy that had been born with two heads. Now that was tailor-made for a sensationalist and patriotic headline, complete with picture: *Two-headed bulldog takes on the Nazis*. But he favoured the one about the duchess. Stories of adulterous sex involving the upper class were always a winner, and the additional attraction in this case was the footman's angry wife. Angry wives who wanted to get back at their husbands were always responsive to a touch of flattery and a bit of rumpy-pumpy. He was just looking up the number of the footman's wife – Mrs Edie Boot, a very appropriate name, he thought – when a cough made him look up into the concerned face of Wes Morgan.

'What's up, Wes?' he asked. 'You look like you've lost a shilling and found a tanner.'

'Did you hear about St Paul's?' asked Morgan.

'No,' said Marsh. 'What about it?'

'It got hit in last night's bombing.'

Marsh looked at him, shocked. 'Badly hit?'

Morgan shook his head. 'Amazingly, no. I heard

that twenty-eight incendiaries were dropped on it but somehow the fire crews kept the damage down. There was a great photo taken of it, which will be in all tomorrow's papers. The cathedral wreathed in masses of thick smoke, but with that famous domed roof still standing.'

'Who took it?'

'Herbert Mason from the *Daily Mail*, but they've agreed the picture's so important they're letting the other papers have it.' He shook his head sorrowfully. 'The truce, if there really was one, is well and truly over. They reckon the bombing raids last night caused more damage by fires across London than the original Great Fire of London. 1666. So, the worst for nearly three hundred years. Those bastard Germans.' Morgan was just about to move on, when a thought struck him. 'By the way, you know that bloke Grigor Rostov you were after.'

'Yes?'

'He's dead. He was stabbed yesterday.'

Marsh looked at him, momentarily stunned, then his face lit up with pleasure. 'That's brilliant!' he said, delighted.

'Brilliant?' asked Marsh, bewildered.

'First the sister, now the brother. There's a *real* story here!'

A report on the threatening letter was waiting for Coburg when he arrived at Scotland Yard. The only fingerprints on the letter were those of Coburg and Rosa. The envelope had multiple fingerprints on it, but the technical staff believed that the person who wrote the actual letter had been wearing gloves.

'No luck?' asked Lampson, seeing the disappointment on his boss's face as he read the report.

'No,' said Coburg. 'Whoever wrote the letter wore gloves, so no fingerprints.' He put the letter in his drawer and took out Svetlana's box of client cards. 'Right,' he said. 'Let's go through these and see if any of them might be worth talking to.'

When Bert Marsh called at the house in Paddington where Priscilla Rostov lived, he found not just a grieving widow but a furiously angry one. When he introduced himself and told her he was from the *Daily Globe*, she reached inside the house, picked up a broom where it had been propped up just inside the front door and began to beat him with it.

'You had my husband killed!' she shouted as she lashed at him. 'That stuff you wrote saying he was hiding something made someone think it was true and they killed him!'

'No!' he pleaded, putting his hands and arms over his head to protect himself, which led to Priscilla using the broom to hit him in the body instead. 'That wasn't me! Someone else added that! I want to find out who killed him. Bring his killer to justice.' As she hit him again, he blurted out in desperation, 'The police are the ones! They knew his sister had been murdered; they should have guessed he might be in danger as well.'

Priscilla stopped hitting him and looked at him suspiciously.

'Did he tell you that?' she demanded.

Marsh hesitated, his instincts telling him that she knew something. Something that would put him on the right track.

'He hinted at it,' he lied. Then he looked at her in appeal. 'Please, talk to me about him. We might be able to find out who did it.'

Priscilla hesitated, then leant the broom back against the wall.

'Alright, you can come in. But be quiet. My baby daughter's asleep. At the moment my mother's with her, but she wakes up if there are loud noises.'

Like you shouting at me and smacking me with a broom, thought Marsh, but he forced a grateful smile and stepped in.

Coburg and Lampson had made a list of the forty clients on Svetlana's cards, and then divided it into two separate lists of twenty names.

'This way we can get through them quicker,' said Coburg. 'You take one list; I'll take the other.'

Svetlana had put down the addresses of the clients,

so at Lampson's suggestion they had put the ones with expensive addresses on one list, which was to be for Coburg to investigate, while Lampson would talk to the others.

'I'm not sure if this is the right way to do it,' commented Coburg doubtfully.

'It's the only way, guv,' said Lampson. 'Whether you like it or not, you being the Hon. Saxe-Coburg will have clout with the ones in Kensington and Knightsbridge; they'll talk to you much more than they will to me, some lower-class oik from Somers Town. Especially if it's delicate stuff about their lifestyles, which I bet it will be if a fortune-teller's involved. You know the way these fortune-tellers work; they get the mark talking about themself and their family so they can make up something that sounds real.'

'You sound like you disapprove of fortune-tellers.' Coburg smiled.

'I had an aunt who used to do it, reading tea leaves,' said Lampson. 'At least, that was what she told people she was doing, but the truth was she made it all up depending on what she'd found out about them.'

'So she was a con artist?'

'She was indeed, and very good at it. But it taught me not to trust anything like that.'

'I had a slightly different experience when I was in France during the First War,' said Coburg. 'A French gypsy woman came round offering to read the men's fortunes. For money, obviously. And some of her predictions were surprisingly accurate.'

'She'd been making enquiries about them,' said Lampson.

'I'm not sure if she had the time,' said Coburg. 'She arrived and just set up.'

'With her crystal ball?' Lampson grinned.

'No, she read people's palms and felt the bumps on their heads.' Coburg smiled. 'As it was a war situation, some of the men had more bumps than others. But she did predict that some would be coming into money, and those did when it came to the nightly card games we played in the trenches in between enemy attacks.'

'It's all a con,' said Lampson. He looked at the lists. 'Some of these people look to be quite important people. You wonder how they got suckered into this?'

'Most people are looking for something,' said Coburg. 'Some go for religion. In a way I suppose astrology is no different from most other religions. It's all based on belief and taking things on trust.'

'Like I say, the ideal con,' said Lampson. 'No real proof to back it up.'

Marsh sat on the sofa, notebook and pencil in hand, as Priscilla Rostov told him about Stalin's assassination squads.

Not a bad looker, he thought. A bit on the scrawny side; his preference was for bustier women with bigger hips, hips he could get hold of, but women of any size or shape were fine by him. He'd noticed they were especially vulnerable to his approaches when they'd just had bad news, as Priscilla Rostov had. The friendly comforting arm around their shoulders, them laying their head on his chest to cry. In need of sympathy and solace. A comforting cuddle that gradually developed into something else as they unleashed their grief and his hands slid inside their blouses to find their bra, his lips finding theirs.

Looking at Priscilla Rostov and listening to her anger being vented, he knew it was too soon to try anything on with her at this moment, but later, he was sure she'd respond to his expressions of deep sympathy as so many had before her. Not everyone, of course. There'd been women who'd been so shocked they'd struck him, and in one case a woman had sent her brother to the offices of the *Daily Globe* to sort him out, and Marsh had only been saved from a bad beating by the newspaper's security staff. Marsh had protested his innocence, of course, claiming the woman had misinterpreted his friendly, sympathetic arm around the shoulder in her time of grief, but it had taught him to be careful about if and when he made his move. He took his eyes off her tantalising small breasts and nodded as he put on his 'listening attentively' face. She was talking about Stalin and what she said Grigor had called his assassination squads.

'They're killing the families of Stalin's victims to stop them avenging their murders. After they killed his sister, Svetlana, Grigor knew it was likely he'd be next. He begged the police for protection, but that Detective Inspector Coburg did nothing. And now Grigor's dead.'

'So you think the Russians killed your husband and his sister?'

'Yes.'

This is gold dust, thought Marsh as he wrote the words 'Stalin's assassins' in his notebook. *This was worth a raise.*

'Her name's Priscilla Rostov,' Rosa told Doris. 'Her husband was murdered recently. She's got a young baby and I was wondering if she knows anyone that could help her. You know, if she's got family. My husband was worried if she'd be able to cope on her own.'

Rosa and Doris were at the ambulance station giving their ambulance a clean, using a bucket of soapy water and a sponge and a cloth each.

'You say she lives in Paddington?' asked Doris.

Rosa nodded. 'It's possible her baby was born locally. I wondered if you could make enquiries because you know the area.'

'She's Russian, you say?'

'No, she's English. Her husband was Russian.'

Doris nodded. 'I'll ask around, and check out at the hospital.'

'Thanks,' said Rosa.

'Rosa!'

They looked around and saw Chesney Warren looking at them through the open window in his office. He held up the telephone receiver. 'It's the BBC!'

'I hope they haven't changed their mind about having me on the show,' Rosa said to Doris, concerned, as she hurried into the building. 'Maybe their first choice has recovered from whatever was wrong with them.'

'It's that Mr Fawcett,' whispered Warren as he handed the receiver to her.

'Hello, Mr Fawcett,' said Rosa.

'I'm terribly sorry to disturb you at work,' apologised Fawcett. 'But I've been talking to Henry about tomorrow's show, and we've got a suggestion we'd like you to consider. On your second number, "The Saints", how would you feel if, after you've done the first two verses and choruses, Henry and the orchestra came in to back you, along with the orchestra's singers. We thought this would give a really rousing version of the song. And, if you're agreeable, we thought we'd use it to close the show. The big finale.'

The finale? Rosa felt a sense of excitement at the words, but she also realised it would reduce her own solo spot to just one number. It was as if Fawcett could read her mind, because he then added, 'Because that would mean it would leave you with just one number on your own solo spot, we'd be happy for you to select a second to follow "Stardust". As we'll be doing the rousing "Saints" at the end, the other song doesn't have to be an up-tempo number. We'll both be happy with whatever you choose.'

'Mr Fawcett, I'd be delighted. You're sure that's alright with Henry?'

'Oh yes. In fact, he suggested it. He's a great fan of yours. Oh, and I've arranged for your husband's ticket to be waiting for him at the box office.'

Rosa steeled herself before asking her next question. She'd been planning to phone Fawcett but she'd been unsure how he'd react to her request. The last time she'd asked for tickets for a broadcast for a friend it had been when Dennis Main was producer, and he'd been quite curt in his response. 'We don't do that sort of thing,' he'd told her sharply. 'No favourites. Everyone has to go through the ticket office.'

'Actually, Mr Fawcett, I've had another request for a couple of tickets. Edgar's brother is the Earl of Dawlish and he'd love to come and see the show with his companion.'

'No problem!' said Fawcett. 'The Earl of Dawlish, you say? Excellent!' There was a note of regretful apology in his voice as he added, 'However, I think that might have to be it. If word got out . . .'

'It won't, I promise you,' Rosa assured him. 'Thank you so much, and I promise there'll be no more requests from me.'

It was with a sense of relief that Rosa replaced the receiver.

'Still on for tomorrow, then?' asked Warren.

'Yes,' said Rosa. 'Even better, I get to do three numbers, one of them with me and the Henry Hall Orchestra to finish the show.'

'That's stardom!' Warren beamed. 'I shall be listening tomorrow, along with my wife and her family, and I can proudly say to them: "I work with her."' He looked at her quizzically. 'Unless, of course, you can arrange tickets for us for the show.' He laughed when he saw the look of alarm on her face. 'I was joking, honestly. I heard what you said just now about not asking for more tickets. I couldn't resist winding you up.'

Rosa gave him a rueful smile. 'At least after tomorrow it will mean there'll be no more phone calls from the BBC interrupting things here.'

'You don't know that,' said Warren. 'You might get a flood of offers.'

'If so, I'll tell them to write to me at our flat. The occasional phone call from Mr Fawcett may be just about acceptable because of the short notice, but the ambulance work is what's important.'

CHAPTER TEN

Tuesday 31st December 1940

Lampson was waiting outside his terraced house when Coburg arrived to pick him up the following morning. He handed his inspector a newspaper as they changed seats, Lampson getting behind the wheel.

'The *Daily Globe*?' said Coburg. 'The rag we had the other day?'

'This time it's got a piece about Grigor Rostov being killed,' said Lampson.

He put the car into gear and they moved off, while Coburg read the piece in the paper.

'This is outrageous!' Coburg burst out. 'He blames me for Grigor Rostov's death.' He read aloud, his voice showing his annoyance: '"According to Grigor Rostov's grief-stricken widow, her husband told DCI Coburg he and his sister had been under threat of death by order of the Soviet dictator Josef Stalin. Grigor pleaded with DCI Coburg for protection after his sister had been murdered, but the chief inspector refused, and now Grigor Rostov himself has been stabbed to death, killed the same way his sister was."'

'He didn't ask us for police protection,' said Lampson, equally outraged. 'He told us he thought the Russians were responsible for his sister's death, but he never said anything about himself needing protection from them.'

Coburg scowled.

'I suppose he was asking us in an oblique sort of way,' he admitted. 'If the Russians killed his sister because they were worried she might do something vengeful after their father was executed, then it follows they might do the same to him.'

'*If*,' stressed Lampson. '*If* the Russians killed his sister.'

Coburg let out a sigh.

'The trouble is, the way the paper puts it, questions will be asked. I think I'm going to be in the firing line over this.'

'*We're* going to be in the firing line,' Lampson corrected him. 'We saw him together.'

'Thanks for the support, Ted, but it's the senior officer who's responsible. That's the way the top brass will see it.'

It was indeed the way the top brass saw it, as Coburg discovered when they got to Scotland Yard and the chief inspector was summoned to Superintendent Allison's office. Allison brandished a copy of the *Daily Globe* at him.

'Have you seen this?' he demanded.

'I have, sir,' said Coburg.

'So have the commissioner, and the Home Secretary. They are furious, Coburg. Is it true? Did Rostov ask you for police protection?'

'No, sir. He told us he thought one of Stalin's assassination squads were responsible for his sister's death because of what had happened to their father.'

Coburg then related the recent history of the Rostovs, their father's execution and their escape to Britain.

'Have you investigated whether these assassination squads exist?' asked Allison.

'I intend to talk to MI5 about them.'

'It's a pity you didn't talk to them before this Grigor Rostov was killed,' said Allison angrily.

'Yes, sir,' said Coburg, chastened. It would be no use trying defend himself by saying that it was just one line of enquiry, or that he hadn't had time to talk to MI5. Two people, both Russian immigrants, had been killed and the police had been blamed for the second murder in print. Detective Chief Inspector Edgar Saxe-Coburg had been named and shamed as the person responsible. The big question for Coburg was, was the *Daily Globe* right? Had he been lax in not giving Grigor Rostov police protection?

Martin Higgins was making for the bus stop on his way to work when he saw the placard attached to the newspaper stand: *Another Russian Murdered in*

London. He bought a copy of the *Daily Globe* and read the story on the front page as he walked to the bus stop. So Lady Za Za's brother was dead, stabbed to death the same way as his sister, and by Stalin's assassins, according to the paper.

He stuffed the paper in his pocket as he neared the stop and saw his bus approaching, taking the paper out again once he'd found a seat. He wondered what Bidlow's reaction would be when he saw the story. Would he believe the stuff about Stalin's assassins? If he did then he wouldn't pay Higgins. He might even sack him for trying to use a lie to blackmail him. But if Bidlow tried that, Higgins had Krupp up his sleeve. Higgins had seen the exchanges of letters between the German arms company and Bidlow authorising the MP to act for them, including keeping them informed of Britain's military and weapons requirements. The first of these exchanges had been in 1937 and 1938, before war was declared, but the later ones since September 1939 were evidence of treason.

Higgins had recently managed to get into the cabinet in Bidlow's office where the correspondence was kept, but he discovered that all the correspondence and any other documents relating to the relationship between Bidlow and Krupp had gone. Bidlow had obviously destroyed that evidence. But one lot of evidence he couldn't destroy: his bank accounts showing payments from Krupp to Bidlow.

Higgins knew that Bidlow kept his bank accounts in his safe at home, but that didn't matter. Higgins would threaten to tell the authorities about the deal and tell Bidlow that if he did that, they'd demand the accounts from Bidlow's bank. And that would be the end for Bidlow. Not just of his political career but maybe his life. Treason was a capital offence.

For the moment, Higgins decided to keep up the pretence that it had been him who'd killed Grigor Rostov because he was sure that Svetlana had passed on information to her brother. He pondered over asking Bidlow for a further five hundred for killing Grigor, but decided against it. He'd leave it at the same five hundred for both of them. And if Bidlow balked at paying, then he'd throw in the Krupp business. Either way, Bidlow was going to cough up.

'All ready for the big broadcast today?' asked Doris as Rosa arrived at the ambulance station.

'I am,' said Rosa.

Doris looked around the yard, at the parked-up vehicles, and said, 'It must be so different from working here. I mean, all those people in the theatre listening to you, and the thousands listening at home.'

'Both satisfying in their different ways,' said Rosa. 'In fact, I'm not sure that I don't prefer this. It's definitely more satisfying feeling you're saving lives than being in front of an audience.'

'I couldn't do it,' said Doris. 'Standing in front of all those people? I'd be terrified.'

'It's what you get used to,' said Rosa.

'By the way, that Mrs Rostov you asked me about,' said Doris. 'You don't have to worry. I asked around about her and it seems she's got a mum and family who live near here, so she'll be alright. They'll be looking after her.'

'There's a change of plan today,' Coburg told Lampson unhappily. 'Instead of talking to Svetlana's clients, we've got to check with Inspector Hibbert at MI5 about these Soviet Russian assassination squads.'

'The superintendent's orders?' asked Lampson.

Coburg nodded.

'D'you think they might be right?' asked Lampson. 'That the Russians did it?'

'I don't know,' admitted Coburg. 'It's possible because whoever killed them did it very professionally. A slim knife in the right spot, between the ribs and into the heart. That doesn't sound like an upset client of an astrologer, but who's to say? Hopefully Inspector Hibbert will have some information for us.'

They drove to St James's Street, where MI5 had taken over part of a former MGM building as their London sub-office, having been forced to move from their former temporary base at Wormwood Scrubs prison after it had been badly damaged by bombing.

'I preferred being at the Scrubs rather than this place,' complained Inspector Hibbert as he walked them through a maze of corridors towards his office. 'Alright, we got bombed, but so's every place in London getting bombed. At least at the Scrubs we were away from all the top brass so we hardly ever saw them. Here at St James's Street we're right in the middle of them all, the Admiralty, the Cabinet, the Home Office, who all want to poke their noses in.' Then he added with a rueful sigh, 'Though it could be worse; I could have been sent to join the rest of them at Blenheim Palace. That's where most of them have gone.'

'I would have thought Blenheim Palace would have been preferential. Out in the country in Oxfordshire, away from the bombing.'

'Not for me,' said Hibbert. 'I like London.' He pushed open a door and ushered them into his office. 'So, what can I do for you? I don't expect this is a social visit.'

'There have been two murders recently, a Russian brother and sister.'

'The Rostovs.' Hibbert nodded. 'I saw it in the paper.'

Coburg looked at him, amused. 'The only paper I saw that featured the murders was the *Daily Globe*. I'd have thought you'd be more of a *Times* or *Telegraph* man.'

'In this business we need to check all the papers. You never know when someone's using them to send coded messages. So, what do you need from me? As far as I know, neither was a security risk.'

'We saw Grigor Rostov after his sister was stabbed to death, and he told us about their life in Stalin's Russia, and how they had to escape after their father, a general in the Red Army, was found guilty of treason and executed.'

'Along with many thousands of others,' said Hibbert. 'Stalin's as bad as Hitler. They make a right pair, tied up with their treaty.'

'According to Grigor, Stalin has assassination squads out across the globe killing off people related to the ones he executed because he's paranoid they might take revenge on him.'

'Yes, that's what we heard,' said Hibbert. 'Look at the way he had Trotsky bumped off.'

'That was in Mexico,' said Coburg. 'Do you know if any of Stalin's assassins are operating here?'

'Not as far as we know,' said Hibbert. 'Though that's not to say they aren't. There are all manner of spies and seriously dodgy people inside the Soviet Embassy. I have to admit our concentration has been on trained killers working for the Germans and Italians, and those would be after Churchill and our top people. We've come across a few of those and neutralised them. But Russian assassins?' He shook his head. 'Not as far as I know. Mind, in view of what's happened to the Rostovs, I'll alert our people to the possibility.'

Martin Higgins knocked at the door of Henry Bidlow's office, and at the command 'Come!' entered and placed the copy of the *Daily Globe* on Bidlow's desk.

'What are you bringing that rag in for?' demanded Bidlow.

'For the continuation of the story.' Higgins smirked.

Bidlow read the story, then looked at Higgins, bewildered.

'They say it's Stalin's people,' he said.

Higgins winked.

'And as long as they think that, we'll be alright,' he said.

Bidlow's expression changed to one of horror. 'You don't mean that you . . .?'

Higgins put a finger to his lips to silence the MP, then winked again. 'It was possible that the lady we talked about had said something to him. Better safe than sorry, that was my feeling. I'm sure you'll agree.' He bent down and whispered, 'I assume you'll be making a withdrawal from your bank very soon?'

Bidlow gulped. 'Look, it's not that easy,' he blustered.

'I'm sure it is for a man in your position.' Higgins smiled. Then he leant in closer and whispered, 'Krupp.'

With that, he picked up his copy of the *Daily Globe* and left, taking satisfaction in the look of agony on Henry Bidlow's face.

Bella Wilson stood in the shadowy area of the building directly opposite the block of flats where Coburg and Rosa lived. She'd been here for half an hour, waiting to see if Rosa would be heading for Finsbury Park. Wilson had pulled the hood of her coat over her head in an attempt to hide her henna-red hair. Along with the tattoo of a spider on one side of her forehead, which she'd had done some years before, these would make her stand out in a crowd, hence the necessity of the hood. She didn't want Rosa spotting her.

Once upon a time the name of Bella Wilson had been lauded in jazz clubs up and down the country. There'd been appearances on the wireless. Adulation whenever she stepped onto a stage and sang, her voice raspy, but adored by the people who loved Billie Holiday. It was true that Wilson had copied the immortal Billie, but that was because there was no one else in Britain singing Lady Day. They said Billie's voice was the result of alcohol and heroin, and so Wilson had roughened her voice with gin, brandy, whisky, vodka, whatever was on hand. But not heroin. Heroin was a step too far, she'd known too many people die, and she wanted to live and savour success. But then, one day, success began to slip away. Maybe the alcohol had made her voice too rough, or maybe the audiences in England wanted something more than a shadow of Billie H. Wilson could date it to the arrival on the scene of Rosa Weeks. Weeks played piano, and well, and when she sang there were echoes of Ella Fitzgerald's sweetness of tone. As time went by, Wilson began to lose gigs. Admittedly, some of these losses were due to her problems with alcohol. Hell, she was only doing what

Billie had been doing: turning up late or not at all because she was out of it. That's what jazz fans wanted, someone with a dysfunctional life. Then she began to be aware that when she lost a gig it was often Rosa Weeks who replaced her. And some of them had been big gigs, gigs that could kickstart her career. Like this Henry Hall one. That had been hers. The producer had called her to have lunch and told her it was hers. And then, out of the blue, she'd had a call to say there were problems with the contract and they regretted she wouldn't be able to appear.

What problems? she'd asked. But they never got back to her. And the next thing she knew it was in the paper that her spot in the show was now being taken by Rosa Weeks.

For Wilson, it had been the last straw. This past year – no, longer than that – as her career languished in the toilet, that bitch Rosa Weeks had risen, riding to success on Wilson's bad luck. But had it just been bad luck, or had Weeks had something to do with it? A whispered word in a producer's ear, slagging Wilson off?

Yes, there had to be something like that going on. Well, this is where it ended. She'd sent a warning: cancel the Henry Hall gig or die. Now was the time for the truth. Was Rosa going to go to Finsbury Park, or had she pulled out? If Rosa appeared, Wilson would follow her. There was no direct bus from Piccadilly to Finsbury Park – she'd need to change – so if Rosa appeared and went to the bus stop, it was all about if she caught a second bus to Finsbury Park. If she did, then her fate was sealed. Wilson's fingers settled on the handle of the knife in her pocket, a knife with a long slim blade. It would be very simple. Creep up behind her and strike, the blade sliding in between Rosa's ribs and into her heart, that was the plan. The only question was: when? On the second bus?

Her heart gave a jump as Rosa appeared and walked to the bus stop. Wilson crossed the road and followed her. A bus pulled up and Rosa got on, Wilson letting others follow Rosa before she got on herself and took a seat four behind Rosa.

The telephone was ringing as Coburg and Lampson entered their office. Lampson picked it up and said, 'DCI Coburg's office.' He listened for a few seconds then held out the receiver towards Coburg. 'It's the Earl of Dawlish.'

Coburg took the receiver. 'Magnus,' he said. 'What can I do for you?'

'What time are you leaving for Finsbury Park?'

'I'll be heading there straight from work. I shall be leaving at a quarter to five to allow for traffic and other hold-ups, along with finding a place to park. I want to make sure I'm in my seat well before the show starts. I understand it actually begins with a compère coming on a quarter of an hour before the actual live broadcast, just to get the audience in the mood.'

'In that case we'll pick you up,' said Magnus.

'Malcolm will drive us. That way we can bring Rosa home in the Bentley rather than that police car of yours. Otherwise people might think she's being arrested. If you're agreeable to that, I'll see you in the main reception at Scotland Yard at a quarter to five.'

Coburg thought about his proposal, then said, 'Yes, thank you for that, Magnus. I'll see you at a quarter to five.'

He hung up and took the car keys from his pocket and put them on Lampson's desk.

'It seems my brother's arranging transport for Rosa's appearance this evening, so I'll leave you with the car. Can you pick me up at the flat in the morning?'

'No problem,' said Lampson, smiling as he picked up the keys. 'I might even take Terry out for a short run in it. That'll make his day.' He looked at the clock. 'It's one o'clock. What's the plan for the rest of the afternoon?'

Coburg tapped the copy of the *Daily Globe* lying on his desk.

'I think a visit to this Bert Marsh is in order.'

The bus pulled to a halt and Rosa got off, Wilson following. Rosa crossed the road to another bus stop; Wilson continued to follow her. She looked up at the list of the main destinations for buses from this stop, and saw the words 'Finsbury Park'. So, Rosa was going there after all.

Wilson's fingers tightened around the handle of the knife. Do it now, before Rosa got on the bus? But no, there was too big a crowd by the bus stop.

A bus pulled up and Rosa got on. Wilson let others get on, then boarded the bus.

It would have to be when they got to Finsbury Park. Once Rosa had got off the bus and was walking along the street towards the theatre, that would be the time to move in for the kill. Rosa had been warned and decided to ignore it, so this was her fault.

When the bus pulled up at Finsbury Park, Rosa stepped off, Wilson keeping a safe distance behind Rosa, her fingers on the knife. Any moment now, once they'd turned the corner into St Thomas's Road.

Rosa turned into St Thomas's Road and Wilson followed, closing in on her target. Then Wilson stopped. Instead of an empty street, the pavements, and even the roadway, were filled with people all making for the Finsbury Park Empire. As Rosa neared the ornate façade of the theatre, she was surrounded by people thrusting autograph books at her.

Damn! thought Wilson. *I should have thought of that. Whenever there's a BBC show being broadcast live, people gather near the venue to get a sight of, and autographs of, the celebrities appearing.*

Angrily, she stopped and made her way back to Seven Sisters Road. The moment would just have to wait until after the show had been done and the crowds had gone.

Rosa would be alone then. That would be the answer. Catch her as she came out of the theatre and making for the bus stop to go home. That would be the time.

Coburg and Lampson stood by the entrance doors to the reception area of the *Daily Globe* and watched as a door at the back of the area opened and a bulky man in an ill-fitting suit appeared. He went to the reception desk. The receptionist pointed towards Coburg and Lampson, and he came towards them, suspicion writ large on his face.

'You wanted me?' he asked warily.

'If you're Bert Marsh,' said Coburg.

Marsh nodded, still wary. The two detectives produced their warrant cards and showed them to him.

'DCI Coburg and DS Lampson from Scotland Yard,' said Coburg.

'The police, eh,' said Marsh, suddenly defiant. 'I thought you'd be after me sooner or later. Come to drag me off to Holloway for revealing the location of Churchill's underground bunker?' He sneered at them. 'My editor will fight it if you try. The point is that everyone knows about it, so it's not like I was really revealing a state secret.' He held out his hands to them. 'But slap the handcuffs on me, let's make a big show of it. The might of the police sent to crush the little man.'

'We're not here to talk to you about what may or may not be Churchill's secret bunker, as you call it. We're interested in the murder of Grigor Rostov and your allegation that I was to blame. That's libel.'

'That wasn't my view, that was his widow's. All I did was report it. I can't be sued for reporting what someone else says.'

'Don't you think it's more likely that your story was the reason he was killed? All that insinuation that he knew something.'

'Maybe he did. And you can't hang his death on me. I was only doing my job. You were the ones who failed to protect him.' He sneered and scowled as he added, 'It was the Russians who did it.'

'Do you have proof of that?' asked Coburg. 'I ask because we checked with MI5 and they have no knowledge of Soviet hit squads operating in Britain.'

'I've got what his widow told me,' said Marsh. 'The same as Grigor told you. About Stalin's assassination squads. I suppose you're going to try and gag me from writing any more about him being killed?'

'Not at all,' said Coburg. 'I believe in the freedom of the press. That's one of the reasons we're fighting this war.' Then he added thoughtfully, 'Of course, there's always the danger that if it was the Russians who killed Grigor, they may wonder if you're hiding anything about the conversation you had when you interviewed him.'

'I never interviewed him,' snapped Marsh. 'He refused to talk to me.'

'But you talked to his widow,' said Coburg. 'They may want to know how much you found out from her about what he said. And how dangerous it might be to them.'

Marsh's mouth opened in alarm as what Coburg was implying sank in.

'You mean *I* might be in danger?' he asked hoarsely.

'That depends what you write,' said Coburg.

He and Lampson turned to exit to the street, but Marsh rushed forward and barred their way.

'I demand police protection,' he said agitatedly.

Coburg nodded. 'We shall consider your request,' he said, and headed once more for the door.

'If you don't give it to me now, I'll write in the paper that you refused to protect me!' shouted Marsh.

'Which might make the killer wonder what you know that makes you so desperate for the need for protection,' said Coburg. 'Goodbye, Mr Marsh.'

As they left the building, Lampson chuckled. 'I thought he was going to have a heart attack when the penny dropped about what you said about him being a possible target. Do you think he might be at risk?'

'I don't know,' said Coburg. 'It depends on why Svetlana and Grigor were killed. In view of what happened to Grigor, I'll put a small team on him to see if anyone goes after him.'

'Are you going to tell him?' asked Lampson.

'No,' said Coburg. 'I think someone like him needs to understand that saying something in print can have a bad effect on people's lives. He might think twice about that in future.'

CHAPTER ELEVEN

Tuesday 31st December 1940

Magnus was waiting for Coburg in the main reception at Scotland Yard on the dot of a quarter to five.

'I'm glad you weren't late,' said Magnus as they walked out to the waiting car. 'Malcolm has been worried that you'd be caught up in some police business. He said if you weren't here on time, we should go without you. He's one of Rosa's greatest fans.'

'I know he is,' said Coburg. 'And so am I, which is why I was determined to be there for this show.'

The roads were surprisingly clear and with Malcolm's skilful and speedy driving, they pulled up in a parking space at the kerb outside the Finsbury Park Empire at a quarter past five.

'You made good time,' Coburg complimented Malcolm.

'He usually does,' said Magnus as they got out and made for the doors of the theatre.

Inside, they found that three tickets had indeed been left for them at the box office as promised, something that Coburg had been concerned about as he had often found that bureaucracies such as the BBC were not as efficient as they should be.

'Malcolm, if you wouldn't mind going in and making sure no one takes our seats. I need to have a word with Edgar,' said Magnus.

'Of course,' said Malcolm.

Magnus held out his hand. 'If I can borrow the keys,' he said. 'We'll be more comfortable in the car.'

Malcolm handed over the keys and said, 'Don't be too long. They won't let you in once the show's started.'

Coburg looked enquiringly at his brother as they returned to the car.

'What's going on?' he asked.

'I'll tell you in the car,' said Magnus.

'Won't Malcolm think this strange?'

'I told Malcolm that I wanted to have a word with you in private,' said Magnus. 'I wasn't sure if it would be before or after the show.'

'I didn't think you and he had any secrets from one another,' said Coburg as he and Magnus got in the car and pulled the door shut.

'Except this one,' said Magnus. 'I want your word that what I'm about to reveal, you don't pass on to anyone. And that includes Rosa.'

Coburg frowned. 'This sounds very serious.'

'It is. I was entrusted with it on the promise I told no one. But I see in the papers that you're in charge of this Russian woman who got murdered. The fortune-teller.'

'Along with her brother,' said Coburg. 'He was found stabbed to death on Sunday. One paper accused me of being responsible for their deaths.'

'The thing is, Edgar, I get the impression that the papers are putting the blame on the Russians. Stalin's secret assassins.'

'Yes,' said Coburg.

'I just wanted to mark your card. There's a lot of prejudice against the Russians, and much of it has come about because they killed their royal family.'

'Tsar Nicholas, his wife and five children.' Coburg nodded. 'Shot and bayoneted to death.'

'There's always been a lot of talk that the British government offered to take the Tsar and his family as refugees, and the Russians at first agreed but then reneged on it and then the Bolsheviks killed them.'

'Yes,' said Coburg. 'That's what I heard. Another reason not to trust the Russians.'

'In fact, it's not true,' said Magnus.

'No?' said Coburg, surprised.

'As it seems as if you'll be dealing with the Russians over this latest case of yours, I wanted to tell you what really happened so you won't have too prejudiced a view of them.'

'How do you know what really happened?' asked Coburg suspiciously. 'You can't have been there; you were in the trenches in 1917, along with Charles, fighting the Germans. And I've already been told a lot about the Russians that reinforces the view of them as ruthless, corrupt and not to be trusted by the son of one of Stalin's victims.'

'Ah yes, Stalin.' Magnus nodded. 'Indeed, a bad lot. But they're not all like that. Or, rather, they weren't when I was involved in the rescue of the royal family from Russia.'

'You? Like I said, you were in the trenches in France when the Romanovs were killed.'

'That's true, but I received an order to go with two of my men to Murmansk on the north-west coats of Russia on a secret mission. I think I was chosen because of a recommendation by Churchill. I served with him when he went into the trenches following the disaster at Gallipoli. I was told that the Russian royal family were being kept prisoner at the Tsar's Siberian residence, Tsarskoe Selo, but that an agreement had been reached with the Soviet minister of foreign affairs for the Romanovs to come to Britain. A cruiser was going to be sent to the port of Murmansk. I and my two men were to go to Tsarskoe Selo and escort the Tsar and his family, and his household entourage, to the cruiser. It was felt that having British soldiers there escorting them to the ship would reassure them that they would be safe, it wasn't a trick by the Soviets to cause them harm. We'd been given an official letter confirming our safe passage through Russia signed by the Russian minister of foreign affairs, Pavel Milyukov.

'We were about to set off for Murmansk – this was in April 1918 – when we were suddenly told our mission had been cancelled, and we'd be returned to the trenches. The letter of safe passage was taken off me. We assumed, as did everyone else, that it was the Russians playing games, and when the Romanovs were killed by the Bolsheviks in July 1917 we all took it as a slap in the face to the British government. But in fact, it wasn't so. I only got the full story many years later from Churchill, who heard it from Arthur Balfour, who was secretary of state for foreign affairs at the time.

'It seems there had been an exchange of letters between Pavel Milyukov and the British ambassador to Russia, Sir George Buchanan. Milyukov proposed sending the Tsar and his family to Britain, and Sir George reported this to the then Prime Minister, David Lloyd George, and Arthur Balfour. The government responded positively and instructed Sir George to advise Mr Milyukov that a cruiser would be sent to Murmansk to bring the Tsar and his family to Britain. As I've said, we were ordered to travel to Murmansk to ensure their safe boarding of the cruiser, and then our journey was cancelled.

'In the event, no cruiser arrived at Murmansk. In Sir George Buchanan's memoirs, he claimed the Russian had reneged on it rather than risk trouble with the hard socialist left politicians in Russia. However, according to Churchill, the truth was that the Tsar and his family were prevented from coming to Britain by the intervention of no less a person than the king himself, George V. Lord Stamfordham, the king's private secretary, wrote a letter to Arthur Balfour in which he said: "The King must beg you to represent to the Prime Minister that from all he hears and reads in the press, the residence in this country of the ex-Emperor and Empress would be strongly resented by the public and would undoubtedly compromise the position of the King and Queen from whom it would generally be assumed the invitation had emanated." I know the wording so well because Churchill showed it to me to prove what he was telling me was true.

'He also told me that the reason Buchanan blamed the Russians for the Tsar not coming to Britain in his memoirs was because he was warned that if he revealed the true reason he would be charged with a breach of the Official Secrets Act and he'd lose his pension.'

'So it was the king who abandoned his cousin and effectively sentenced him to death,' said Coburg, stunned.

'Yes,' said Magnus. 'You're the only person I've ever told this to, and I'm only doing it to warn you that whatever murky goings-on you encounter as you get into this case, do not necessarily believe all the bad things you hear about the Russians. Yes, Stalin is evil, there's no doubt about that, but not every Russian can be tarred with the same brush. Milyukov did his best to help the

Romanovs escape, but it was the British government acting under orders from the king who left the Tsar and his family to their fate.' He looked at his watch. 'Twenty to six. We need to go in or Malcolm will start to worry.'

As they returned to the theatre and took their seats, Coburg was in a state of shock because of what Magnus had told him. Three grandsons of Queen Victoria, each of whom became the monarch of their country: King George V in Britain, Kaiser Wilhelm in Germany, and Tsar Nicholas II of Russia. Of the three, George and Nicholas had been almost identical, more like twins than cousins. And when George had had the opportunity to save the life of his cousin, he had rejected it. Left him to be butchered to death. Not just Nicholas; the others who died were the Tsarina, Alexandra, the couple's five children – Olga, Tatiana, Maria, Anastasia and Alexei – along with the court physician Eugene Botkin, who cared for the sickly Alexei; Alexandra's lady-in-waiting, Anna Demidova; the footman, Alexei Trupp and the head cook, Ivan Kharitonov. Eleven people who had been waiting for the British cruiser to arrive and take them to safety, as agreed between the Soviets and the British government. Instead, a party of Bolsheviks had arrived at the house where they had taken sanctuary, shot them, bayoneted them, then took their naked bodies into the woods where they were buried, their bodies being disfigured with grenades in an attempt to prevent them being identified.

When news of their deaths reached Britain, there was a public outcry at the fact that this had happened, that the Soviets had reneged on their safe passage agreement and murdered the Russian royal family. Yet the truth was that it hadn't been the Russian authorities who'd betrayed the Romanovs, it had been Nicholas's own cousin, King George V of Britain. A truth so terrible that it had been hushed up, and remained a secret even to this day rather than the British public finding out that it was the present king's father who'd abandoned the Romanovs to their deaths.

Fortunately, at that moment, the house lights in the theatre dimmed and those at the front of the stage came up, and a round, chubby man in a garish white and blue suit bounced onto the stage and leant into the microphone.

'Good evening, ladies and gentlemen, and welcome to the Finsbury Park Empire for tonight's live broadcast of *Henry Hall's Guest Night*. My name is Fred Lively and I shall be your compère for the night. Before we start, I just want to mark your card. You are here tonight to enjoy yourselves, and I know you will. We have Henry Hall and his fantastic orchestra tonight, and some amazing guest stars: Dickie Henderson, a brilliant comedian who always has people in stitches – as the surgeon said to the bishop – plus that amazing young ventriloquist Peter Brough, and the wonderful Rosa Weeks. Ladies and gentlemen, this is a roster of talent to delight you. But it's also on radio, so the audience at home won't know you're enjoying it unless you make the right kind of noises to let them know how much fun you're having. So, lots of applause, nice and loud. Let's hear those hands clapping together as a kind of warm-up to hear how good you are at it. So, all together now, clap, and keep clapping.'

With that, Fred Lively began to clap his hands together, persuading the audience to join in. Magnus was not alone in keeping his hands in his lap. 'This is moronic,' he muttered to Coburg, who had joined in the applause, as had Malcolm.

'Hold it! Hold it!!' said Lively, holding his hands up to stop the audience. 'Call that a clap?' he said disparagingly. 'I've heard better than that from the sea lions at the zoo. Let's try it again, and this time . . . LOUD! Let 'em hear it up the road at Highbury. The Arsenal might think it's them getting some applause for a change.'

Once again, Lively began to clap his hands together, fast and enthusiastically, and this time the audience responded, sending a loud wave of applause around the auditorium, with some members of the audience even adding a shouted 'Bravo!'

Lively held up his hand to stop them, smiling broadly all the while.

'Fantastic!' he said. 'You're brilliant! Better than the last lot we had. I'll ask the producer if we can have you every week. And now, I'll introduce you to the stars of our show, the wonderful, the brilliant, the magnificent . . . Henry Hall and his orchestra!'

At that, the stage curtains parted to reveal a full orchestra, each musician behind a glittering placard with the letters HH on, and in front of them the tall figure of Henry Hall himself, baton raised. He brought his baton down, and the orchestra burst into life for three bars, before muting their tone, continuing at a lower volume as Henry Hall strode to the microphone. Coburg noticed that a light bulb on a stand beside the microphone had come to life just before the orchestra had begun to play, and now Henry Hall said, 'Good evening, listeners. This is Henry Hall speaking, and welcome to my Guest Night coming to you live from the Finsbury Park Empire in London.'

With that, he turned to the orchestra and flourished his baton, and immediately the volume level from the musicians was raised again, and the show was under way.

The rest of the show was wonderful to Coburg's eyes and ears. And not just his, to judge by the genuine warmth and extent of the audience's applause, especially for Rosa's solo spot where she did Hoagy Carmichael's 'Stardust' followed by Rodgers and Hart's 'Manhattan', and then showed she could really belt out a rocker when she and the full Henry Hall Orchestra did 'The Saints' to close the show, and the whole audience rose to its feet, stamping, clapping and whistling.

'That was magnificent,' said Magnus in the car as they drove to Coburg and Rosa's flat in Piccadilly. 'You were superb, Rosa, but I liked that young ventriloquist as well. I think he could go far.'

'If you like that sort of thing,' commented Malcolm rather sourly. 'It's always seemed odd to me, people believing a lump of wood is a real person.'

'That shows you how good he is,' said Rosa. 'It takes a good one to keep the illusion going.'

When Malcolm pulled the car up outside their block of flats, Rosa said, 'Please, won't you both come in? After a night like that, I think a celebratory drink is in order.'

'Yes, please,' said Magnus. 'We can relive the whole show as we talk about it.'

'I thought the orchestra were good,' said Coburg as they mounted the stairs to their flat. 'It worked so well with them on "The Saints", anyone would have thought you were part of the band.'

'If Henry Hall ever needs a second pianist . . .' began Rosa. Then she stopped.

The four of them looked at the doll pinioned to the front door of their flat with a long-bladed knife.

'My God!' exclaimed Malcolm, shocked. 'What on earth is that?'

'It's a long story,' said Rosa sadly.

'And it's no longer a joke,' added Coburg angrily.

CHAPTER TWELVE

Wednesday 1st January 1941

At 8 a.m., Lampson knocked on the door of his parents' flat as he regularly did to hand over his young son, Terry, prior to heading off to pick up Coburg.

'Morning, Mum!' He beamed as his mother opened the door. 'Happy New Year!' And he kissed her on the cheek.

'Not a lot to be happy about,' grumbled his mum. 'The air raids the last few nights have been amongst the worst we've had. We spent it in the Tube station. Luckily, someone had a wireless they were able to plug in so we could hear Rosa on *Henry Hall*.'

'Is that Ted and Terry?' called Bert Lampson from the kitchen.

'Here we are, Dad!' called back Lampson and he and Terry walked into the kitchen, where his father was cooking breakfast.

'We thought you might be joining us in the Tube station,' said his dad. 'The bombing's getting worse.'

'That's what I just said,' said Mrs Lampson. She elbowed her husband aside and took over the frying pan. 'You're burning the fried bread,' she complained.

'It's supposed to be burnt,' said Mr Lampson. 'That's why they call it fried bread.'

'Not that burnt,' said Mrs Lampson, and she flipped the browned slices of bread onto a plate.

'Me and Terry went to stay overnight at a mate of his,' said Lampson.

'Oh yes?' said Lampson suspiciously. 'Who was she?'

'Nothing like that,' Lampson told him. 'Benny Roberts had to go on night duty, so he asked if me and Terry could stay over and keep little Joe company. Benny's got a cellar and he's made it up like a mini air raid shelter. He's got a wireless in there so we were able to hear Rosa on *Henry Hall* last night. Mum said you heard it down at the Tube station. Good, wasn't it?'

'Stunning,' said Mr Lampson. 'Especially that "Saints Go Marching In" they did.' He looked enquiringly at his son. 'Did you hear the announcement afterwards? Herbert Morrison, the Home Secretary.'

'No,' said Lampson. 'I turned it off after *Henry Hall* was finished so the boys could get to sleep.'

'They're setting up a Civil Defence Home Guard.'

'We've already got a Home Guard,' said Lampson.

'This is a Civil Defence Home Guard, to deal with fires. Since this so-called Christmas truce, we've been hit by more bombing than ever, and much of it has been fire bombs. Incendiaries. So much so that the fire brigades can't get enough water to fight them. They've been taking it out of the Thames, but that only works if the fires are near enough to the river. Water mains have run dry. So what the government's doing is setting up a fire watch, with properly organised groups to keep watch when there's a raid and alert the fire brigades so they can attack the fire quickly before it gets really going. I'm volunteering.'

'You?' said Lampson.

'Why not? I'm fit and able. And this needs men.'

'They said on the wireless that women can sign up too,' added Mrs Lampson.

Lampson stared at his mum.

'You're not going to be doing this as well, are you?' he asked, stunned. 'I mean, you've got that gammy leg of yours. You won't be able to run around hauling buckets of water.'

'No, but I can watch out for fires and get warnings out.'

'You ought to sign up,' Mr Lampson said to his son. 'It's got to be more than just volunteers. They said on the wireless it's gonna be compulsory. Everyone has to join up.'

'Compulsory?' said Lampson.

'Well, not at first,' admitted Mr Lampson. 'They said it'll take time to put the regulations in place, so in the meantime it's about people volunteering. Shall I put your name down?'

'Er, yes,' said Lampson awkwardly.

'Good.' Mr Lampson smiled. He looked at the clock. 'You'd better get off otherwise your boss will wonder where you are. You're supposed to pick him up this morning, ain't you?'

'Yes,' said Lampson.

'Then you ought to come earlier if you want to keep talking. We'll see you later and I'll let you know about the fire-watching.'

Over breakfast, Coburg and Rosa talked about the previous evening. Not so much about the Henry Hall show, but the threats to her, now made manifest by the doll stuck to their flat door.

'I'm going to be looking into this as soon as we get to work,' Coburg assured her as he finished and pushed his plate away. He looked at the clock. 'Ted should be arriving any time now to take me to the Yard.'

The doorbell rang as Coburg was putting on his coat.

'That'll be Ted,' he said. 'At least, I hope it is.' He took Rosa in his arms. 'You sure you're going to be alright?' he asked.

Rosa nodded. 'I'm going to the ambulance station. Doing something will help take my mind off it.'

'I'm going to find out who did it,' he promised her fervently. 'I'll have them behind bars and off the streets. I'm not going to let anything happen to you.'

'Can you give me a lift to Paddington?' she asked. 'I'm still a bit shaky after what happened. At least that way I know I'll get to work safely.'

'I was going to suggest it anyway,' Coburg told her.

If Lampson was surprised to see Rosa accompanying Coburg, he didn't show it. Instead, he waxed enthusiastic. 'What a fantastic show last night!' he said. 'I listened to it with Terry, and my mum and dad heard it in the shelter at the Tube station. They reckon it was the best thing they'd ever heard on the wireless. I bet there wasn't one listener who wasn't over the moon with it.'

'Unfortunately, there was at least one,' said Rosa with a forced smile that was belied by her giving a little shudder.

Lampson looked at them, puzzled. As they got into the car, Coburg told him what had happened after the show: the knife pinning the doll to the door, the threatening letter beforehand.

'Bloody hell!' exploded Lampson. 'A lunatic, you reckon?'

'If so, one capable of finding out where we live and sticking a knife through a doll in our front door,' said Coburg.

Lampson dropped Rosa at the St John Ambulance station at Paddington, and Coburg kissed her goodbye and gave her another hug of reassurance.

'The Yard, guv?' asked Lampson as Coburg pulled the door shut.

'No. Make for Maida Vale. The BBC studios. I want to have a word with the producer of last night's show, see if he can throw any light on who we might be dealing with.'

'Does Rosa know you're doing this?'

'No,' admitted Coburg. 'I didn't tell her because I thought she might get upset at my bothering her producer, and she'd tell me not to.'

'This way, if she doesn't know what you're up to she can't say anything?' Lampson grinned.

'Oh she'll have something to say about it once she finds out,' said Coburg. 'But by then I hope I'll have the information I need.'

Lampson parked in the car park at Maida Vale, while Coburg made for the main reception where he showed his warrant card to the woman at the reception desk.

'Detective Chief Inspector Saxe-Coburg from Scotland Yard to see Mr John Fawcett. I believe he's based here.'

He'd decided to go the whole hog with his name and rank because he knew from experience that often receptionists saw their primary job as keeping any callers from gaining entry to the building and the people who worked there. The two words 'Scotland Yard' usually punched a hole through that without further discussion. That was the case here as the receptionist picked up the phone and dialled an extension number and had the briefest of possible chats before replacing the receiver and telling Coburg, 'Mr Fawcett will be with you shortly.'

In fact, Fawcett arrived in the reception area in less than four minutes. He greeted Coburg with a friendly, relaxed smile. 'How wonderful to meet you, Mr Coburg. I hope you enjoyed last night's show? Your wife is a wonderful performer.'

'She is indeed,' agreed Coburg. 'But it's not about last night's show I need to talk to you.'

'It's not?' asked Fawcett, puzzled, and also slightly worried.

'Is there anywhere we can talk privately?' asked Coburg.

'Of course. My office,' said Fawcett.

Coburg followed the producer down the stairs to the next level and along a plushly carpeted corridor until they came to an office with the name 'J. Fawcett' on a board outside the door.

Fawcett seated himself behind his desk and gestured for Coburg to take a seat.

'Mr Fawcett, I need to know the name of the person who originally was on the bill at the Finsbury Park Empire, the one that Rosa replaced,' said Coburg.

Fawcett looked uncomfortable.

'I'm very sorry, Chief Inspector, but that kind of

information is highly confidential. The BBC—'

'Someone has threatened to kill my wife,' Coburg interrupted. 'I believe it's to do with whoever she replaced.'

'Kill?' echoed Fawcett, horrified.

'Soon after it was announced that Rosa would be in the show, she got an anonymous letter threatening to kill her if she went ahead with it and appeared. She did appear, and when we got home after the show there was a knife stuck in the door of our flat, pinning a doll to the wood. I believe the person who made that threat is serious and a danger to her. Either it's connected with the person who Rosa replaced, or someone who wanted to make sure that no one filled that spot.'

'Yes, I see.' Fawcett nodded unhappily. 'Of course, in the circumstances, you need to know. The person we had to let go was a singer called Bella Wilson. I don't know if you know of her?'

'Dyed red hair?' asked Coburg.

'Yes,' said Fawcett. He hesitated, then said, 'I had a meeting with her about the show, just as I always do with every artiste who's appearing. Unfortunately, Miss Wilson was inebriated. *Very* inebriated. It wasn't just the smell of drink, it was the fact that she slurred her words and seemed unable to stand or move without falling over. I realised it would be a disaster if she were to appear and was in that state. I couldn't take a chance on her. *Henry Hall's Guest Night* is a live broadcast, for heaven's sake.'

'Yes, I understand,' said Coburg. 'Thank you, Mr Fawcett. Do you have an address for Miss Wilson?'

Fawcett took a contacts book from his desk, found the address and wrote it down for Coburg.

'Thank you,' said Coburg, getting to his feet.

'I hope this won't mean unpleasant publicity for the show,' said Fawcett, looking very concerned.

'We'll do our best to avoid publicity of any sort,' Coburg assured him.

Lampson was leaning against the car when Coburg returned to it.

'I've got the name of our possible suspect,' said Coburg. 'A woman called Bella Wilson.'

'Bella Wilson?' Lampson frowned. 'We had an encounter with her not long ago, didn't we?'

'We did.'

'So, are we going to pick her up?'

'First, I want to let Rosa know we've tracked who did it,' said Coburg. 'Then we'll call on her.'

'So, back to the St John Ambulance at Paddington?'

'Indeed.' Coburg nodded.

When they arrived at the station, Rosa, in her St John Ambulance uniform, was just walking across the yard towards an ambulance, accompanied by a short, plump woman in her fifties, who Coburg assumed to be Doris.

'Edgar!' exclaimed Rosa in surprise. 'Doris, this is my husband, DCI Coburg.'

'A pleasure to meet you,' said Doris, shaking Coburg's hand. 'I've heard so much about you.'

'As I have about you.' Coburg smiled. He turned to Rosa. 'I've got some information.'

'I'll see you at the ambulance, Rosa,' said Doris, and walked off.

'She's nice,' said Coburg.

'She is,' agreed Rosa.

'Are you off on an emergency?'

'No, this is just running someone to hospital for an appointment. They're in a wheelchair and can't get there any other way. What's the information?'

'I've found out the name of the act you replaced at Finsbury Park Empire on the Henry Hall show.'

'Who?'

'Bella Wilson.'

'Bella?'

'And we know how she feels about you. I have no doubt it was her who wrote that threatening letter and stuck that doll to our door with a knife. I've come to tell you to be on your guard. She's dangerous, and I suspect mad. She's certainly mad with hatred and jealousy of you.'

'You're not going to send me away again?' asked Rosa unhappily. 'Last time you thought my life was in danger I was hidden out at Dawlish Hall.'

'Which you absolutely loved,' Coburg reminded her. 'Being cossetted and made a fuss of by Magnus and Malcolm and Mrs Hilton.'

'Yes, but—' she began, but she was interrupted by Coburg.

'No,' he said. 'At that time, we didn't know where the threat was coming from. Now we do. Bella Wilson. I'll put out an alert for her and have her picked up.'

'How did you find out who it was?' asked Rosa.

'By asking questions,' said Coburg.

'But who did you ask?'

He winked at her. 'Call it a trade secret,' he said.

The postman rang the doorbell again, and heard it buzzing from inside the terraced house where Bert Marsh lived. Normally he'd have just left the parcel he was delivering inside the door on the mat, especially as the front door was partly open, but this particular parcel had to be signed for. Registered post. The fact that the door was partly open meant that Marsh was somewhere inside, possibly on the toilet or in the kitchen.

He pressed the bell again, and this time he pushed the door open wider.

'Mr Marsh!' he called.

Then he saw the figure of Marsh lying face down in the passageway.

'Mr Marsh?' the postman asked. Tentatively he stepped in and approached the prone man. *Heart attack?* he wondered. He bent down and touched him. No sign of movement. Then he saw the blood beneath Marsh's head spread over the carpet, and saw the damage to the back of the head and realised that the white splodges in Marsh's hair were bits of bone and brain.

He stood up and scrambled back from the dead man, shocked. Then he rushed to the telephone on a small stand in the passage and dialled 999.

'Police!' he said urgently when the operator answered. 'A man's been murdered. Beaten to death by the look of it.'

CHAPTER THIRTEEN

Wednesday 1st January 1941

As Coburg and Lampson drove to the address they'd been given for Bella Wilson, Lampson asked Coburg if he knew anything about the new Civil Defence Home Guard.

'No,' said Coburg.

'My dad said that the Home Secretary made an announcement about it on the wireless yesterday evening.'

'We were otherwise engaged yesterday evening,' Coburg reminded him.

'Yeah, so was I,' said Lampson. 'According to my dad, they're setting up these local fire-watching units. Everybody has to sign up for it. Compulsory, he said Morrison had said. My dad's already volunteered and he's asked me to sign up.'

'Will you?' asked Coburg.

'If it's going to be compulsory, I won't have any choice.' He frowned as he added, 'I suppose you'll get roped in on it as well if it's compulsory.'

'*If*,' said Coburg doubtfully. Then he added,

'Although I can see the sense of it. These fire bombs the Germans are dropping, the incendiaries, alongside the heavy bombs, are destroying the city. I read that the fires on the 29th December were the biggest the city's ever seen, with the destruction being even worse than the original Great Fire of London. The one in 1666.'

'The one they teach you about in school?'

'Yes,' said Coburg. 'This was far worse than that, and it's happening every night. It makes sense to try and stop the smaller fires from spreading to stop it becoming this giant inferno. As I understand it, the problem is the lack of water.'

'Yes, that's what my dad said.'

'What will you do?' asked Coburg. 'Will you sign up, or wait till it becomes compulsory?'

'I don't have much choice, with my dad being one of those who'll be organising our local fire-watch,' said Lampson. Then he brightened as he added, 'Mind, I've often said I ought to be doing more for the war effort. This will be it.'

When they arrived at Bella Wilson's address, they learnt from her landlady, Mrs Glover, that Bella Wilson had left three days before and hadn't been back.

'She went off owing me two weeks' rent,' Mrs Glover told them, her angry expression showing her deep displeasure at having been robbed in this way. 'When you find her, I want my money.'

'We'd better put out an alert for Bella Wilson,' said

Coburg as they walked back to their car.

'Leave it to me, guv,' said Lampson. 'I'll find a photograph of her and get it sent out. We can't have this maniac on the loose after your missus.'

As they reached their car, they heard their radio calling: 'Control to Echo Seven. Control to Echo Seven. Come in, please. Over.'

Coburg pulled open the car door and picked up the microphone. 'Echo Seven to control, over.'

'Echo Seven: message for DCI Coburg. Inspector Saunders needs to talk to you urgently. Over.'

'Echo Seven to Control. Is Inspector Saunders in his office? Over.'

'Confirm that, Echo Seven. Over.'

'Echo Seven to Control. Advise Inspector Saunders I'm on my way to Scotland Yard and will see him there shortly. Over.'

'Copy that, Echo Seven. Over and out.'

When they arrived back at Scotland Yard, Coburg sent Lampson to check for messages while he went to see Inspector Peter Saunders in his office.

'I've just come from the scene of a murder,' Saunders told him. 'I got the shout, but it's someone you've had dealings with lately, so I wondered if you might want to take it?'

Coburg's heart sank. *Dear God, let it not be Priscilla Rostov!*

'Who was it?' he asked, preparing himself to hear the worst.

'A bloke called Bert Marsh,' said Saunders. 'He's a journalist on the *Daily Globe*. He'd been beaten to death in his house. A postman found him. He was trying to deliver a registered parcel to him and the front door was ajar. The postie pushed the door open and there was Marsh lying in the passage with his head caved in.'

Coburg stared at him, stunned.

'Ted Lampson and I were talking to him just yesterday at the *Daily Globe* offices,' he said, his face showing his astonishment.

'What about?'

'About a story he wrote about the Rostovs who were killed.'

'Oh yes, the brother and sister.'

Suddenly Coburg remembered Marsh's last words of appeal. 'He asked me for police protection,' he said. 'He thought his life was in danger.'

'Why did he think that?' asked Saunders.

Because I hinted to him it was, thought Coburg bitterly. Aloud, he said, 'We'll have to look into it.'

'But you'll take it on?' asked Saunders.

'Yes,' said Coburg. 'Leave it with me.'

As Lampson drove them to the offices of the *Daily Globe*, both Coburg and Lampson's thoughts were filled with mental images of their last encounter with Bert Marsh: his anguished plea for police protection and his desperation as he threatened to publicise Coburg's refusal to give it, to which Coburg had responded with a curt, 'Which might make the killer wonder what you know that makes you so desperate for the need for protection.'

And now Marsh was dead, murdered.

Was it connected to the murders of the Rostovs? If so, then Coburg was responsible for Marsh's death.

When they got to the *Daily Globe*, they were shown into the office of the editor, Steve Blewer, who was in a state of shock. 'I was expecting an Inspector Saunders,' he told them after they'd introduced themselves. 'He telephoned me to tell me about Bert and said he'd be coming to talk to me.'

'Inspector Saunders has passed the case to me,' said Coburg.

'A chief inspector,' said Blewer. 'So it's something serious? Something complicated?'

'We don't know yet,' said Coburg. 'We're trying to find out what sort of motive there could be for killing him. Did he have any enemies that you know of?'

'A good investigative reporter always makes enemies,' said Blewer. 'People who are being investigated about something they want to be kept secret sometimes try to stop a journalist digging around.'

'By violence?'

'It has been known.'

'Did it happen to Bert Marsh?'

Blewer hesitated, then said, 'We did have an incident at the office not long ago.'

The awkward way he said it told Coburg that there was more to this than initially met the eye.

'Someone took exception to what he was writing?'

'Not exactly,' said Blewer.

'Then what exactly?' pressed Coburg.

Blewer looked uncomfortable. 'It wasn't actually to do with anything he was working on, and I'm only telling you in case you hear it from someone else here and get the wrong impression.'

'And what is the wrong impression?' asked Coburg.

This time Blewer took even longer over deliberating how much to say, before he muttered, 'Sometimes Bert let himself get unnecessarily involved.'

'With who? Or with what?'

'Women,' said Blewer awkwardly.

'There's nothing wrong with that, surely,' said Coburg. 'It's what men and women do.'

'Yes, but it was who the women were.'

'And who were they?'

Blewer hesitated again before saying, 'Sometimes he'd go and see someone who'd recently lost their husband. A soldier or a sailor killed in the war. He did our human-interest stories.'

'And he took advantage of their human interest?' said Coburg sarcastically.

'Now and then. He was a bit of a chancer like that, was Bert. On this occasion he came on to this woman whose husband had just been killed. He said he was just trying to show her sympathy. That was his defence. But most people here knew what he got up to; he even used to brag about it sometimes.'

'He sounds like a bit of a rat,' said Coburg.

'He was a good reporter,' Blewer defended him. 'This was like his Achilles' heel.'

'Women who were vulnerable, having just lost their partner. Or their son. Or a brother,' said Coburg.

Blewer nodded. 'I tried to warn him that one day it would come and bite him, but he shrugged it off.'

'So what happened with this incident at the office?'

'One of the women he tried it on with told her brother. He was a soldier on leave. Built like a brick wall. He turned up here and said what he was going to do to Bert. Luckily we had security on duty and they intervened, but not before he'd given Bert a bit of a kicking.'

'Was the man charged with assault?'

'No. That would've been bad publicity for the paper.'

'Did the man come back again?'

'He came back again, but Bert wasn't here.'

'How long ago was this?'

'About two months.'

'I need the name of the man, and also the woman Bert tried it on with.'

'I don't know the bloke's last name, but the woman's name and address will be in Bert's notebook. She lived in Clapham. A Mrs Walters. I only remember that because the bloke who turned up said he was here for what Bert had done to his sister, Ethel Walters.'

'Did Marsh keep his notebooks here at the office?'

'No, he kept them at his house. He came into the office every day to deliver his copy, but mostly he worked from home.'

As Coburg and Lampson drove to Marsh's house, they talked about his murder.

'I know everyone will think it's got to be connected, but I've got my doubts that it's the same people who did the Rostovs,' said Lampson. 'Both of them were stabbed, each one a very neat job. This one's messy. Violent. Brutal.'

'A crime of passion.' Coburg nodded. 'So we need to talk to this Mrs Ethel Walters. Let's hope Marsh's notebooks are easy to find.'

CHAPTER FOURTEEN

Wednesday 1st January 1941

Rosa pulled the ambulance into the yard at the St John station.

'Time for a cuppa,' said Doris, climbing down from the cab. 'I'll put the kettle on while you park up.'

Rosa manoeuvred the ambulance into a space between two other vehicles and then jumped down from the cab. She was just heading towards the office building when she realised someone was barring her way. With a shock she recognised Bella Wilson. Wilson's face was twisted in deep hatred. In one of her hands she clutched a knife. She began to advance towards Rosa.

'Bella!' exclaimed Rosa, shocked.

'Shut up, you bitch!' snarled Wilson. 'Don't talk to me!'

With that she made a run at Rosa, but she suddenly stopped as Doris appeared behind her, grabbed Wilson by the shoulders and smashed her head hard against the side of the ambulance. Wilson stumbled back. Doris was still holding on to her and she smashed

Wilson's head against the side of the ambulance again. This time Wilson collapsed.

'I saw this woman coming towards here and I saw she was holding a knife,' said Doris. 'After you told me about that doll stuck to your door, I thought there might be a connection, so I hurried back.'

'Thank God you did!' said Rosa. 'She was going to kill me!'

Coburg and Lampson found Bert Marsh's notebooks in the drawer of the sideboard in his front room. There were four of them, three full and one half-filled.

'He's been helpful,' commented Coburg, flicking through the most recent one. 'He's put rings round certain names. All of them women. There are notes after each one: brother dead. Merchant navy. Convoy struck, with a date after it. Addresses.'

'This one's got the same,' said Lampson, looking through one of the other notebooks.

'So, we make a list of the women whose names he ringed and see which of them were offended by him trying it on,' said Coburg. 'Offended enough for them to tell their male relatives.'

'Or take action themselves,' observed Lampson. He gave a groan. 'We'll have a list of these women and their relatives, then that list of Lady Za Za's clients. It'll take for ever to talk to them all.'

'You never know, we might get lucky early on,' said Coburg.

They locked Marsh's house up and made for their parked car. They'd just got in when the radio crackled into life: 'Control to Echo Seven. Do you read? Over.'

'Echo Seven to Control. Receiving you. Over.'

'Echo Seven. Message for DCI Coburg. His wife has been attacked by a female wielding a knife. Mrs Coburg is unharmed. The assailant is under restraint at Paddington St John Ambulance station.'

'Received, Control. Echo Seven out,' said Coburg. He turned to Lampson, who'd already started the engine. 'Let's go, Ted. Put the bells on.'

Rosa was in the yard at the ambulance station, watching out for them as the police car pulled in. Coburg leapt out of the car and hugged her to him.

'Are you alright?' he asked.

'Thanks to Doris,' said Rosa. 'She overpowered her.'

'Where is she? I assume it was Bella Wilson?'

'It was. She's in the storeroom, tied to a chair. Mr Warren and Doris are keeping an eye on her.'

Bella Wilson was indeed tied to a chair, her ankles fixed to the legs, her wrists tied to the wooden struts of the back of the chair. She was also gagged and glared venomously at Coburg and Rosa as they walked in.

'I gagged her because her language was so foul,' explained Warren. He pointed to a knife on a nearby packing case. 'That's what she tried to stab Rosa with.'

Coburg took a bag from his pocket and dropped the knife into it. He then removed the gag from Wilson's mouth and said, 'Bella Wilson, I am arresting you on a charge of attempted murder.' He then read her her rights about staying silent, but anything she did say would be taken down and might be used against her. 'I'm taking you to Scotland Yard. I can either have you untied and put in a police car, or we can unload you tied to the chair as you are into the back of a van. That depends on you. If we untie you from the chair, will you co-operate?'

Wilson scowled, but nodded.

'If you'd untie her ankles,' said Coburg to Warren. 'And untie her wrists from the back of the chair and I'll put handcuffs on her."

'She might cause problems in the car,' said Doris. 'I'll go with you if you like.'

Coburg became aware she was clutching a heavy metal starting handle.

'Thanks,' said Coburg. 'But I think we have to make this official personnel only.' He smiled at Doris. 'Thanks for what you did, Doris.'

'Bitch!' Wilson spat venomously at Doris.

'Watch your mouth,' Doris snapped at her, and waved the starting handle menacingly towards her. Wilson shut up.

Warren had untied the ropes and Coburg put handcuffs on Wilson's wrists.

'Do you want a hand to take her to your car?' asked Warren.

'It might be a good idea,' said Coburg. 'Thank you.'

Coburg and Warren each took hold of one of Wilson's arms and lifted her up, then walked her out of the storeroom and towards where Lampson was waiting in the car. The sergeant got out of the car as he saw them approaching and helped Coburg put Wilson in the back, Coburg getting in beside the prisoner.

'I'll see you at home later,' Coburg said to Rosa. He gave last thanks to Warren and Doris, then pulled the door shut and Lampson put the car into gear and they moved off.

Coburg half-expected Wilson to try something in the car, lash out with her feet or try and headbutt the back of Lampson's head, but the journey was without incident.

They took Wilson to an interview room, where Coburg once again read Wilson her rights, before asking, 'Why did you try to kill Rosa?'

'Who said I tried to kill her?' demanded Wilson.

She sat, looking venomously at Coburg. Now he could study her properly for the first time, Coburg took in the small spider's web, complete with spider, tattooed on the right-hand side of her face, half hidden by her hair. He was also aware of the decorative rings she wore on the fingers of her left hand, one with a small skull set in it, others with occult carvings on them. Together they made a useful knuckleduster, Coburg reflected.

'The witnesses, and the knife you were carrying,' replied Coburg. 'Plus the threatening letter you sent saying you were going to kill her if she appeared on the Henry Hall show.'

'You can't prove I wrote that.'

'I don't need to prove it; the main thing is the evidence of eyewitnesses and the knife you dropped. The letter is just evidence to back the charge.'

Wilson glared at him. 'Your wife assaulted me. She smashed my head against that ambulance.'

'Actually, I believe it was her co-driver who did that after you attacked Rosa with a knife, intending to kill her. As I say, attempted murder.'

'She did it to me!' burst out Wilson angrily.

'Attempted to kill you?' said Coburg, intrigued.

'She killed my career. Every time I did a gig, everyone kept on going about how 'Rosa Weeks was here last week. She was fabulous'. You think I like that? And then this Henry Hall gig. That was mine and she stole it from me!'

'And so you tried to kill her.'

'I'm saying nothing,' snapped Wilson defiantly.

'Book her and put her on remand,' said Coburg to Lampson.

'I have to have a solicitor!' shouted Wilson.

'And you will,' Coburg told her. 'We'll arrange for

167

one to see you at Holloway.'

She stared at him, shocked. 'You're putting me in jail?!'

'That's what we normally do with people accused of attempted murder,' said Coburg. 'And they stay there until they come to trial.'

She leapt to her feet and made as if to rush at him, but the table between them stopped her.

'I can't go to prison!' she said. 'It was just a joke, that's all.'

'Which I'm sure you'll tell your solicitor when he comes to see you,' said Coburg. 'Take her away.'

As Lampson moved towards her, she suddenly lashed out at him with her feet, but Lampson dodged nimbly aside and pushed her so that she fell back down on the chair. The duty constable in the room with them took hold of her shoulders to stop her getting up. She twisted in his grasp.

'This is police brutality!' she screamed.

As Lampson joined the constable in restraining the struggling Wilson, Coburg made for the door, saying, 'I'll get some WPCs. They can take care of her. And I'll arrange for a van to take her to Holloway; the cells in them are nicely secure.'

As he left the room, he heard her shouting obscenities, along with 'I'll get you, you bastard! And that bitch wife of yours! This isn't over.'

CHAPTER FIFTEEN

Thursday 2nd January 1941

Steve Blewer looked up at the knock on his office door and it opening, and his secretary, Emma, looked in.

'Excuse me, Mr Blewer, but there's a woman to see you?'

'A woman?' He frowned. 'I don't think I've got any appointments booked.'

'No, Mr Blewer. This is a Mrs Rostov, who wants to talk to you about Bert Marsh.'

Oh no, groaned Blewer inwardly. *Another widow come to complain that he's tried to get off with her.*

'Shall I tell her to make an appointment?' asked Emma.

No, thought Blewer firmly. *If we send her away she's likely to go to another paper and tell them the story, about Marsh trying it on. That's the last thing we need.*

'No, you can bring her in,' said Blewer, forcing a smile. One he didn't feel. He hoped she wasn't too angry, like some of the previous women had been. 'But would you ask security to send someone to stand outside my office, in case I need them?'

Emma nodded and disappeared, closing the door after her. Blewer got to his feet and went to the mirror hanging on his wall and began to practise looking sincere and sympathetic; he didn't want to make this woman any more upset than she already was.

The door opened and Emma ushered in a young woman in her early twenties.

'Mrs Rostov,' she announced, and then withdrew.

Blewer approached her, looking sympathetic, his hand held out.

'Mrs Rostov,' he said. 'I'm so sorry for your loss.'

'I'm here about Mr Marsh,' she said, her face grim.

Blewer gave her an apologetic look. 'If you have a complaint about him—' he began, but she cut him off, surprise on her face.

'Complaint?' she echoed. 'Why would I have a complaint?'

'The thing is, Mrs Rostov, tragically, Bert Marsh died yesterday . . .'

'Yes, I know, that's why I'm here.'

Blewer looked at her, bewildered. Her attitude wasn't what he'd been anticipating. He gestured her to the chair on the other side of his desk, and sat down in his as she settled down.

'I saw it in the paper that he'd been killed,' she said. 'I've come to tell you who killed him.'

'Oh?'

'The Russians.'

'The Russians?'

She nodded. 'I told Mr Marsh when he came to see me the other day, after my husband was murdered.' She then went on to tell him everything she'd told Marsh: Stalin's assassination squads, the execution of her husband's father in Russia, the identical way that Grigor and his sister had been killed. 'Mr Marsh wrote about it in your paper, about the Russians, and the fact that my husband told that detective chief inspector about it, warning him, but he did nothing to save him. And now my husband is dead, and your reporter who wrote about it is dead. It's the Russians shutting people up by killing them. They're here and killing people, British people, and no one's doing anything about stopping them.'

Coburg and Lampson sat in the office compiling a list of the women named in Marsh's notebooks. Ethel Walters was there, along with details of her late husband, Wally, who'd died serving on a merchant navy ship that had been torpedoed by a German U-boat. Various other women were in the book, some with a ring round their name.

'Why the ring?' asked Lampson.

'Possibly to mark a sexual conquest,' mused Coburg. 'There isn't one around Ethel Walters's name, and we know he had no success there. But it could mean anything.'

'There are fourteen women named in his notebooks,' said Lampson. 'With those and the forty cards we got from Svetlana's stash, that's fifty-four people to talk to.'

'Let's narrow it down, at least for starters,' said Coburg. 'Like you, I think we're dealing with two separate murderers here. The same person killed both Svetlana and her brother, but someone else killed Bert Marsh. Let's take a guess that whatever happened to cause two different people to commit murder is likely to be something that happened recently.'

'Not necessarily,' cautioned Lampson. 'Sometimes people are killed because of something that happened ages ago. Either the person who did it has only just found out about something that happened, or they've been dwelling on it, sometimes for years.'

'True.' Coburg nodded. 'And that may turn out to be the case here, but we have to do this in stages. I think we start by concentrating on things that might have happened in, say, the last four months. So we talk to the women Marsh mentions who he talked to since the start of September.'

'That brings it down to five,' said Lampson after checking the dates in the notebooks.

'I assume the prices written on the backs of the cards are what they paid. It's interesting how they vary. Most of them are for ten shillings, but there's one for a pound, and one for five pounds.'

'Remember Alphonse told us she charged by what she thought people could afford,' said Coburg.

'In which case there's one here, a Captain Bradley, who paid nothing,' said Lampson.

'Worth looking into that one, I think,' said Coburg.

They'd decided that Ethel Walters would be the first one Lampson would talk to as her brother had had the violent confrontation with Marsh that Blewer had reported to them. Ethel Walters lived in a flat in Southwark in a dull grey concrete block not dissimilar to the small block of flats where Lampson's parents lived in Somers Town. When Lampson called, she was wearing an apron and holding a wiping-up towel and she regarded him suspiciously as if she suspected he was a hawker selling worthless tat, as so many people seemed to be doing lately.

'Good morning, Mrs Walters,' he greeted her. 'I'm Detective Sergeant Lampson from Scotland Yard.' And he held out his warrant card for her to look at.

'Scotland Yard?' she repeated, bewildered. 'What do Scotland Yard want with me?'

'We understand you had a problem with a Mr Bert Marsh, a reporter with the *Daily Globe*.'

'That filthy man!' she said, her face showing her distaste. 'He came round to see me to ask me about my husband who'd been killed. Said he wanted to write about him in the paper. Something they were doing called Heroes of the Nation, so I invited him in. At first he was all politeness, asking about Wally and writing it down, but then – when it was time for him to go – he tried to cuddle me. And worse! He put his hand on my bum and started squeezing it!'

'Disgusting,' said Lampson sympathetically. 'May I come in?'

'No,' said Walters firmly. 'After what happened with that pig, I don't allow men I don't know in, even if they've got a warrant card or whatever.'

'Made you suspicious.' Lampson nodded sympathetically.

'Worse than that,' said Walters indignantly. 'Disgusting it certainly was. Me, just widowed! Well, I pushed him away and let him have a right hander round his ugly face. He fell over on my settee and sat there looking up at me in shock. "I was only being sympathetic," he said. "I know what you were doing, you filthy pig," I answered him. "Now get out of my house before I call the police on you."'

'And did he go?'

'He did, because he knew what he'd get if he tried it on again.' She looked enquiringly at Lampson. 'But what's this about? Has he put in a complaint against me? Because if he has . . .'

'No, no,' said Lampson. 'Mr Marsh was killed either early yesterday morning or some time the night before.'

'Killed? How?'

'He was beaten to death in his house.'

She stared at him, shocked. 'Who by?'

'That's what we're looking into. I'm here because we understand your brother went to the offices of the *Daily Globe* and sought out Mr Marsh to get retribution for what Mr Marsh did to you?'

She stared at him, stunned, then her expression turned to righteous anger as she said, 'Jim did nothing to him. He went there to warn him off from doing anything like that again.'

'Nevertheless, we understand that security had to be called to protect Mr Marsh from your brother.'

'Jim was angry, that's all. He never actually touched him. If you think that Jim beat that pig to death . . .'

'No, we're just looking into it as one possibility.'

'Well, you can look elsewhere. Try the families of some of the other women I bet he tried it on with.'

'We will, but we still need to talk to your brother.'

Ethel Walters studied the sergeant, then said, 'Early yesterday or the night before, you say.'

'That's what the medical people have told us.'

'Then it can't have been Jim. He's been with his regiment at Catterick camp this last week.'

'We'll still need to talk to him. What's his name?'

'Adams. Jim Adams. He's in the Engineers. And he's a decent man.'

* * *

175

Captain Bradley was a man in his sixties, living in a small terraced house in King's Cross not far from the railway station. He was short but with a rigid straight back, which suggested either a military background to go with his title, or a man who suffered from severe back pain.

'Captain Bradley?' enquired Coburg, and he held out his warrant card to the man. 'Detective Chief Inspector Saxe-Coburg from Scotland Yard.'

'Saxe-Coburg?' Bradley frowned. 'That was the royal family's name before they changed it to Windsor. Are you related to them? To Their Majesties?'

'I'm afraid not,' said Coburg. 'Their name was Saxe-Coburg-Gotha. Our family are one hyphen away.'

'Close, though,' said Bradley.

'Indeed,' said Coburg. 'May I come in?'

'Why?' asked Bradley.

'We're investigating a rather difficult case and your name has come up.'

'My name?'

'Along with many other names. We're talking to everyone.'

'Yes, well, I suppose so,' said Bradley.

He stepped aside to let Coburg in, then led him through to a small sitting room, which was decorated in late Victorian style, with dark wallpaper and ornate furniture. Coburg noticed a photograph of a younger Bradley in the uniform of the Scots Guards on a dresser. There were no photographs of any women on display, so no Mrs Bradley, Coburg assumed.

Bradley gestured for Coburg to take a seat, then settled himself down in an armchair.

'So,' he asked, 'what's this about?'

'We understand you consulted a fortune-teller called Lady Za Za,' said Coburg.

'So?' demanded Bradley, his tone and posture aggressively defensive. 'It's not illegal, is it?'

'No it's not,' said Coburg. 'However, Lady Za Za, or to give her her proper name, Svetlana Rostova, was found stabbed to death.'

Bradley stared at him, shocked and bewildered.

'Stabbed?' he repeated.

'And as part of our investigation we're talking to everyone who had a consultation with her.'

'Am I a suspect?' demanded Bradley. 'Because I can assure you I did nothing except see her that once. I certainly did not harm her in any way.'

'You just talked?'

'That is correct.'

'On her cards she wrote down the amount different people paid. I note on your card you paid her nothing.'

'Again, that is correct.'

'May I ask why?'

'Because she was a fraud. A charlatan. That's what I do: I track down these criminals and expose them for the frauds they are.'

'Is there a reason you do this?'

'There is. My mother was cheated by one. He wormed his way into her life after my father died. Told her he could communicate with the dead. Total tosh, of course, but she believed it. He went on to telling her he could tell her future. I warned her against him, in no uncertain terms, I can tell you. Unfortunately, she backed him against me. Her own son! After she died, I discovered he'd taken most of her money. She was left penniless. I went to the police, but they refused to do anything about it. Said there was no proof a crime had been committed because holding séances and telling people's fortunes isn't against the law. But it bloody well ought to be!'

The next name on Lampson's list was Vera Truscott. Truscott was a large and jolly middle-aged lady of healthy proportions. Lampson remembered that it had been her brother, Sid, who'd died three months previously. He explained the purpose of his visit, and Truscott invited him in warmly.

'Come into the parlour,' she said. 'It's more comfortable than the kitchen. Can I get you anything? Tea?' She smiled. 'Or something stronger? It's quite cold out there today, and a little nip to warm you up wouldn't go amiss.'

'No thank you,' said Lampson, settling himself down on a settee. 'Thank you, but not while I'm on duty.'

'Maybe later? What time do you get off?'

'Not for some time,' said Lampson warily. 'I've got a lot of people to talk to, I'm afraid.'

'I bet you have,' sighed Truscott wistfully. 'Yes, I saw it in the paper that someone had killed Bert. Dreadful. But then, in a way, I wasn't surprised, not living the way he did.'

'Oh?' asked Lampson.

'The women,' she explained. She chuckled. 'He was a one for the women. Not that I complained; I've always taken my men where I find 'em, with no strings.' She eyed Lampson and gave him a wink. 'If you get my drift. Although I have rules. No married men. Are you married?'

'Widowed,' said Lampson.

'Yeah, well, that's alright. I'm a widow myself. His merry widow, Bert used to call me.' She chuckled again. 'No ties. No strings. Take your fun where you can find it, especially in these times when you don't know if you're going to be alive tomorrow.'

'When did you meet Bert?'

'After my brother was killed in action. Bert turned up on my doorstep and said he'd like to write a piece about him, his bravery giving up his life for his country, that sort of thing. Well, I told him, I loved my brother, but Sid was no hero. He'd never done anything heroic in his life. He signed on for the navy because he didn't fancy going into the army. He was doing his job. It was just his bad luck the ship he was on got torpedoed.'

'Did Bert write about him?'

'Oh yes, and a nice piece it was, too. Our mum cut it out of the paper and got it framed and hung it on her parlour wall to show the neighbours.'

'And you saw Bert after that?'

'I did.' She gave a wistful smile. 'He was fun. We used to go for walks, and sometimes he'd come back here, and a couple of times we went to his place for a bit of what you fancy.' She looked at Lampson, a risqué smile playing on her lips as she added, 'I expect you do the same thing yourself, being a widower and footloose and fancy-free.'

Lampson avoided the obvious invitation and asked, 'When did you stop seeing him?'

'Stop?' She frowned, remembering, then said, 'It was after that madwoman had a go at me. Threatened me.'

'What madwoman?'

'I never found out her name. I didn't ask. There was a knock on my door and I opened it and there was this woman standing there, absolutely furious. "Stay away from my man!" she said. "Who?" I asked. "What man?" "Bert Marsh," she said. "He's my man and you'd better stay away from him if you know what's good for you." With that, she stormed off. Well, of course, I had it out with Bert. "I told you I don't go with married men," I said, "and that includes men

180

who are engaged or committed to someone else."'

'What did he say to that?'

'He said he wasn't committed to anyone else. He asked who this woman was who'd come round, and I said I didn't know, she never gave her name. Just gave me a mouthful of abuse. He asked me to describe her, so I did, and he nodded and said, all very grim-like, "She's nothing to me. I'm not tied up with her. We had a bit of a fling, that's all, but it's over now." "Not in her head it ain't," I told him. I told him it was over between us. "I don't want mad women turning up and chasing after me in the street," I told him.'

'Can you give me a description of this woman?' asked Lampson.

'I'll give you the same one I gave Bert,' she said, and she proceeded to describe the woman as Lampson wrote the details down in his notebook: in her fifties, greying hair, medium height, on the plump side, dowdy-looking, her clothes ordinary, not expensive but not tatty, quiet voice with a working-class accent. 'She wore a long winter coat and flat shoes. Just like any ordinary middle-aged woman in any street. When I described her to him, Bert recognised her right enough, but he never told me her name. Not that I wanted to know who she was. Like I said, I didn't want her in my life.'

* * *

CHAPTER SIXTEEN

Thursday 2nd January 1941

Sadie Morris was the next on Coburg's list of Svetlana Rostova's clients. Sadie was a cleaner at The Dorchester hotel and had just finished her shift when Coburg called at The Dorchester.

'I saw her card on the table when I came to work one day,' she told Coburg. 'I've always had an interest in that sort of thing. I've been to other fortune-tellers, you know, so I had something to compare her with. I went to one who did something called the I Ching, where they throw coins the air and the way they fall is supposed to tell you what path to take.' She shook her head. 'It was interesting, but not my kind of thing. Lady Za Za did things more scientifically. She cast horoscopes depending on your date and time of birth. She also read my palms, and explained to me what the different lines meant.'

'Did she ask you much about yourself?' asked Coburg.

'Not really. It was mainly me asking her. She had this accent, you see, and I asked her where she came from, and she told me she came from Russia. She'd had a fascinating life.' She gave a sad sigh. 'It's terrible to think someone killed her. Why would anyone want to do that?'

Emily Winstone was a small, thin woman in her fifties, living in a small third-floor flat in the Angel, Islington. Lampson introduced himself and showed her his warrant card, but as soon as he mentioned the name Bert Marsh, her eyes flared with anger and she glared at Lampson.

'Someone killed him, you say?' she said, tight-lipped.

'Yes,' said Lampson. 'We're talking to everyone who had anything to do with him to try and find a motive.'

'I can give you a motive,' she said.

'In that case, can I come in?' asked Lampson.

She opened the door and led him through to a sparsely furnished, tiny living room. Lampson settled himself down in one of the two armchairs and took out his notebook and a pencil, Winstone sitting down in the other. Lampson reflected that although she appeared to be a frail, almost bird-like woman, there was something in the set of her jaw and in her eyes that indicated a woman of emotional, if not physical, strength.

'I believe Bert Marsh came to talk to you about your brother, Edward?'

She nodded, her face still showing her anger. 'That's what he said he was calling for, but I soon discovered what he was really after. He started by telling me how sorry he was about Edward. Edward was ground crew at Manston Airfield in Kent and he was killed during a raid. I made him a cup of tea, and it wasn't long before he started to get fresh with me.'

'How did he go about it?'

'He started by going to put his arm around me, pretending to be comforting, but I'm not that simple. I told him to go, but instead he kept on, trying to cuddle me. And he would have kept trying if I hadn't hit him.'

'You hit him?'

She nodded and showed Lampson her clenched fist. 'I may be small but I've got strong bones. I used to have play-fights with Edward when we were kids. He was quite a useful boxer and he showed me the moves and different sorts of punches. I landed Marsh a hard one right in the face. That soon put a stop to him. When he saw I was building up to letting him have another, he grabbed up his hat and he was off like the rat he was.'

'Have you seen him since? Or heard from him?'

She shook her head. 'No. He knew he wasn't wanted. There was no chance of him coming back here ever again.'

* * *

Coburg returned to the Yard in case Lampson had come back, but there was no sign of his sergeant. Instead, Coburg picked up his telephone and asked the switchboard to get him the number he'd noted down from Svetlana's card with the contact details of Eleanor Bidlow. He recognised the address on it as being that of Henry Bidlow, a member of parliament he'd met some years before. Remembering that encounter and disliking the man, Coburg decided to telephone Mrs Bidlow first, rather than just turn up and knock on her door. For one thing, he didn't fancy coming into contact with Henry Bidlow again, so he hoped to fix it up so he saw Mrs Bidlow on her own.

When the call was connected and he found himself speaking to Mrs Bidlow – who came across as a rather nervous woman – he introduced himself, and asked if he could come to see her.

'What's it about?' she asked, her tone wary.

'It's just a police procedure,' he said, trying to sound reassuring. 'I promise I won't take up much of your time.'

Thirty minutes later he was entering the rather grand house in Knightsbridge where Henry Bidlow and his wife, Eleanor, lived. Coburg was relieved to discover that Henry Bidlow was out – 'He's at the Houses of Parliament,' explained Eleanor Bidlow – and surprised to note that the MP's wife sported a black eye. Mrs Bidlow saw him looking at it and gave a rueful smile. 'I'm afraid I walked into a door,' she said.

Of course you did, thought Coburg sceptically.

She invited him into the parlour and once they were both sitting down she asked him how she could help.

'We're investigating the death of a fortune-teller who called herself Lady Za Za,' he told her. 'Her real name was Svetlana Rostova. We believe you consulted her.'

Eleanor Bidlow shook her head. 'No,' she said. 'I don't recognise the name.'

Coburg took the card with Eleanor Bidlow's name on it from his pocket and passed it to her. 'This is the card we collected from Svetlana's card index,' he told her. 'It's just one of many such cards, so there's nothing to be embarrassed about. If you turn it over you'll see that you paid her five pound for the consultation.'

She turned the card over, then returned it to Coburg.

'Yes, I remember her now,' she said apologetically. 'You say you're investigating her death. How did she die?'

'She was stabbed. Unfortunately, it seems to be murder.'

'But who'd want to murder her?' she asked, shocked.

'That's what we're hoping our enquiries will lead us to,' said Coburg. 'May I ask why you gave her five pounds? It seems quite generous as most of her other clients paid her around ten shillings, sometimes a pound, but rarely more than that.'

She hesitated, then said, 'She told me that she was homeless and I took pity on her. She seemed to have had a difficult life.' She waved her hand around the opulent décor of the room they were sitting in. 'As you can see, my husband and I have quite a good lifestyle. It seemed unfair that we should have so much and she – who I thought was a lovely and genuine person – should have so little.'

'That's very commendable, Mrs Bidlow,' said Coburg. 'May I ask how your husband felt about you seeing a fortune-teller?'

She hesitated, then asked, 'Do you know my husband, Chief Inspector?'

'I met him some time ago during a case,' said Coburg.

'Then you know that he can be quite cynical about some things.'

'Including fortune-telling?'

'Yes.'

'Does he know you had a session with Lady Za Za?'

'Yes,' she said. 'I told him. I must admit, I hadn't intended to, but it sort of slipped out.'

Which is where you got your black eye, I expect, thought Coburg. Aloud, he said, 'What did Svetlana – Lady Za Za – tell you about your future?'

'Nothing major,' she answered. 'She said I'd had some difficult times recently, but they would improve.'

She gave a light laugh. 'But then, I think the same could be said for all of us with this war going on as it is.'

'What form did her fortune-telling take?' asked Coburg. 'A crystal ball? Tarot cards?'

'She read my hands. She also drew a horoscope based on my date of birth. It was very interesting. She spent quite a lot of time on it, so I thought that the five pounds I paid her was actually a fair rate for what she did. The time she spent.'

'How long was she here?'

'About an hour. Possibly longer.'

'And during that time she obviously told you quite a bit about herself.'

'Yes.'

'And, of course, she would have been interested in you and your life. It must have been nice to find someone you could talk to.'

'Yes, it was,' she said rather awkwardly. 'Not that I told her much. Mostly I listened to her story.'

'Of course,' said Coburg. He stood up and produced a card from his pocket, which he gave her. 'Thank you, Mrs Bidlow, you've been very helpful. This is my card with my contact details. If you think of anything that might be helpful in us finding the person who hurt Svetlana, don't hesitate to give me a call. If I'm not there, my sergeant, Sergeant Lampson, is usually in the office.'

CHAPTER SEVENTEEN

Thursday 2nd January 1941

Coburg returned to Scotland Yard and found Lampson already in the office.

'How did you get on, guv?' asked Lampson.

'Not very well,' admitted Coburg with a sigh. 'Although I had one interesting talk with an Eleanor Bidlow, the wife of Henry Bidlow MP. I thought the name Bidlow was familiar when I saw it on the list. What was interesting was Eleanor Bidlow's black eye.'

'A black eye?' echoed Lampson, shocked. 'You reckon her old man's knocking her about?'

'I do. Some years ago I had a call to go to the House of Commons after some papers had gone missing. It was suspected that someone in Henry Bidlow's office might have been involved.'

'And were they?'

Coburg nodded. 'A secretary. She was being paid by some opposition politician to get any dirt she could on Henry Bidlow. There was an election coming up and they wanted to take that seat from him.'

'So, political skulduggery and shenanigans.'

'Yes. However, when I met Henry Bidlow as part of my investigation I took a strong dislike to him. He was a bully. He bullied his staff, and he tried to bully me, until he found out about the Saxe-Coburg name, and my being an Honourable and my brother the Earl of Dawlish. He soon backed off, worried that I might know important people and say bad things about him.'

'But his wife's black eye?'

'Yes. It sounds like he hasn't improved his behaviour. I think I might dig a little deeper into Henry Bidlow MP.'

'To upset him?' asked Lampson with a grin.

'Partly,' admitted Coburg. 'But there is a possibility that Mrs Bidlow may have told Svetlana something her husband would rather not be known, and he wanted to make sure it didn't go any further.'

'Such as?'

'I have no idea,' Coburg said. 'But when I met him I got the impression he was completely untrustworthy and quite liable to be involved in corrupt practices.'

'So he's a suspect?'

'At the moment he's a person of interest,' said Coburg.

The telephone rang and Lampson picked it up.

'DCI Coburg's office,' said Lampson. 'DS Lampson speaking.' He listened, then looked enquiringly at Coburg. 'It's reception, guv. Sir Vincent Blessington of the Foreign Office is here and asking if he can see you.'

'Sir Vincent Blessington?' Coburg frowned. 'What can he want?'

'My guess is it's something to do with the two dead Russians,' offered Lampson.

'Yes, I expect you're right. Tell reception to send him up.'

'The boss says to send him up,' said Lampson.

A few moments later the tall, elegant figure of Sir Vincent Blessington was shown into the office. Coburg shook his hand, then gestured for him to take a chair.

'You remember Sergeant Lampson?' he asked.

'Indeed I do,' said Blessington with a friendly smile.

'What can we do for you?' asked Coburg.

Blessington held out a copy of the *Daily Globe*.

'I don't know if you've seen today's edition of this?' he asked.

'No,' said Coburg. 'It's not my newspaper of choice, especially after they accused me of being responsible for the death of Mr Grigor Rostov, a Russian immigrant and employee of the Railway Executive Committee. I assume that's why you're here?'

'Yes, and then again, no,' said Blessington. 'If you read the story it will make it clear.'

Coburg read the story, which was in banner headlines on the front page. '"A Soviet Russian assassination squad killed Svetlana Rostova. Then they killed her brother, Grigor. Now they've killed our reporter Bert Marsh, who exposed the truth about their actions. How much longer are we going to allow these allies of the madman Hitler to walk freely around our country killing our citizens?"'

Coburg passed the newspaper to Lampson to look at the story.

'Very emotive stuff,' he commented. 'To the point of being incendiary.'

'Which is exactly what happened,' said Blessington, concerned. 'This morning some youths attacked the Soviet Embassy, throwing bricks, smashing the windows, and shouting "Murderers!" This sort of thing creates problems with the Russians. This kind of allegation works up anti-Soviet fever.'

'They are our enemies in this war,' Coburg pointed out.

'Technically they are neutral,' said Blessington. 'They have a non-aggression pact with the Germans, but that's not the same as being on the Germans' side, as is the case with Mussolini and the Italians. At the moment we've been able to put a lid on this situation over the attack on the embassy. The youths who did it have been cautioned, so there'll be no court appearance, which means it won't get in the papers. The last thing we want is anyone else copying them and doing the same.'

'Why is it so important we keep on the side of the Russians?' asked Coburg. 'You can call it a non-aggression pact, but basically they favour Hitler.'

'That could change,' said Blessington. 'If it does, we'll need them on our side.' Awkwardly, he added, 'I know you're not fond of the Russians after what happened, with your wife getting shot—'

He was cut off by Coburg snapping sharply, 'If you're going to tell me it wasn't the Russians who shot her, I'm well aware of that. Just as I'm aware that the Russians were involved with the people who *did* shoot her, and it happened outside the Russian Embassy as we were being taken in there against our will. Despite what various people have told me – including a particular one I have great respect for – I don't trust the Russians, and everything that Grigor Rostov told me makes me sure that I'm right not to. I'm not saying they killed Grigor and his sister, or Bert Marsh, but there's a possibility, and sooner or later I may have to go and question them.'

'If you have to, that might be better done on neutral ground. With an observer present.'

'You?'

'Or someone else from the Foreign Office.'

After Blessington had left, Lampson asked, 'Does this mean we switch our attention to the Russkies?'

'No,' said Coburg. 'Let's finish what we've started. You carry on with Marsh's women and I'll go and see the last few on my list. Then we'll meet back here and compare notes.'

The next woman from Bert Marsh's notebooks on Lampson's list was Betty Meadows, a plain woman in her mid-fifties. As he had with the previous women he'd visited, Lampson explained the reason for his visit and asked if he could come inside and talk about Bert Marsh.

'I didn't really know him,' she said. 'He came round once to ask me questions about my husband, Paul, who was killed. That was all.'

Lampson gave her a friendly grin. 'That seems to be the same with most people we've talked to, but then I suppose it's only to be expected of a newspaper reporter. They pop in and they pop out.'

Grudgingly, it seemed to Lampson, she allowed him to come in and showed him into the parlour. As he was about to settle himself down on a chair, his eye caught the two photograph displays on the sideboard, one of Betty Meadows on her own, obviously taken by a professional photographer in a studio, and in the other she was smiling and standing beside a man who looked to Lampson very much like Bert Marsh. Surprised, he turned to Meadows and asked, 'That's you with Bert Marsh, isn't it?'

Meadows looked discomforted. 'No,' she said. 'That's me and my late husband. Paul.'

'He looks like Marsh,' said Lampson, going to the sideboard and looking closer at the photo.

'Does he?' said Meadows. 'I never noticed it. But then, he wasn't here long. And I was still in shock about Paul being killed when he came.'

'How did you get on with him?' asked Lampson. 'Marsh, I mean.'

She shrugged. 'He was just a man. He came and asked me about Paul. Said he was writing a thing about him and the other brave men who died. Paul was killed when his ship was sunk. He was in the navy.'

'When did Marsh call on you?'

She thought. 'Paul was killed towards the end of October. It must have been early in November.'

'Did he just call that once?'

She hesitated, then said, 'No. He came back a week later. Said he needed to check some facts.'

Lampson nodded and made a note in his notebook, then asked, 'Forgive my asking, Mrs Meadows, but when Marsh was here, did he make any improper advances to you?'

She stared at him, indignation writ large on her face.

'No he did not!' she burst out. 'How dare you? What sort of woman do you think I am?'

'It's not the sort of woman you are, Mrs Meadows, it's the sort of man Bert Marsh was. We've had reports that he made improper suggestions to some of the women he talked to, especially those he came to interview about their husbands' tragic death. Taking advantage of them, so to speak.'

'Well, he didn't do it with me!' snapped Meadows. 'Now I'll trouble you to leave. It's upsetting enough for me to be reminded about what happened to my poor late husband, without having that muck thrown at me.'

Lady Deirdre Pitstone lived in a large, luxurious-looking house in Kensington. The door was opened to his ringing the doorbell by a short, chubby teenage girl wearing a maid's uniform.

'My name's Detective Chief Inspector Saxe-Coburg from Scotland Yard,' said Coburg, holding out his warrant card. 'Is it possible to see Lady Pitstone?'

'If you wait here, I'll go and see,' said the girl. She drew back and shut the door. *Now to see if Ted Lampson's idea that the Saxe-Coburg name opens doors of titled people*, mused Coburg to himself.

The door was opened and the young maid reappeared. 'Lady Pitstone will see you,' she said.

Coburg entered and followed her to a large and luxuriously decorated room adorned with early paintings from the Victorian and Edwardian eras. A woman in her mid-fifties sitting on a settee smiled genially at Coburg as he entered the room. She endeavoured to get up, but then found the effort too much and sat down again heavily.

Lady Pitstone was almost elegantly dressed. *Almost*, because some of the buttons of her dress had been done up wrongly and the pearl necklace she wore hung slightly to one side rather than straight down. When she spoke with a genial 'A policeman! What fun!', Coburg realised that if she wasn't actually drunk, she was close to it. As he sat, she picked up the brandy glass from the small table next to her and took a gulp.

'Thank you, Debbie,' she said. 'You may go.'

The maid bobbed a small curtsey, then left the room.

'To what do I owe the pleasure of your visit?' asked Lady Pitstone.

'We understand that you consulted a fortune-teller, a Lady Za Za,' said Coburg.

Lady Pitstone frowned, digging into her depths of memory, then her face brightened and she said, 'Yes, I did!' She frowned again as she asked, 'Why? Is anything wrong?'

'I'm afraid to tell you that Lady Za Za was stabbed to death at some time on Christmas Day.'

'No!' exclaimed Pitstone, shocked. 'Why? Why would anyone do that? She was a delightful creature.'

'That's what we're trying to find out. We're working on the possibility that the murderer might have thought Lady Za Za had gained information from one of her clients that they didn't want known.'

'What sort of information?'

'Again, we don't know, and at the moment it's just a theory. To be honest, we're groping in the dark and looking for any piece of information we can find that might help us. What sort of things did Lady Za Za ask you?'

'She didn't really ask me anything. She just told me things. You know, what the future held for me.'

'And what did she say the future held for you?'

Lady Pitstone smiled. 'She told me I would find love again. I'm a widow, you see. My late husband, Lord Pitstone, died falling off a horse two years ago. Or it may

197

have been three. He hunted, you know. Do you hunt?'

'No,' said Coburg.

'Nor do I,' said Pitstone. 'It seems so pointless and cruel, chasing some poor deer halfway across the countryside. I'm a vegetarian, you see. No meat passes my lips.'

With that, she took another swig of brandy and topped her glass up from the nearby bottle, her hand shaking enough to spill a drop.

'I thought she was terribly clever,' said Lady Pitstone, lifting her glass, 'She didn't use a crystal ball or anything, just did it using the lines she saw on my hands. Palmistry, she said it was.'

There was a gentle tap at the door and they both turned towards it as it opened and the small maid entered.

'Excuse me, mum,' she said. 'Your brother's here.'

'Sean!' cried Lady Pitstone delightedly. As before, she made an attempt to rise up, then decided against it and fell back on the settee as a man in his thirties entered the room. He was tall and thin, dark-haired, bespectacled, and when he saw Coburg he gave him a look of puzzled enquiry.

'Sean, this is Detective Chief Inspector Conway,' said Lady Pitstone.

'Coburg,' Coburg corrected her gently as he rose to his feet and held out his hand towards the newcomer, who shook it.

'Yes, of course. Coburg,' said Lady Pitstone with a rueful smile of apology.

'A detective chief inspector?' queried Kennedy.

'From Scotland Yard,' added Lady Pitstone, impressed. 'This is my brother, Chief Inspector. Mr Sean Kennedy.' She smiled affectionately at Kennedy. 'He's something important in the Irish High Commission. Secretary to the high commissioner himself, John Welby . . .' She frowned as she struggled to remember the name.

'John Whelan Dulanty,' said Kennedy. 'So, what does a Scotland Yard chief inspector want with my sister?'

Coburg recognised the trace of an Irish accent, but one muted by many years of standard English. He guessed that Sean Kennedy was a product of some English public school.

'He's looking into the murder of Lady Za Za,' said Lady Pitstone.

'Lady Za Za?' asked Kennedy.

'The fortune-teller,' she said. 'You remember, you met her.'

'No, I don't think so,' said Kennedy thoughtfully.

'Yes you did. You called when she was doing a session with me. The Russian woman.'

Kennedy thought some more, then said, 'Oh yes. Though I only saw her briefly. When I saw you were busy, I left.' He turned to Coburg. 'Did you say she's been murdered?'

'She has indeed, I'm afraid to say,' said Coburg.

'And have you found her killer yet?' asked Kennedy.

'We're still looking,' said Coburg.

'I hope you don't think I killed her!' Lady Pitstone laughed suddenly, the shrill sound slightly unnerving to Coburg. And, he saw, unnerved her brother.

Kennedy threw a concerned look at Coburg and whispered, 'You must excuse my sister, Chief Inspector. She sometimes doesn't realise when a joke can be misinterpreted. My sister wouldn't hurt a fly.'

'I didn't mean it, you silly goose!' said Lady Pitstone, and she let out another hearty laugh, managing to rise to her feet this time before swaying and then toppling down onto an armchair.

Kennedy gave Coburg a look of apologetic embarrassment. 'Really, Deirdre,' he said in tones of gentle yet firm chastisement.

Kennedy turned to Coburg and muttered awkwardly, 'I'm afraid my sister isn't really herself at the moment, Chief Inspector. Perhaps it would be better if you could call back later, when she's more in the mood for answering questions. I'd be very happy to be here with you and her, if you feel that might help. I could ensure she's not in such an . . . ah . . . excitable state.'

'I'm in the mood now!' said Lady Pitstone petulantly.

Coburg turned to her and smiled genially. 'Perhaps your brother's right, Lady Pitstone. Next time I'll make an appointment.'

'I'll give you my telephone number,' offered Kennedy, and he produced a pasteboard visiting card, which he handed to Coburg. 'This is the number for the Irish High Commission. It's at Regent Street, overlooking Piccadilly Circus. Just give me a ring when you want to call.'

'Thank you,' said Coburg, pocketing the card.

'I'll just show the chief inspector out, Deirdre,' said Kennedy.

In the passageway, beside the ornate front door, Kennedy leant in to Coburg and whispered, 'I'm sorry about my sister. You must take everything she tells you with a pinch of salt. I'm afraid she can be indiscreet when she's had too much libation.'

'I understand.' Coburg nodded.

'What did she tell you?'

'Not a great deal,' said Coburg. 'We'd only just started talking when you arrived.'

Kennedy nodded. 'Don't forget my offer,' he said. 'Next time you plan to visit my sister, do be sure to give me a call and I'll pop round.'

CHAPTER EIGHTEEN

Thursday 2nd January 1941

Lampson called at the offices of the *Daily Globe*, showed his warrant card to the receptionist, and asked, 'Do you have a photograph of Bert Marsh? Your reporter who was murdered?'

'Yes. We keep photos of all our regular reporters because sometimes we use them to let readers see who's reporting their news. Readers like to see who they are.'

'Can you let me have a copy of his photo? I promise I'll bring it back.'

'That's alright, we've got some spare. We do that because sometimes fans want a signed photo of their favourite journalist.'

She left the desk and returned a few moments later with a photograph of Bert Marsh, which she handed to Lampson.

'Thanks,' said Lampson.

'Have you any idea who did it?' asked the receptionist. 'Killed him?'

'We're still looking into it. But this will be a great help. I'm hoping it might even lead us to his killer.'

* * *

Lampson returned to the street where Betty Meadows lived, but instead of calling on her, he knocked at the door of the neighbouring house. A short, elderly lady in her sixties looked out at him. 'Yes?' she asked.

Lampson showed her his warrant card and introduced himself.

'Scotland Yard,' she said, impressed. 'Well well! What's it about?'

'We're looking into a man who's vanished, and we're checking the local area.'

'Who is he? Would I know him?'

'Albert Smith,' lied Lampson glibly. He produced the photo of Bert Marsh and offered it to the woman. She took it and studied it thoughtfully. 'I've seen him, but not for a while. It was a few weeks ago. He used to call on Betty next door.'

'Was he a regular caller?'

The woman thought about it. 'I saw him knocking at her door about four or five times, and they'd go out together. I don't know where they went.' She grinned. 'He even stayed over a couple of nights.' She gave a smile as she added, 'But then she's a widow and life is short these days, so you can't condemn her. People have to find comfort where they can. And I thought it was nice for her to meet someone she got along with, after that misery of a husband of hers.'

'Her husband?'

'Yes. He was in the navy. He was killed when his

ship was sunk. Miserable git, he was.'

'What did he look like?'

'Paul? Short, thin, with a face like a weasel. Never smiled.'

'So he didn't look like this bloke?' asked Lampson, pointing at the photograph.

'Paul?' The woman chuckled. 'That rat. No. Far from it. Like I said, he was short and thin. This bloke was big and cheerful.'

Coburg and Lampson sat in their office and reported on their experiences of talking to the different people on their lists.

'The most interesting was my call on Lady Deirdre Pitstone,' said Coburg.

'A toff, eh.' Lampson smiled. 'In what way, interesting?'

'She was drunk,' said Coburg.

'At that time of day?' said Lampson, scandalised.

'To a true alcoholic there is no separate time of day for a glass or two. Or ten.'

'Let me guess, she came on to you?'

Coburg shook his head. 'No, I didn't get the impression she saw me in that way. The interesting thing was the arrival of her brother.'

'He protected you from her?' Lampson chuckled.

'I got the impression he was protecting himself from her,' said Coburg.

'Eh?' said Lampson, puzzled.

'Nothing concrete was said, but it was his manner. When she mentioned I was there investigating the murder of Lady Za Za, there was a look in his face. Almost alarm, though he did his best to hide it. And he then went on to suggest that his sister wasn't in the right frame of mind to answer questions. At least, not lucidly, in which he was quite right, and he said it might be a good idea that the next time I came, he was there. He suggested it was because he could stop her drinking before I arrived.'

'But you see it differently,' said Lampson, intrigued.

'Yes,' said Coburg. 'I think he wanted to be there to monitor what she said, and make sure there were some things she didn't say.'

'Such as?'

'I've no idea,' admitted Coburg. 'And I might be wrong, but I got the impression he didn't want me talking to her.'

'Did he mention Svetlana?'

'Only to deny that he'd met her. Then when his sister reminded him he'd met Svetlana when she was having a session with her, he said he vaguely remembered her, but he didn't stay.'

'So what d'you reckon's going on? Why wouldn't he want his sister talking to you?'

'Because she drinks, and when she drinks I get the impression she talks without inhibition about things.'

'Things he doesn't want you to know?'

'It's just a hunch. A gut feeling,' said Coburg. 'I may be totally wrong. He might just be concerned for his sister.'

'But you'd still like to look into him?'

'And her,' said Coburg. 'Both of them. Because maybe she knows something that Kennedy doesn't want made public, and he's concerned she may have said something to Svetlana. After all, it's known that some rather dubious fortune-tellers ferret out information from their clients in order to use it and impress them. How about you? How did you get on with Marsh's women?'

'I think I might have got something.'

'Oh?'

'A woman called Betty Meadows. I'm pretty sure she was having an affair with Bert Marsh.'

'I doubt if she was the only one,' commented Coburg. 'He seems to have tried his luck on every woman he came into contact with.'

'Yes, but I got the impression this was different. Some just saw it as a bit of fun in what are uncertain times, never knowing what's going to happen. But I think she was serious about him. She had a photo of him and her together on her sideboard, looking every inch the happy couple. When I asked her about it, she said it wasn't Marsh, it was her late husband. But I talked to her neighbour about her late husband, Paul, and the neighbour described him as someone who looked completely different from Marsh.'

'So you reckon this Betty Meadows got involved with Marsh and . . . what? Someone got jealous of him and her and bumped him off?'

'No, I think she may have done it. I met this other woman called Vera Truscott who cheerfully admitted to having a fling with Marsh, until she was threatened by this woman who fitted the description of Betty Meadows. This woman warned her to "stay away from my man".'

'So you're thinking that Betty Meadows found out that Marsh was still having various flings with different women and killed him in a jealous rage?'

'I am,' said Lampson. 'I also canvassed the houses opposite Bert Marsh's house, and one of the people who lives there gave me a description of a woman who entered Bert Marsh's house on the evening of Tuesday 31st December, and it sounds like Betty Meadows. I just need the use of the car to clinch it. I thought I'd take this Vera Truscott to Betty Meadows's house then knock on the door and say I've got to double-check something with her. Something simple she can answer at the door. Then I ask Mrs Truscott if she was the woman who threatened her. If she is, Betty Meadows may well be the one.'

Coburg nodded and stood up. 'Good work, Ted. Let's go and pick up this Mrs Truscott and test it.'

* * *

207

They picked up Vera Truscott and made for Betty Meadows's house. Leaving Coburg in the passenger seat, and Mrs Truscott in the back, Lampson walked to Betty Meadows's house and knocked.

Of course, she could be out, he thought. *In which case this will have been a waste of time and we'll have to do it all over again later.*

He was relieved to hear the door catch opening and then Betty Meadows was looking out at him, wariness on her face.

'Sergeant Lampson,' he reminded her.

'Yes, I remember you,' she said.

'I'm sorry to trouble you again but I just want to make sure I've got the details right, then I'll clear off. Your late husband's name was Paul Meadows?'

'That's right,' she said.

'And he was in the Merchant Navy?'

'No, the Royal Navy,' she corrected him. 'He was a stoker.'

Lampson made a note in his notebook. 'Thanks, I'm sorry to have troubled you, but my guv'nor's a real stickler for details.'

He tipped his hat, then walked to the waiting police car. Behind him, Betty Meadows closed her door.

'Well?' asked Lampson as he climbed into the passenger seat of the car.

'That's her alright,' said Vera Truscott. 'Was it her? Did she kill Bert?'

'We don't know,' said Coburg. 'We need to talk to her properly. But thanks for that, Mrs Truscott. Your help has been invaluable.'

They returned Vera Truscott to her own home, then made their way back to Betty Meadows's. This time it was Coburg who knocked while Lampson stood just behind him. Betty Meadows opened the door and stood looking at him.

'What's going on?' she demanded indignantly. She glared at Lampson. 'What was all that about my husband?'

'Mrs Meadows, my name is Detective Chief Inspector Coburg and I have to ask you some questions about your relationship with Bert Marsh.'

'There was no relationship between me and Mr Marsh,' she said angrily. 'And I've already answered all the questions I'm going to. Now go away.'

And she started to shut the door, but Coburg swiftly put his boot in the way.

'Mrs Meadows, this is a murder enquiry,' he said. 'We can have this conversation here or we can have it at Scotland Yard.'

Meadows hesitated, then reluctantly opened the door to let them in. They followed her through to the living room where Lampson had interviewed her previously. As Meadows and Coburg sat down, Lampson walked to the sideboard.

'I see that photograph of you and the man you said

was your husband has gone,' commented Lampson. 'It was there on the sideboard when I was here before.'

'I spilt tea on it so I had to throw it away,' said Meadows.

'Where did you throw it?' asked Coburg.

'Why?'

'Because I'd like to see it.'

'I tore it up and flushed the bits down the loo.'

'Why?'

'Because it hurt me to see it all wet and stained with tea.'

Coburg took the photo of Bert Marsh from his pocket. 'The reason I'd like to look at it is because my sergeant told me that the man in the photograph looked very similar to this man, Bert Marsh. Whereas the descriptions we've been given of your late husband are very different from the man in that photograph.'

Meadows said nothing, just sat with her head down.

'We've also had a positive identification of you by a woman who said that you told her to stay away from your man, who you told her was Bert Marsh. She said your attitude was threatening. Do you have any comment to make on that?'

Still, Meadows kept her head down, refusing to answer.

'In that case, Mrs Meadows, I must ask you to accompany me to Scotland Yard . . .'

At this her head jerked up and she glared angrily at him as she shouted, 'No!'

'It's just to talk, Mrs Meadows,' said Coburg.

'We're talking now,' she said flatly.

'I'm afraid it has to be an official interview. If you would get your coat . . .'

'No,' she repeated firmly.

'Very well,' said Coburg. He looked at Lampson. 'Could you get on the radio to Control, Sergeant, and request a couple of WPCs to assist in taking Mrs Meadows to Scotland Yard. As soon as possible.'

'Yes, sir,' said Lampson, and he left the room and the house.

Betty Meadows remained sitting where she was, her face betraying nothing of her feelings.

CHAPTER NINETEEN

Thursday 2nd January 1941

When they reached Scotland Yard, Coburg led the way into the building while the two WPCs followed, escorting Betty Meadows. Lampson brought up the rear, ready to swing into action if Meadows suddenly became violent. Meadows had been reluctant to enter the police car, and was equally reluctant about walking into the building. But the firm pressure the two WPCs maintained on her upper arms kept her moving. Meadows's head hung down; there was an air of shameful defeat about her, a posture she maintained while she was processed, her fingerprints taken, before being escorted to one of the interview rooms. The two WPCs stayed with them, watching Meadows once she had sat down at the table with Coburg and Lampson sitting opposite her. Lampson had his notebook open to take notes of the interview.

'Did you ever spend time with Bert Marsh at his house?' asked Coburg.

Meadows remained silent, resolutely keeping her head down, refusing to look at the two detectives or even around at her surroundings.

'Do you have a solicitor that we can contact to be here with you?' asked Coburg.

She shook her head.

'If you wish, we can arrange for a duty solicitor to be present at this interview to represent your interests.'

Again, she kept her head down and once more shook her head.

Coburg and Lampson exchanged looks of resignation; this was going to be a hard one. Then Coburg spoke.

'Mrs Meadows, we have reason to believe that you were in a relationship with the late Bert Marsh. My sergeant, Detective Sergeant Lampson, saw a photograph of you with a man who looked like Bert Marsh on your sideboard. You told him that was of you with your late husband, but we have been reliably informed that your late husband, Paul Meadows, was very different in appearance from Bert Marsh. You subsequently got rid of that photograph.

'A woman who was also in a relationship with Bert Marsh has identified you as the woman who warned her from associating with him, you telling her that Marsh was your man.

'We've now taken your fingerprints and we expect to find them in the entrance hall and passage of Mr Marsh's house. My sergeant canvassed the houses opposite to Mr Marsh's and you were identified as entering his house on the evening of Tuesday 31st

December, New Year's Eve, and leaving about an hour later. According to our medical examiner, Mr Marsh died during that evening.

'On this evidence alone we have enough to charge you with the murder of Bert Marsh, but before I do I'd like to give you the opportunity to say something in your defence. There could be extenuating circumstances.'

He looked at her, but she continued with her silence, her head down.

'Mrs Meadows, I believe that when Mr Marsh approached you to interview you about your husband, he acted with great sympathy towards you, and you welcomed that sympathy. I believe that sympathy developed into something else, a relationship, which you believed to be genuine on his part. Then you discovered that you were not the only woman he was having a relationship with. This came as a terrible shock to you. Is that a fair summing-up of what happened?'

Slowly, she raised her head and looked at him, and he could see tears rolling down her face.

'He said he loved me,' she said quietly. 'He told me he wanted to marry me. He was so different from Paul, who wasn't loving at all.' She took a deep breath. 'He told me I was the only one for him, but when I found out about that other woman . . .' She shook her head, upset. 'I saw the pair of them together. Bert had told

214

me that other women were always chasing after him and she was one of those, but he had nothing to do with her. I went to see her, to warn her off. When I told her he was my man, she laughed at me. "He's any woman's man," she said. She told me I was just one of a string he had on the go. So I kept a watch on him. Started following him, and sure enough there were other women. So I went round to his house to face him with it.'

'Did you go intending to kill him?' asked Coburg.

'No. I just wanted to know if he meant what he'd told me, about wanting to get married. I wanted to know if I'd been taken for a fool.' She dropped her head again as she continued. 'While I was at his house, the telephone rang. He went to answer it and I listened, and I could tell it was another woman, though he told me it was about work. While he was on the phone, I went into his living room and opened a drawer of his sideboard and I found these photographs. All of them of women, and some of them were nude. I remembered he said once he'd like to photograph me without clothes on, but I wouldn't let him.

'When I saw them, I felt sick. I knew he'd fooled me just so he could get me into bed. I was disgusted with myself, and with him. I was so angry. When he came back from talking on the phone I showed him the photographs of these women, the nude ones, and demanded to know what he was planning to do with me. Well, he began to bluster, telling me these women had sent him these photographs, and the more he talked and the more he lied, the angrier I got. I turned and started to leave, but he came after me. It was when he grabbed me and started trying to kiss me that I snapped. It was like a red mist came down. There was a boot scraper just inside the door, a heavy metal one. I picked it up and hit him with it to make him leave me alone, and once I'd hit him once I just kept hitting him. I couldn't stop myself.'

As Ted Lampson made his way to the local school where his father had arranged for the inaugural meeting of the Somers Town Fire Guard Defence, he thought about Eve Bradley, Terry's teacher. He guessed his father had asked Miss Bradley if he could use her classroom at the school because it had a blackboard, and Lampson knew his father was just itching to act the part of the main organiser and write things on the blackboard: names, instructions, rules, anything so long as he could write things in chalk on it.

Eve Bradley was co-organiser with Lampson of the Somers Town boys' football club, in which Terry was a main player. Lampson had started the team to give Terry something to do when he seemed at risk of getting in with the wrong crowd in Somers Town, boys who stole and caused trouble. The football team was now benefitting boys other than Terry, from the compliments Lampson had received from other parents. The team had been going for about a month and played competitive games with other local teams, although it wasn't as yet part of any league. Usually they played on a Saturday afternoon when Lampson wasn't working and he could take charge, but on one occasion when he hadn't been able to make it, Eve Bradley had been in charge. Not only had the team won, but they'd behaved themselves. Mind, it could be because – as Terry had said – 'she's a real dragon. She frightens the kids, even the really tough ones.'

Lampson didn't find her frightening; he knew she had to act tough because Somers Town had some of the toughest and potentially dangerous kids in any London borough and it was her job to keep them in line if she was going to teach them. Soft teachers suffered in Somers Town.

Lampson's big dilemma when it came to Eve Bradley was how to move their so-far friendly running of the football team into hopefully something more. Inviting her out on a date and seeing if she'd agree.

There were two problems with this. The first was that he didn't know if she felt like that about him. The second was his son, Terry, and how Terry would react if it became common knowledge that his father was going out with his teacher. So far, that alone had stopped Lampson from even asking Eve Bradley out, but he'd decided to ignore the Terry aspect. Yes, Terry would be upset because of the ribbing he'd take from the other kids in his class – *Miss Bradley's* class. But Lampson had his life to lead. He'd been a widower for six years, and although he'd had some relationships during that time, mainly with widows who were also looking for company, none had got under his skin the way Eve Bradley had. He really liked her, and he hoped she liked him. But he didn't know. The only way to find out was to ask her out somewhere. He'd decided on the pictures. It was safe and conventional. He'd spent a long time deciding which film might attract her, and had decided on *Gone With The Wind*. It was said to be a film very popular with women. Lampson would have preferred going to see John Wayne in *Stagecoach*, but he could see that another time, and also take Terry, which would go some way towards appeasing his son if Terry got upset about Lampson going to the pictures with Miss Bradley.

Having reached that decision, Lampson had decided that this evening he would ask Eve if she'd like to go to the pictures with him. At worst, she could only say no. No, he thought sombrely, at worst she could decide not to keep working with him on the football team. But that was a chance he had to take. Today was the day for the important question.

He reached the school and saw there were already a few people, mostly men, walking in through the school entrance. Lampson followed them to Eve Bradley's classroom. Inside, the room had been prepared: the small desks pushed to the back of the room and adult chairs set out in rows facing the blackboard, where Lampson's father was writing the names of the people as they came in. Bert Lampson winked at his son as he walked in and added his name to the list.

Lampson spotted Eve Bradley sitting in the front row, the chairs on either side of her filled up, so there was no chance of him spending the time being able to chat with her. He opted for a chair near the back, and reflected that the back row was where he'd spent most of his time at school as a pupil.

A few more people came in and settled themselves down. Bert Lampson wrote the name of the latest arrival on the board, then turned to address the room.

'Thank you all for coming to this first meeting of the Somers Town Fire Guard Defence. And I'd like to thank Miss Bradley for letting us use her classroom.

'My name, for those who don't know me, is Bert Lampson. Later on we'll be electing a committee, but for the moment my job is to set out what the Fire Guard Defence is about, and how we're going to handle it.

'You may have heard the Home Secretary, Herbert Morrison, on the wireless talking about the recent fires that have been tearing this great city of ours apart. It's the incendiary devices – the fire bombs – that the Germans are dropping that are causing most of the damage, even more than the heavy bombs. The trouble is a small fire starts, and pretty soon it becomes a big fire, and once it's big it needs more and more firemen to fight it. And we haven't got enough firemen, and we haven't got enough water. So our job is to stop the small fires before they get out of control.

'What the government's done is split every part of London into smaller areas, and it's local people who'll be responsible for their own area. So at the moment, although there ain't many of us, we're the Somers Town Fire Guard Defence unit. The hope is that more people will join in once word spreads. What the government is saying is that volunteers need to do forty-eight hours a month at night, because it's at night that the Germans attack.'

'That's twelve hours a week!' said Sid Potter doubtfully. 'And all at night!'

'It is,' agreed Mr Lampson, 'but the more there are of us, the shorter time we can spend.'

'Twelve hours a week!' repeated Potter, unhappily. 'There'll be many days when we won't have slept at all. Work in the day, fire watch at night, work the next day, fire watch again the next night.'

'Yes, Sid,' said Mr Lampson. 'We get your point. But a lot of people are doing that already. The blokes fighting overseas. Those RAF boys. The navy. Hospital workers. Look, no one's going to ask people to do the impossible. I'm just telling you what the government have said they want. But we're in charge here, so we'll sort out how we do it.'

'I thought on the wireless they said it was compulsory,' put in Jim Jones.

'It will be compulsory, but right now they just want to get something in place to stop London burning, otherwise we could all fry in our beds.'

There were some unhappy and uncomfortable looks exchanged at this.

'Look,' said Mr Lampson, 'let's get on to what we're going to do and then we can sort out how we're going to do it. The first part of it is the fire-watchers. Their job is to watch out for incendiary devices coming down and sound the alarm. It's suggested they be on the roofs of buildings so they get a good view and when they see something dropping they phone the fire brigade.'

'From the roof of a building?' queried Jones.

'The buildings will be the big ones with a telephone on the next floor down. Like Maples repository,' said Mr Lampson.

'Sounds a bit dangerous,' said Sid Potter. 'Being on the roof.'

'You've got to be where you can see the bombs falling.'

'Say one lands on that roof,' said Jones.

'Then this is where this comes in,' said Mr Lampson, and he proudly gestured at what looked like a sort of bicycle pump with a long piece of hose attached poking out of a deep bucket. 'It's a stirrup pump. There'll be water in the bucket and you start pumping and it sprays water through the hose on whatever's burning.' He pointed at a piece of metal poking out from the bottom of the bucket. 'You have to pump it hard so you put your foot on that to stop it toppling over.' He then pointed at the other instruments beside him. 'The garden rake. That's if the device drops on straw or combustible material so you can drag it off before the fire gets going.'

He then pinned a picture to the wall beside the blackboard. It was of a metal cylinder with a three-finned metal tail at one end.

'So you know what we'll be dealing with,' he said. 'This is one of them incendiary bombs. It's about a foot long and three inches in diameter, and it's lethal. It's filled with thermite, which is an incendiary compound. There's a needle inside the device, which, when it hits something, is pushed into an ignition cap and that ignites the thermite, starting a fire. The whole thing sets alight, and the heat this stuff gives off burns so strong it can melt steel.'

For the next hour the men and women sat and watched and listened as Mr Lampson went through the various pieces of equipment they'd be using, along with the organisational structure of the Fire Guard Defence unit.

When the session finished, Lampson walked over to Eve Bradley.

'That was hard going,' he said with a sigh, but making sure his father didn't hear what he was saying.

'It was good, though,' she said. 'I thought your dad did well. He's a bit of natural leader.'

Lampson gave a grin. 'He's in his element,' he said. 'He hated it when he retired. He was a foreman on building sites and he loved ordering people around. This gives him the chance to do it all again. And, even better for him, he's in charge.'

'I gather from the list of names he put on the board that he's roped you in as one of the volunteers.'

'Yeah, well, I could hardly say no,' said Lampson ruefully. 'Look, changing the subject, and I know it's a bit of a cheek, and I don't want you to think I'm being forward but I wondered how you felt about coming to see *Gone With the Wind*? It's said to be a good film and usually I take Terry to the pictures, but I don't think it's his sort of film.'

He saw the look of disappointment on her face and mentally kicked himself. *She doesn't want to go out with you*, he thought miserably. *She doesn't see you like that.*

'Actually, I'd love to,' she said awkwardly, 'but I promised my sister I'd go with her.'

'Oh, that's alright,' said Lampson, thinking to himself: *At least she's not going with some other bloke*. But it was her next words that took him by surprise.

'But why don't I join you on the roof for when

you're doing your stretch of fire-watching?'

'You?' he said, surprised.

'I heard the announcement on the wireless, and they were asking for women to sign up as well, not just men. When are you doing your session?'

'Tomorrow night,' said Lampson. 'I said I'd do six to midnight, then my dad will take over until six the following morning.'

She nodded. 'Six o'clock tomorrow night. Which roof is it going to be?'

'Maples repository,' said Lampson. 'It's the highest one.'

'Right, I'll see you there.'

'Wear something warm,' Lampson advised her. 'It gets cold up there at night.'

CHAPTER TWENTY

Friday 3rd January 1941

'Fire-watching?' asked Coburg quizzically.

'Yes.' Lampson nodded as he drove the car towards Scotland Yard. Coburg had just picked him up outside his house and Lampson was doing the driving, as was their regular practice. He'd just told Coburg about asking Eve Bradley out, something that Coburg had been urging him to do for some time, reminding him that there was a war on and no one knew what the future held in store, and warned Lampson that if he didn't ask her out then someone else was likely to.

'It's not exactly what I'd call romantic for a first date,' commented Coburg.

'Maybe it's not intended to be,' said Lampson. 'I did suggest going to see *Gone With the Wind* at the pictures, but she's arranged to see it with her sister. So she suggested we do fire-watching together.'

'Interesting woman,' said Coburg. 'And she plays football.'

'What are you implying?' asked Lampson defensively.

'I'm not implying anything,' said Coburg. 'I'm just saying it's refreshing to find someone who doesn't conform to known stereotypes.'

'She ain't like that, if that's what you're suggesting,' said Lampson grumpily. 'She was engaged. Her fiancé was killed at Dunkirk.'

'I'm not suggesting anything like that at all,' said Coburg. 'I'm glad you asked her.' He gave a sigh. 'I suppose I'd better get myself involved in this Fire Guard Defence. After all, if everyone's doing it and it's compulsory, the last thing I want as a detective chief inspector is to be charged with non-compliance of the law.' Suddenly a thought struck him. 'Change of destination,' he announced.

'Oh? Where to?'

'The Foreign Office,' said Coburg.

'What's there?'

'Sir Vincent Blessington,' said Coburg.

'About the Russians?' asked Lampson. 'He was very keen to make sure they're protected.'

'No, this is about Sean Kennedy. Lady Pitstone's brother, who works for the Irish Commission.'

'How does he fit into this?'

'His sister was one of Svetlana's clients.' He frowned. 'I can't put my finger on it, but there's something there. The way he wanted to get me away from his sister. He was obviously worried she was going to say something.'

'What about?'

'That's what I'm hoping Sir Vincent Blessington might be able to throw some light on.'

Henry Bidlow hurried down the steps of the Houses of Parliament and made his way to where the usual line of taxis was waiting. He'd quickened his pace when he'd seen Martin Higgins hovering in the long corridor from the chamber, waiting at the foot of the stairs from the MPs' offices. Bidlow had taken to keeping away from his office as part of avoiding meeting Higgins. The man was mad! But was he mad enough to have murdered that damned fortune-teller, Lady Za Za? And her brother? No, it was a bluff. It had to be.

But say it wasn't?

He leapt into a taxi and gave the cabbie his address, then sat back and ran the problem through his mind as the cab meandered through the busy streets.

The problem was that he'd told Higgins why he wanted him to buy that Russian woman's silence, because he was fairly sure Eleanor had mentioned Krupp to her. She knew he was worried that someone might find out about his connection to the German company – which had done them both a great deal of good for years, put good money in their pockets – and if that happened, his political career would be over. He should have cut his ties with Krupp in

1938 when the writing about a forthcoming war with Germany was on the wall, but he had been sure that Chamberlain would save the day, keep Britain out of whatever conflict was going to happen. But instead the fool had blown it. And now here he was, Henry Bidlow, adviser and shareholder to Krupp, Germany's major weapons manufacturer. He should never have told Eleanor about it, but he'd been so pleased at the coup he'd pulled off back in 1937, landing the highly paid extra-curricular job to his being an MP that he couldn't resist letting her know what a very clever husband she had, and how grateful she should be to him.

He was still thinking these thoughts when he walked into their house and found his wife sitting at a table crying, a handkerchief pressed to her face. *Oh God, what now!*

'What the hell's the matter with you?' he demanded.

Eleanor looked at him, her face streaked with tears. 'That fortune-teller I saw, Lady Za Za. She's been murdered.'

Is that all? thought Bidlow sourly. *I know that already.* It was her next words that struck fear into him.

'A policeman came to tell me. A detective chief inspector from Scotland Yard.'

'A policeman? What in hell did you say to him?'

'Nothing, honestly!'

'Did you tell him you'd met this woman?'

'I told him I didn't know her, but he produced this card she'd made out with my name on it and the amount I'd paid her. Five pounds.'

'So he knows you talked to her?'

'He forced it out of me.'

'For God's sake! Who was he, this detective?'

'His name's Saxe-Coburg.'

Bidlow frowned. 'Saxe-Coburg? I met him. He gets these cases where top people are involved. He cracked the murder at The Ritz, and at The Savoy, and God knows where else.' He groaned. 'This is a disaster!'

'Why? What can he do? He's looking for the person who killed Lady Za Za, not anything else. That German firm you told me to keep quiet about . . .'

'Shut up! Don't even mention their name!'

'I didn't!'

But Higgins would, thought Bidlow nervously. Oh God, this was the worst thing! If any of this got out, any chance he had of political advancement would be gone. *Political advancement?* he thought bitterly. He'd have no political life at all. He might even get tried for treason.

He'd have to attend to Higgins. Shut him up. But how? He didn't have five hundred pounds to spare!

Then he remembered a social event he'd attended the year before, before the Blitz had started. It had been organised by one of his fellow members and was in aid of some local North London charity to help the poor protect their homes in the event of air raids. At least, that was the official purpose. As Bidlow realised once he was there, his fellow MP who'd organised it had another purpose in mind: to introduce important people to two well-known local businessmen, the Bell brothers, Dennis and Danny. The Bell brothers seemed to have fingers in lots of pies, and it soon became apparent that many of these pies were illegal. Protection rackets, the black market, prostitution, thefts on a grand scale, all of which contributed to a very wealthy crime empire run by Dennis and Danny Bell. The purpose of this social event had been to make connections: people with influence on government and its institutions, including the law, to form relationships with the Bell brothers, who were prepared to amply reward such people for protection against the instruments of the state.

Many of the members of parliament who had been present had opted not to embark on such relationships, but quite a few had, and they'd definitely benefitted financially. At that time Bidlow hadn't got involved, mainly because he knew as a very minor member of parliament he had little of value to trade. Also, he was already quite comfortable thanks to his association with Krupp. It was only when things became difficult when trading his Krupp shares that he found himself having to watch his spending.

He remembered reading in the newspapers some months earlier that one of the brothers, Dennis Bell, had been shot dead, leaving Danny Bell in control of the outfit. It had been Danny Bell that Bidlow had spent some time talking to at the social event. Danny Bell had struck Bidlow as the more civilised of the two brothers, the one that he could possibly do business with if he decided to engage in that world.

Bidlow opened his desk drawer and rummaged through it until he found the business card Danny Bell had given him. It gave the address and phone number of the Merrie Tumbler pub in Tudor Street, just off Fleet Street, where the Bell brothers could be contacted. That social event had been held at the Merrie Tumbler.

Bidlow reached for the telephone. It was time for him to return to the Merrie Tumbler.

Fortunately, Sir Vincent Blessington was in and available when Coburg called at the Foreign Office. Ever since he'd first met Blessington, Coburg had got the impression that the diplomat quite enjoyed chatting with him. Coburg guessed that it made a change from the more formal and rather cautious exchanges Blessington was forced to make with his departmental colleagues.

'I've come to pick your brains,' Coburg told him, 'about the Irish High Commission. In particular the senior members of the staff. John Whelan Dulanty and his assistant.'

'As far as we're concerned, Dulanty is one of the good people,' said Blessington.

'An Anglophile?' asked Coburg.

'Oh, most definitely. It was Dulanty who was instrumental in getting Churchill back into parliament at the 1906 election. He supported him in gaining the seat in Manchester.'

'That was as a Liberal, as I recall from my history lessons,' commented Coburg.

'Yes,' said Blessington. 'He'd sat as a Tory MP after being elected in 1901, but in 1904 he crossed the chamber to become a Liberal, and it was as a Liberal he was re-elected in 1906, which he said was largely due to the support he received from Dulanty. The two men have been close ever since.'

'So you would describe Dulanty as pro-British?' asked Coburg, pushing the matter.

'I would. He held quite a few senior positions in the British Civil Service until he resigned over the issue of Irish independence.' Then, thoughtfully, he added, 'Even though one could describe him as pro-British, he's even more pro-Irish.'

'But not anti-British? I ask because there are quite a few members of the Irish government who seem to favour a German victory in this war.'

'There are some, but the majority are sympathetic

to Britain and the Allies and very much opposed to Hitler. Officially, of course, Ireland is neutral in this war. And not just in this war. Article 49 of the 1922 Constitution of the Irish Free State states: "Save in the case of actual invasion, the Irish Free State shall not be committed to participate in any war without the assent of the Oireachtas, the Irish Parliament."'

'What about Dulanty's assistant, Sean Kennedy?'

'Ah, there you have a different personality. By all accounts he's definitely of the United Ireland faction, North and South coming together as an independent Irish nation, ruled by the Irish. That faction resents the fact that de Valera agreed for Ireland to be part of the Commonwealth, with the king as their official head.'

'Is Dulanty aware of Kennedy's views?'

'I'm sure he must be, but how aware of just how deep Kennedy's nationalist views are is another matter. I don't believe Kennedy makes a point of airing his views to all and sundry, at least not here in London.'

'And that faction would like a German victory?'

'I believe the German government has promised support for a united Ireland in the event of their winning this war.'

In her cell in Holloway Prison, Bella Wilson let out a scream of pain and rolled into a ball on the bunk in her prison cell, writhing in agony. Her cellmate,

Jane, came over to her, worried.

'What is it? What's up?'

'Pain!' groaned Wilson. 'Worst ever! Right in my guts. Call someone. I need a doctor.'

Jane went to the door and banged on it and shouted, 'Help! Prisoner in trouble!'

The arrival of anyone in response seemed to take a long time, during which Bella Wilson let out scream after scream of pain and rolled about on her bunk. Finally the sound of a key turning in the lock was heard and the door swung open and a female warder entered, clutching a long wooden baton. Behind her was a tall, muscular male warder also holding a baton.

'Get back to the wall,' barked the woman warder, and Jane retreated, watched over by the man, while the woman warder bent over Wilson, her baton held defensively ready to strike in case it was a ruse.

'What sort of pain is it?' asked the warder.

'Worst pain ever,' groaned Wilson. 'Here. In my guts. Sharp pain like glass digging in.'

'Sound like appendix,' said the male warder. 'My sister had that.'

Of course it sounds like appendix, you idiot, thought Wilson venomously. She was repeating the symptoms she'd experienced when she'd suffered a burst appendix some years before.

'We need an ambulance to get her to hospital,' said

the man. 'We haven't got the facilities to cope with it here.'

'You stay here, outside,' said the female warder. 'Lock the door. I'll phone the ambulance.'

As Wilson heard the key turn in the lock, she let out another scream, but inside she felt a surge of triumph. It was going to work.

Henry Bidlow sat at the table in the Merrie Tumbler and took a swig of the brandy Danny Bell had ordered for him. It was good brandy. Elegant. Like Bell himself, who sat, smartly dressed in an expensive three-piece suit, regarding the MP enquiringly.

'Long time no see, Mr Bidlow,' said Bell. 'I must admit I was surprised to get your phone call after all this time. Has there been a change in your status?' He gave a sly smile. 'An improvement in your political sphere of influence that you feel might be of mutual benefit?'

'Yes and no,' said Bidlow carefully. 'There could be, but at this moment there's an irritation.'

'What sort of irritation?'

'A man who's threatening me.'

'Threatening you?' said Bell. 'Tut tut, that's nasty. What's he threatening you about?'

'He claims to have knowledge about my business dealings that he says will harm my political career. Absolute nonsense, of course. His allegations are

235

totally untrue. But that won't help my reputation if he sneaks them to some sleazy reporter.'

'What are these allegations?' asked Bell.

Bidlow shook his head. 'I refuse to repeat them, they're so patently false.'

'Have you tried buying him off?'

'I did, but the price he demanded was ludicrous. Especially for such false information that would be laughed at if it appeared in print.'

'But you'd prefer it not to appear in print,' said Bell, 'because there are some in your party, and in power, who might not like the idea of anything detrimental to one of their own being aired.'

'Exactly so,' said Bidlow.

'And you're wondering if something couldn't be done to stop this man spreading this false information,' said Bell.

Bidlow nodded. 'I realise there would be expenses involved—' he began, but Bell stopped him with a wave of his hand.

'Let's not talk of that at this stage,' he said. 'Far better would be to think of this as a mutually beneficial relationship, where we can help one another, now and in the future. I'm sure whatever I could do to assist you in your present awkward situation could be reciprocated in some way by your assisting me should I have any issues of concern in the future.' He smiled and held out his hand. 'Is that acceptable to you?'

'Very acceptable,' said Bidlow, reaching out and shaking Bell's hand.

A result! he thought exultantly. *Problem solved, and at no cost to me.*

Following his meeting with Sir Vincent Blessington, Coburg then made his next call on Inspector Hibbert at MI5, intent on continuing his quest to nail down Sean Kennedy's stance on the question of Irish unity.

'As I understand it, the IRA would prefer Germany to win this war.'

'Yes, that's what we've picked up,' said Hibbert. 'We believe there's some kind of unwritten agreement between the Germans and the IRA that if the IRA help the Germans, then Germans will look to grant their wish for a united Ireland. Ulster back in the fold with Munster, Leinster and Connacht.'

'Could Sean Kennedy be involved in any such pro-German activity?'

'I must admit he's on our watch list, particularly because he's the main courier between the high commissioner in London and Dublin,' said Hibbert. 'As you can imagine, we've got people in Dublin keeping tabs on things. But then, we've always done that, right through their War of Independence and during the Civil War that followed: de Valera's crowd and Michael Collins's lot battling for power.'

'And?'

'Our people reported that on nearly every occasion when Kennedy has gone to Dublin with messages for the Irish government, he's also been seen to call in on some Germans of his acquaintance.'

'The same ones each time?'

'He seems to have two different addresses he calls at.'

'Do you know who these people are?'

Hibbert smiled. 'Of course.'

'And are you going to tell me?'

'That depends on what you intend to do with the information,' said Hibbert. 'If your plan is to send someone blundering and planting your big policemen's feet on them . . .'

'That wouldn't be allowed,' Coburg pointed out. 'The British police have no jurisdiction in another sovereign state.'

'No, but we do know you have a tie-up with certain sections of the Irish Garda, and if they went blundering it would upset a situation we have carefully nurtured for some time over there.'

'You know who they are and can keep an eye on who calls on them and who they go to see?'

'Exactly.'

'And what they talk about when they meet?'

'That's not so easy. They tend to go for walks in parks and other open spaces, and as we never know which one they're going to use for their open-air ambulations in advance, it's impossible to listen in. But now and then we pick up whispers.'

'And what do these whispers say about Kennedy and the Germans?'

'We get the impression that Kennedy is passing on secrets.'

'Secrets from the Irish government?'

Hibbert laughed. 'He doesn't need to do that. The Irish are passing on their own policies to the Germans direct. No, secrets from inside the British government about their intentions for the war.'

'How would Kennedy get hold of that information?'

'A respected political adviser from a neutral country talking to other political advisers in a genial fashion, friend to friend.'

'Are these people that gullible?'

'Of course they are. That's how this whole business of espionage works. They do it, we do it. At this moment I expect one of our people is chatting in Brussels to an old friend of his, a German diplomat who he went to school with.'

CHAPTER TWENTY-ONE

Friday 3rd January 1941

The ambulance pulled up outside the Royal Northern Hospital in Holloway Road. The trolley Bella Wilson was on was unloaded from the ambulance and wheeled towards the entrance to Accident and Emergency. The tall, muscular figure of Warder Ernie Heston followed the trolley. To be honest, he was glad to get out of the jail for a bit, even if it was just to the local hospital to keep an eye on the prisoner.

Bella was equally relieved when she recognised the Royal Northern building. She knew it from when she'd lived in a crummy bedsit in Seven Sisters Road and had spent time in the Accident and Emergency rooms there, usually as the result of falling down in the street and injuring herself. Her plan was that if she could get in there and keep up the pretence of being in pain there was a good chance she could get out. The hospital was always busy, especially with the war on, and with a bit of luck she'd be able to get lost in the crowds. So far, phase one had gone to plan. The other people waiting in Accident and Emergency looked on sympathetically as she was wheeled in on the trolley by the two ambulance crew, accompanied by the tall figure of Heston in his prison officer's uniform.

The ambulance crew transferred Bella Wilson onto a hospital trolley, then left, taking their own trolley with them back to their ambulance. During the transfer, Wilson had kept up a series of blood-curdling shrieks and moans and now she writhed on the trolley. Heston stood beside it, stone-faced, his focus on her as she writhed in pain, while the people watching looked at him in deep disapproval.

'Cruel, that's what it is,' muttered one woman.

Wilson writhed, every now and then letting out a shriek of pain as she clutched her stomach. All the time Heston did his best to remain impassive, but his face showed the uncomfortable embarrassment he was feeling.

'Can't you find out when someone's going to look at me?' Wilson begged him. 'I could die here.'

Heston looked doubtful. 'Alright, but I'm going to have to handcuff you to the trolley while I find someone,' he told her, taking a pair of handcuffs from his belt.

'Please, no,' she begged. 'I can't go anywhere, I can't move.'

Suddenly she let out a muted scream and began to roll and writhe about on the trolley.

'Is she alright?' asked an elderly woman, coming over.

'I'm in terrible pain and he's going to handcuff me to this trolley,' moaned Wilson, writhing.

The woman looked at Heston, outraged.

'Handcuff her?' she said.

'She's a prisoner,' explained Heston. 'She's got to be handcuffed to something if she's out of my sight.'

Another woman joined them, her face showing her indignation.

'I think that's disgusting,' said the new arrival. 'It's like the bloody Gestapo.'

'I'm only following orders,' defended Heston.

'Yeah, that's what the Nazis say. Bloody disgusting to see it happening here. And in a hospital!'

Wilson let out a cry of pain and writhed some more.

'Look, I'm going to see if I can find a doctor or nurse for her,' Heston said to the hostile faces glaring at him. 'Will you keep an eye on her?'

One of the women nodded. 'And we'll do it without handcuffing her,' she snapped.

Heston moved off. As soon as she saw him go, Wilson writhed again, then pushed herself up. 'I got to go to the toilet,' she said. 'Can you give me a hand?'

The elderly woman looked doubtful. 'I think they might be calling me any minute,' she said.

'I'll give you a hand,' said the newest arrival. 'Put your arm round my shoulder.'

Wilson tentatively put her feet on the floor, moaning and groaning all the time, then rested her arm on the woman's shoulder. The woman eased her off the trolley and then moved slowly in the direction of the toilets, Wilson hobbling along, resting on her, and almost doubled over in apparent pain.

'I'll be alright from here,' said Wilson when they reached the door to the toilets. 'You'd better get back in case they call your name.'

'I'm here with my sister,' said the woman. 'She's waiting to be seen.'

'You'd better get back in case she's called,' said Wilson. 'Thanks for getting me here. I'll be OK from now. Honest.'

The woman hesitated, but when Wilson pushed open the door to the toilets and staggered in, albeit with some difficulty, the woman departed.

Wilson waited a few more seconds then walked back out of the toilets, no longer struggling but moving easily.

She made her way along a corridor towards the dispensary where she knew, from her previous visits, there was a door to an open yard at the rear of the hospital.

Five minutes later she was moving through the narrow alleyways off Holloway Road, parallel with Seven Sisters Road. There was someone she hoped was still living in a bedsit in a tatty house off Seven Sisters Road. Someone who owed her a favour.

* * *

Coburg walked into his office as the telephone was ringing.

'DCI Coburg,' he said.

'We have a call for you from the governor of Holloway Prison, sir,' said the operator.

'Put him through,' said Coburg, wondering why the governor was calling him.

'Chief Inspector,' said the voice of James Carnley. 'I regret to report that the remand prisoner you sent to us has escaped.'

'Remand prisoner?' repeated Coburg. 'Do I understand you to mean Bella Wilson?'

'Yes,' said Carnley.

'How?' asked Coburg. 'I assume she was kept in her cell.'

'She was, but she was taken to the Royal Northern Hospital with suspected appendicitis. She appeared to be in great pain. While there, she managed to slip out of the hospital.'

'Wasn't she under guard?'

'She was, but the warder who accompanied her went to find out when she would be treated as she appeared to be in great pain. While he was away, she disappeared.'

'Didn't he handcuff her to something to prevent that happening? I thought that was standard procedure. And why was only one warder accompanying her? I thought two was the minimum with a dangerous prisoner.'

'I'm afraid we're short-staffed due to the war; we could only spare one warder. And she did appear to be in great pain. The warder attempted to handcuff her to a trolley, but he was prevented from doing so following protests by members of the public. It seems that after the warder left Miss Wilson, she asked a member of the public to assist her to the toilet. And it was at that time that she made her escape.'

'Miss Wilson is a very dangerous person,' said Coburg in firm tones. 'She tried to kill my wife.'

'I know, that's why I'm telephoning you personally,' said Carnley. 'Every effort is being made to recover her. The local police station has been alerted. I can only say how sorry I am this has happened. The warder responsible has been disciplined.'

When Coburg hung up, he immediately put through a call to the St John Ambulance station at Paddington.

'St John Ambulance, Paddington. Chesney Warren speaking.' said Warren.

'Mr Warren, this is DCI Coburg. Is my wife there?'

'She's out on a call at the moment,' said Warren. 'A traffic accident. I'll get her to call you as soon as she returns. Or is there something I can do for you?'

'Yes. Bella Wilson, the woman who tried to kill Rosa, and who you and Doris overpowered. It seems she's escaped from Holloway prison. I'm worried that she might try to attack Rosa again. I shall be sending some uniformed officers to your station to watch out for her, but I thought you ought to know so you can be on your guard. When Rosa returns, can you ask her to phone me here at Scotland Yard.'

'Of course,' said Warren.

CHAPTER TWENTY-TWO

Friday 3rd January 1941

When Lampson arrived at Maples furniture repository at a quarter to six, Eve Bradley was already there waiting for him, her ARP warden's tin helmet on her head and her gas mask in its box dangling from her shoulder.

'I can't see these helmets giving us much protection if bombs start falling on the roof,' she commented as they mounted the stairs to the roof.

'They're mainly to protect against shrapnel,' said Lampson. 'Mind, if a bomb hits the roof I doubt if we'd know much about it. The whole building will likely come down, and us with it.'

'And is that supposed to reassure me?'

When they reached the top floor, they saw the telephone on a small table beside the stairs to the roof. They climbed the last flight of stairs and stepped out onto the flat roof. A stirrup pump in a big bucket of water had been left near the doorway, along with a rake and a large-headed broom. There were other buckets dotted around the roof, all filled with water.

'It looks like your father's been here,' said Eve.

'He loves organising things,' said Lampson. He put down the bag he was carrying. 'I brought a flask of tea and a small bottle of brandy,' he said.

Eve put her bag down beside his. 'And I brought a few sandwiches in case we get hungry. We've got six hours to get through.'

'Yes, I should have thought of that,' said Lampson.

They stood there near the edge of the roof looking out across the darkened city. The blackout was being strictly observed: not one light could be seen, not even the merest narrow chink. As they stood there, suddenly Lampson cocked his head.

'Air raid warning,' he said. He looked up at the night sky, searching for sightings of the bombers that were on their way.

'I can't hear them,' said Eve. Then her tone changed and she was suddenly on the alert. 'Yes I can. Coming from the east.'

Lampson lifted the binoculars he'd slung round his neck to his eyes and aimed them towards the east, but every movement he made just ended up with an enormous barrage balloon appearing in his lenses. The barrage balloons, huge inflatable dirigibles tethered to the ground by stout steel cables, were the last line of defence to prevent the bombers getting too close for accurate bombing, but the giant bombers flew above the barrage balloons and let their weapons drop. It may not have been accurate, but it still had devastating results.

As the sound of the approaching planes grew louder, searchlights sprang to life, their broad powerful beams sending bright light into the night sky, searching for the German bombers. When one was picked out, the anti-aircraft guns in the streets below opened fire, sending a stream of bullets at the incoming planes. The German bombers kept as high as they could, staying out of reach of the tracers of anti-aircraft fire, but the bombs had started to fall, although landing some distance away from where Lampson and Eve stood on the roof and watched. Nearer to them, the incendiary devices were falling, too narrow to be seen in the darkness except when some fell through the beam from a searchlight as it swung to and fro, searching for the bombers. In the near distance they could see small fires suddenly erupting.

'Euston station,' said Lampson.

'I'll go and phone the fire brigade and alert them,' said Eve, and she hurried to the doorway into the interior of the building.

She's brave, thought Lampson admiringly as he watched her disappear through the doorway.

Other incendiary devices were dropping, nearer now, and as he watched one fell on the roof and suddenly exploded into a bright flame. Lampson grabbed the bucket with the stirrup pump in it and dragged it towards the burning device, just as Eve appeared. She ran towards the fire, snatching up one of the other buckets as she did, and dashed the contents of her bucket on the fire, dousing it.

'We're supposed to use the stirrup pump,' said Lampson.

'That was quicker,' said Eve.

Which was true, Lampson had to admit.

They stood there, looking up at the beams from the searchlights, listening to the rapid ack-ack fire from the anti-aircraft guns in the streets, looking swiftly in as many directions as they could, alert for more incendiaries to fall.

Coburg and Rosa were about to tuck into their evening meal when the alarms sounded.

'We could take a chance?' suggested Rosa.

'We could, but it would be just our luck for something to hit the block,' said Coburg, getting up and putting his plate on top of the oven and placing a soup bowl upside down over it.

'It'll still be cold by the time we get back,' commented Rosa, copying him with an inverted bowl over her plate.

They were the first to arrive in the shelter in the basement of their block, which meant Coburg was able to talk with Rosa about the escape of Bella Wilson from Holloway.

'The police are searching for her,' he said. 'Though it's not going to be easy. My guess is she'll find some old conspirator to hide out with. She's always been a bit of an itinerant, from what I can make out, never staying in one place for long.'

'That's the impression I got when I used to run into her,' said Rosa.

'We need to keep you safe over the weekend,' said Coburg.

'You really think she'll try again?'

'I do. I think that's why she escaped from Holloway; she's obsessed with you. I suggest that tomorrow morning I'll drive you to the Paddington ambulance station, and then pick you up from there later. At least you'll be with people who know Bella Wilson and just how dangerous she is.

'I also think on Saturday after I finish work we drive to Dawlish Hall and spend Sunday with Magnus. I can't see Wilson coming all the way there. For one thing, she doesn't drive, as far as I'm aware, and Dawlish isn't an easy place to get to without a car. My hope is that the police pick her up over her weekend, but if they don't I'll get them to redouble their efforts on Monday.'

'I don't want to go away again,' said Rosa. 'I refuse to be made a victim by her.'

She was referring to a previous occasion when her life had been threatened and Coburg had insisted she took refuge at Dawlish Hall, the Saxe-Coburgs' ancestral home, where his brother Magnus lived.

'We'll get her,' Coburg promised her. 'I'm going to start badgering her known associates. Someone will know where she is.' He looked around the small and otherwise empty shelter. 'I wonder where everyone else is?'

'Finishing their dinner, I expect,' said Rosa. 'Also, I'm sure the bombing's started earlier tonight.'

'Ted Lampson's doing fire-watching tonight,' he told her. 'I expect I'll have to sign up for it in this locality. It's going to be compulsory.'

'It's going to be dangerous,' she warned him.

'Not as dangerous as it'll be for Ted. Somers Town is right next to Euston station, and King's Cross and St Pancras, all major targets for the German bombing to disrupt railway traffic. Here in Piccadilly we get off lightly by comparison.'

'We thought we'd get off lightly when we lived in Hampstead, away from central London,' Rosa reminded him.

Coburg gave a sigh at the memory of their small block of flats in Hampstead being completely obliterated. Luckily, they'd been out when the bombs hit.

The door of the shelter opened and William and Mary Stainways from the flat below the Coburgs' entered.

'Good evening.' William beamed at them. 'Jerry's started early tonight.' He opened the case he was carrying and produced a couple of bottles of red wine and some glasses. 'Thought I'd bring some juice along to cheer us up. Fancy a glass?'

No further incendiaries had fallen on the roof of Maples repository; most of Lampson and Eve Bradley's time had been spent identifying where those that dropped in their locality hit and then telephoning the fire brigade to alert them. By nine o'clock the bombing activity around Somers Town seemed to have eased off, the German planes moving to attack other more distant areas, which gave Lampson and Eve the opportunity to pour tea from the flask he'd brought and tuck into the sandwiches she'd provided.

In the far distance, parts of London were ablaze and they could hear the familiar explosions and reverberations of buildings collapsing. As they watched, Eve started to talk about the forthcoming football match between the Somers Town boys' team and a Boys Brigade team from nearby King's Cross. They discussed their own team selection, and then filled in what each had gathered about their opponents.

'Their goalkeeper's a kid called Bert Harper,' said Lampson. 'Got arms like an octopus. He claws the ball out of the air when you're sure it's gonna go past him. He's going to be difficult to beat.'

'We could do with a win,' said Eve. 'The last one was a draw, and the one before that St James's church choir beat us three to one.'

'Lucky, that was all,' grunted Lampson.

'Our right back, Pete Spokes, was useless.'

'He'll get better,' said Lampson. 'He'd been up early helping his dad at his blacksmith's forge. I had a word with his dad yesterday and asked him to give the lad a rest with the game coming up tomorrow.'

'We'll see,' said Eve, but there was no mistaking the fact she wasn't convinced. Then she added, 'I'm sorry about *Gone With the Wind*. My promising my sister I'd go with her.'

'That's alright,' said Lampson. 'I understand. Family has to come first.'

'We could always go and see something else,' she suggested. 'I wouldn't mind going to see *Stagecoach*.'

Lampson looked at her in surprise. 'You like Westerns?'

'I love Westerns,' she said. 'When I was a kid I used to read my brother's cowboy comics. I remember one year I asked my parents for a cowboy outfit for Christmas.'

'Cow*boy*?' queried Lampson.

She nodded. 'Yes. I never saw myself as a cowgirl. All those frills. I wanted to be a cowboy.'

Interesting, thought Lampson, recalling the innuendo Coburg had made about Eve. *Not only does she like football but plays it. Chose fire-watching. Likes cowboy films. Am I barking up the wrong tree here?* he wondered. He looked at her, and she responded with a curious smile.

'You look thoughtful,' she said. 'Penny for them.'

'I was just wondering how many more incendiaries are going to fall tonight,' he lied. 'And if any more are going to land on the roof.'

Bella Wilson rang the bell beside the doorway of the betting shop. The betting shop was closed and the doorbell connected with the small flat above it. She wondered if Sam would be in, or if he'd be at the shelter with everyone else. The neighbouring houses and shops were in darkness and seemed to be empty, as did the local streets. 'Stay off the streets and go to the shelter' was the order. But then, Sam Rodney was never one for following rules.

She rang the bell again, and this time heard footsteps coming down the uncarpeted stairs and then the door opened and Sam looked out at her, astonishment on his face.

'Bella!' he said. 'What the hell are you doing here?'

Just before midnight, Bert Lampson and Chalky White appeared on the roof.

'How did it go?' asked Mr Lampson.

'Not too bad,' said Lampson. He nodded at the

place where the incendiary had landed and left a burnt patch in the roofing. 'One fire bomb, but we put it out.'

'The stirrup pump worked, then?' asked Mr Lampson.

Lampson and Eve exchanged glances, then she said, 'It was perfect. Worked like a dream.'

'Right,' said Mr Lampson. 'Then it's time for me and Chalky to take over. Well done, the pair of you.'

As Lampson and Eve made for the door and the stairs down, Mr Lampson called out, 'We'll see you at the match tomorrow! Let's have a win this time.'

'We'll do our best,' his son called back at him.

As they descended the stairs to the street, Lampson asked, 'After all that, fancy coming back to my place for a fresh cuppa or something?'

She nodded and said, '"Or something" sounds good.'

CHAPTER TWENTY-THREE

Saturday 4th January 1941

Lampson stirred in the bed and opened his eyes to see Eve putting on her clothes.

'You're going?' he said. 'What's the time?'

'Quarter past six. I thought I'd get away before Terry comes home,' she said. 'We don't want to upset him.'

'Who says he'll be upset?'

'I do. His dad and his teacher? He needs time to adjust to that sort of thing.'

'Yes, I suppose you're right,' said Lampson. He pushed back the blanket and got out of bed. 'At least let me make you a cup of tea.'

She shook her head. 'I'd better be off just in case your dad brings Terry home earlier than expected. What time do they normally bring him home when you've been out all night?'

'I'm never out all night unless it's to do with work,' said Lampson. He went to her and took her in his arms. 'That was lovely last night. Really lovely.' He kissed her and grinned as he said, 'We're gonna have to go fire-watching more often.'

Suddenly they froze as they heard the door knocker below banging, and Mr Lampson's voice calling, 'Open up! I've brought Terry home!'

'Bugger.' Lampson scowled unhappily. He pushed Eve gently to one side, then went to the window, half-pulled back the curtains, partly opened the window and shouted down, 'I'll be down in a minute. I ain't dressed yet.'

With that he pulled the curtains shut.

'You'd better go out the back,' he whispered. 'Can you climb over the wall at the end of the yard? You'll be in the back lane.'

'No problem,' she said. She hugged him close and gave him a big kiss. 'I'll see you this afternoon at the rec for the football.'

Then she was gone.

Lampson gave a big smile as he watched her go, then picked up his clothes and started to put them on. Life suddenly felt very good.

Bella Wilson rolled out of the bed and pulled on her clothes. She went to the window and looked out at the day. It was wet and miserable, which suited her fine. She'd be able to wear her hooded jacket, keeping her face and head hidden. The previous night one of the first things she'd done after arriving at Sam's had been to dye her distinctive red hair black, so that ought to throw the police off. The police would be looking for her, making it important for her to get off the streets and somewhere safe as quickly as possible, which was why she'd come to this room above a shop on Seven Sisters Road, where Sam Rodney lived.

She'd known Sam for years. He was a welder and occasional trumpet player, and occasionally her lover. Like last night, when she'd knocked at his door, hoping that he still lived here. It had been two years since she'd seen him. There'd been very little talking; they'd gone straight to bed and made urgent love. No, not love, urgent sex. That was what she'd needed, what she'd been missing.

After, she told him she'd escaped from Holloway where she'd been held on remand on a trumped-up charge.

'They're looking for me, Sam. I need a place to hide out for a day or so.'

'Stay here as long as you want,' he'd told her.

It had been then she'd produced the bottle of black hair dye she'd bought at a local chemist. 'Part of me hiding,' she'd told him.

He'd gone out and bought some fish and chips and a bottle of gin, and after that they'd gone back to bed again.

Now, having slept properly for the first time in a very long time, Bella sat on the edge of the bed looking at the sleeping Rodney. She'd chosen him not just because of the sex, or the gin, or the place to hide, but because Sam Rodney had a special sideline. He dealt in guns, most of them stolen. And what Bella Wilson wanted now was a gun. After the fiasco of her failed knife attack on the bloody bitch Rosa Weeks, her next attempt would be at a safer distance, allowing no one the chance of getting close to her. She'd point the gun and pull the trigger. Bang. That would be it.

Martin Higgins knocked at the door of the address he'd got for Grigor and Priscilla Rostov. He was frustrated and angry at the way Bidlow had been dodging him. Bidlow was going to avoid paying him, that Higgins was sure, so Higgins was desperate to get hold of something that would put the squeeze on the MP. All the paperwork relating to Bidlow's links with Krupp had vanished. Bidlow must have spirited them away somewhere. Higgins's one hope was that Bidlow had been right about his wife passing information about Krupp to Svetlana Rostova. When Higgins had confronted Svetlana about it, she'd avoided answering, but she hadn't refused the twenty pounds he gave her for her silence. Svetlana may have been avoiding telling him anything because there was nothing to reveal; maybe Eleanor Bidlow hadn't said anything about it, but there was always the possibility that she had. In which case, Svetlana may have kept a note somewhere. But Svetlana had been killed at Down Street station.

He'd telephoned the offices of the Railway Executive Committee there and introduced himself as the private secretary to Henry Bidlow MP.

'I'm making enquiries on behalf of Mr Bidlow into the murder of one of his constituents, a Svetlana Rostova. We understand that her brother worked for you and was also murdered. We're trying to locate any papers Svetlana Rostova may have left. We believe she may have deposited them with her brother, and we wondered if they were still in your offices at Down Street?'

'All Mr Rostov's papers and personal effects were sent to his widow,' he was informed.

Which was why he was here, at this small terraced house in Paddington. He was just about to knock again, when the door opened and a young woman looked at him anxiously.

'Mrs Priscilla Rostov?' asked Higgins, putting on what he hoped was a genial smile.

'Who wants to know?' asked Priscilla suspiciously.

'My name's Martin Higgins. I'm the private secretary to Henry Bidlow, the member of parliament.' And Higgins produced his House of Commons pass and the letter of authority from Bidlow naming him as one of his work team, a letter that Higgins kept in order to gain access to places difficult to get into. 'May I come in?'

'Why?' she asked.

'It's about the murders of your husband and his sister. Mr Bidlow is keen to push the investigation forward as it appears the police seem to be making slow progress.'

'It was the Russians,' she said flatly.

'Yes, I saw the interview you gave to the *Daily Globe*,' said Higgins. 'But we feel there may be more to it than meets the eye. May I come in?'

Reluctantly, she stepped aside and let him enter, then led him into a small living room.

'It was the Russians,' she repeated when they were seated.

'That may well be the case,' said Higgins, 'but we've received information that there may be another aspect relating to Grigor's sister's fortune-telling business. There is a possibility that she may have picked up information from one of her clients that certain people didn't want known.'

'Who?' she asked. 'Which client of hers?'

'That's something we're now looking into,' said Higgins. 'I've been told that your late husband's effects, which were held in Down Street, have been sent to you here. Did they include anything of his sister's? Notebooks, for example, where she may have kept a record of her meetings with her clients.'

'No,' said Priscilla. 'The only things that Down Street sent were Grigor's own possessions.'

'Do you mind if I look at them?' asked Higgins. 'In

case any notes of hers had got mixed up with them.'

'You can look if you want,' said Priscilla. 'But there was nothing there that wasn't Grigor's, and it wasn't much. Some books in Russian. They looked like dictionaries.' She left the room and returned with an open-topped box, which she put on the coffee table.

'There you are,' she said.

She sat down and watched him as he went through the contents of the box. There were very few documents, and most of them were in Russian. Similarly, the sheets of paper with handwriting them were mostly in Russian. Higgins held them out to Priscilla.

'Is this Grigor's writing, or Svetlana's?' he asked.

'Grigor's,' she said. 'Svetlana's handwriting was more of a scrawl. Grigor's was neat. He was an organised person, very neat and responsible. She was . . .' She hesitated, but when she spoke Higgins could see from her expression and the tone of her voice that she disapproved of her late husband's sister. 'She was odd in every way. And forgetful. Her writing was a mess, even when she wrote in English.'

'Have you got anything she wrote in English?' asked Higgins hopefully.

'No. If she wrote to him she did it in Russian.' She sniffed in annoyance. 'She did it to cut me out.'

'But she did write some things in English?' pressed Higgins.

'Shopping lists, to practise her English,' said Priscilla.

'Have you got any of them?'

'No. I threw them away after Grigor died. I didn't want anything of hers hanging around. She contaminated him with her madness. If it hadn't been for her, Grigor would still be alive and my daughter Mary would be growing up with her father in her life.'

After half an hour, Higgins gave up. There was nothing of Svetlana's in the papers, The books were all in Russian, but Higgins checked them in case Grigor had hidden anything between the pages.

In the end, he thanked Priscilla and left the house, weighing up his next move. There was always a chance that Grigor had hidden something that Svetlana had written under his desk at the Down Street offices. Stuck it to the underside of a drawer, perhaps.

He made his way to Down Street and used the same ruse and the same explanation of Henry Bidlow having sent him to check for any papers, possibly handwritten, that Grigor or Svetlana might have stashed in his desk, or somewhere else in his office.

He was taken to see Jeremy Purslake, who said the REC would be delighted to help in any way, especially as it was a request from a member of His Majesty's government. Purslake was obviously intrigued by Higgins's request and watched as Higgins took out the drawers of Grigor Rostov's former desk and examined them for signs of anything having been fixed to them. Higgins then examined Grigor's former locker in great detail, but found nothing.

'I didn't expect there to be anything,' Purslake told him. 'The police were very thorough in their search of Mr Rostov's locker and they took away everything that he'd kept stored there for his sister.'

'What sort of things did they take?' asked Higgins.

'They seemed most interested in some cards she had. Cards to do with her fortune-telling.'

'Do you know the names of the officers who took them?' asked Higgins, though he was fairly sure he knew them already. 'The *Daily Globe* had made accusations against Detective Chief Inspector Saxe-Coburg.'

'A Detective Chief Inspector Saxe-Coburg and a Detective Sergeant Lampson,' Purslake confirmed.

As Higgins made his way back to the surface up the spiral staircase, he thought over how to handle this business over the police having got Svetlana's documents. Could he try the same ruse of claiming that his MP employer had authorised him to look at any papers Svetlana or Grigor had left? No, he had to be cleverer than that, otherwise there was a chance the police would check with Bidlow. But somehow he had to get hold of those cards.

CHAPTER TWENTY-FOUR

Saturday 4th January 1941

Coburg took a sip of the cup of tea Lampson had returned with from the canteen, then put the cup down on his desk with a grunt of discontent.

'This tea's getting thinner every day,' he said. 'If it gets any thinner, we'll be drinking hot water.'

'Mrs Sampson in the canteen says she's had to start re-using tea leaves,' said Lampson.

'Maybe we'd better switch to coffee,' suggested Coburg.

Lampson shook his head. 'Mrs Sampson says she's going to start using substitutes because there's going to be a shortage of coffee.'

'What sort of substitutes?' asked Coburg.

'She was talking of chicory mixed with acorns.'

'Sounds disgusting,' said Coburg.

'The longer this war goes on and more things get in short supply, we'll have to get used to lots of changes,' said Lampson. 'Personally, I miss butter. I can't get used to this whale-oil margarine.'

'Neither can I,' said Coburg. He looked at his

sergeant and asked, 'How did the fire-watching go last night?'

'Good,' said Lampson.

'Anything exciting happen?' asked Coburg.

Lampson looked at him warily. 'In what way?'

'Bombs. Incendiary devices. I'm considering signing up for my area so I'm interested to see what I'll be letting myself in for.'

'We had an incendiary device fall on the roof of the building we were on. Luckily we dealt with it.'

'How did Miss Bradley take to it?'

'She was good,' said Lampson. 'She knew what she was doing.'

The telephone rang and it was with a feeling of relief that Lampson picked up the receiver before his boss could ask more questions.

'DCI Coburg's office,' he said. 'Sergeant Lampson speaking.'

'Switchboard here, sir,' said the operator. 'We have a note that you and DCI Coburg are investigating the murders at Down Street, the former Tube station.'

'That's right,' said Lampson.

'We've just had a report that there's been another murder there.'

'At Down Street?'

'Just outside the building, according to the report. The patrol who attended are on site. Can I tell them you'll be attending?'

'You can. Who's been killed? And how? Were they stabbed?'

'No, sir. It seems he was shot. The victim has been identified as a Martin Higgins, a private secretary to Henry Bidlow MP.'

'Thank you. Let them know we're on our way.'

'Who's been shot?' asked Coburg, standing up and pulling on his coat.

'A man called Martin Higgins. He's a private secretary to Henry Bidlow MP. Shot just outside Down Street.'

Coburg shook his head as they made for the door. 'This is getting more complicated than ever.'

When Coburg and Lampson arrived at Down Street, they found a uniformed sergeant and a constable standing guard over the dead body of Martin Higgins just outside the entrance to the former Tube station.

'We're just waiting for the doctor to arrive, sir,' said the sergeant. He gestured at the body of the man lying face-down on the pavement in a pool of dried blood. 'This is how we found him. It looks like he was shot in the back of the head. I took a quick look at the front of his head, but without disturbing things too much. There's no exit wound so we assume the bullet's still in there. We radioed through to Scotland Yard. We also put in a call for the duty doctor to come out.'

'Who found the body?'

The sergeant pointed to a tobacconist's shop just along the road.

'A Mr Hart who owns that tobacconist's. He'd come out to clean his shop window when he noticed someone lying on the pavement. He went to see what was wrong, and realised the bloke was dead and there was blood on the pavement around his head. He phoned 999 to report it, then went and stood by the body until we turned up. He's gone back to his shop if you want to talk to him.'

'Did he hear a shot?'

The sergeant shook his head. 'Not according to him. I then went to that black door there, the entrance to the Railway Executive people, and rang the bell to see if they knew who the bloke was, seeing as he was lying just outside their door. Their duty security man came out and looked at him and said he'd let him out of the building about fifteen minutes before. The guard was the one who'd let him in, so he knew his name. Martin Higgins. Working for this MP, he said. I told them I'd radioed through to Scotland Yard and someone would be out to talk to them.'

'Good work, sergeant.' Coburg nodded. He turned to Lampson. 'Sergeant, if you go and have a word with the tobacconist, this Mr Hart, get his statement, while I go into Down Street and talk to the boss. Hopefully Jeremy Purslake will be available.'

* * *

The tobacconist was obviously keeping an eye on the activity outside the former Tube station because he appeared from his shop and stood in the doorway as he saw Lampson approaching.

'Good morning, sir,' said Lampson, he introduced himself, then asked, 'I understand you were the one who found the body. Mr Hart, isn't it?'

'Gerald Hart.' The man nodded. He was in his fifties and still looked a bit shaken. 'Horrible, it was. The back of his head blown away. I knew straight away he was dead. I was in the First War, you see, so I know what that sort of shot does. Rips the brain apart.'

'Did you touch the body?'

Hart shook his head. 'No. I know you're not supposed to in case you destroy evidence. I just phoned 999.'

'Excellent,' said Lampson. 'Did you see the man anywhere around here at all before you found the body? The people at the Railway Executive Committee say he was in there before he came out and got shot.'

Hart shook his head. 'No, I've been busy checking my stock. It was when I went out to clean my windows I saw him. At first I thought it was just a pile of clothes someone had dumped, then as I got nearer I saw it was a bloke.'

'Did you see anyone else around in the street?'

Again, Hart shook his head. 'No. Everything was quiet.'

'And you didn't hear a shot?'

'No. Maybe I was in the back room when it was done, but I've got pretty good hearing.'

In the offices of the Railway Executive Committee building, Coburg was relieved to discover that Jeremy Purslake was on duty, saving him a lot of introductory explanations.

'I'd never met this man Higgins before,' Purslake told him. 'He said he'd been instructed by his employer, Henry Bidlow the MP, to examine Mr Rostov's desk in case anything had been hidden there.'

'What sort of thing?'

'He was looking for papers that Rostov's sister might have hidden there. The fortune-teller.'

'And did he find anything?'

'No. I told him that all documents and possessions of Mr Rostov had been returned to his widow. He said he'd been to see her but he needed to check in case anything might have been left behind here at the offices.'

'And did he find anything?'

'No. I know that because I was with him the whole time he was searching Mr Rostov's former desk, and his locker.'

'And then he left.'

'He did. It was about twenty minutes later that we were informed that a man had been found dead in the street not far from our main door. The police constable who arrived at the scene knocked at our door and asked the security man if he recognised the dead man. Our security man did. He said he'd let him out twenty minutes before. When asked if he'd heard a shot, he said he hadn't.'

Coburg and Lampson waited until the duty doctor, a Dr Morse, had appeared and carried out his initial inspection of the body, reporting with a resigned sigh, 'Cause of death appears to be exactly what it seems: bullet in the back of the head.' He gestured at the ambulance waiting at the kerb. 'If there's anything more, I'll find it when I get him on a slab, although I doubt if I'll get to him before tomorrow morning.'

'Sunday?'

'Death doesn't take days off,' said Morse. 'We've got quite a backlog of bodies to get through as it is.'

'Where will you be taking him?'

'UCH,' said Morse. He tipped his hat to them. 'You'll have my report as soon as I can get to him.'

Coburg and Lampson watched as the dead body was loaded into the ambulance, then Morse got into his car and the entourage drove off.

'Speculation?' asked Coburg thoughtfully. 'Higgins is inside Down Street, and almost immediately after he comes out of there someone shoots him.'

'So someone was outside waiting for him to appear,'

said Lampson. 'Which means they'd followed him there.'

'From where?' mused Coburg. 'And why?'

'From what Purslake told you, he'd gone there after going to talk to Mrs Rostov. So it's the Russian connection.'

'Not necessarily,' said Coburg thoughtfully. 'Let's go back to the idea that maybe Svetlana and her brother were killed because someone thought that one of Svetlana's clients had told her something that was supposed to be kept secret.'

'And Higgins was at Down Street on behalf of Henry Bidlow MP, whose wife was one of Svetlana's clients. And who got a black eye from him.'

'So he knows she told Svetlana something that he didn't want to get out.'

'But what?' asked Lampson.

'I think I need to talk to Mr and Mrs Bidlow.'

'You want me to come with you?' asked Lampson.

Coburg shook his head. 'No, you've got a football game this afternoon.'

CHAPTER TWENTY-FIVE

Saturday 4th January 1941

Coburg was relieved to discover that Henry Bidlow wasn't at home when he called at the house. He knew he'd have to talk to the man sooner or later, and it really needed to be sooner, but at the moment he wanted to talk to the MP's wife alone, without her husband interfering or trying to influence what she said.

'I'm here because your husband's assistant, a Mr Martin Higgins, has tragically been murdered.'

'Murdered?' she repeated, horrified.

'It's my belief that it may be connected with whatever you may have told Lady Za Za, Svetlana Rostova, about your husband's business.'

'I told her nothing!' protested Eleanor.

'I understand that, but it's possible you may have revealed something to her inadvertently. Throwaway phrases, for example. About your husband's work. I'm sure Svetlana would have been interested in his work as an MP?'

'No!' said Eleanor. 'I didn't say anything about his

work at all. And she never asked. All we talked about was me. My future.'

'And how did she see that future?' asked Coburg gently.

Before she could answer they heard the front door opening, then Henry Bidlow walked into the room. He stopped, almost shocked at the sight of the man with his wife.

'What's going on?' he demanded. 'Who are you?'

Coburg got to his feet. 'I'm Detective Chief Inspector Saxe-Coburg from Scotland Yard.'

Bidlow stared at him, bewildered. 'What the hell are you doing here in my home, bothering my wife?'

'I'm hardly bothering her, sir. I was just talking to her while we waited for you to arrive.'

'Me?' said Bidlow, suddenly alarmed.

'Yes, sir. I need to talk to you about Martin Higgins.'

'No!' said Bidlow sharply. 'Out of the question. I have an appointment at the House shortly. You'll need to make an appointment.'

'I'm afraid I'm going to have to insist,' said Coburg calmly. 'This is a murder enquiry.'

'Yes, I understand some fortune-teller got herself murdered, but it's hardly anything to do with me.'

'We're not here about the murder of the fortune-teller. We're here about the murder of Martin Higgins.'

Bidlow stared at him. Either the MP was a very good actor or his shock at this information was

275

genuine. 'Higgins murdered?'

'He was shot dead outside Down Street, the former Underground station. Jeremy Purslake, the senior executive in charge at the REC there, says Mr Higgins told him you'd sent him there to make enquiries into the murders of Svetlana and Grigor Rostov.'

'Me?' squeaked Bidlow, appalled. 'No! Absolutely not! I never sent him there!'

'But Martin Higgins did work for you?' asked Coburg.

'Yes,' said Bidlow awkwardly. He turned to his wife and said, 'Eleanor, I'll deal with this. You go and busy yourself.' He then turned back to Coburg and said, 'You did say it was me you wanted to talk to?'

'Yes indeed,' said Coburg. He smiled politely at Eleanor Bidlow. 'Thank you, Mrs Bidlow. If we need to talk to you again we'll be in touch to make an appointment.'

As Eleanor Bidlow made her exit from the room, Bidlow asked suspiciously, 'Why would you need to talk to her again?'

'She did have a session with Lady Za Za,' said Coburg. 'It's all part of fact-gathering. We're talking to everyone Svetlana Rostova had a session with. You never met her, did you?'

'No. I don't believe in all this fortune-telling rubbish.' Bidlow gestured for Coburg to resume his seat, then settled himself down in a large armchair.

'You say Martin Higgins was shot?' he said.

Coburg nodded. 'By the look of it, in the back of the head shortly after he left Down Street. How long had he been working for you?'

'About a year,' said Bidlow.

'What sort of duties did he carry out?'

'Odd and ends. Delivered messages. Checked my post. Did research for me on queries and complaints my constituents raise.'

'Was he a good worker?'

Bidlow seemed to think it over before answering with, 'He seemed adequate enough. But now and then he overstepped the role he was supposed to carry out. Like this business of him telling the people at Down Street that I'd sent him to check on this man Rostov's possessions. Absolute nonsense. Why would he make that up?'

'Again, that's something we're trying to find out. Do you have his contact details? His home address? We'll need to inform his family. Was he married?'

'I believe so,' said Bidlow. 'To be honest, I didn't really know much about the man. We didn't socialise with one another. It was simply an employer–worker relationship.'

'Do you have his address?'

Bidlow nodded, got up and walked to a sideboard. From a drawer he extracted a thick address book. He looked up Higgins's address, then wrote the details down and handed them to Coburg. Coburg read the details, then put the piece of paper into his pocket.

'Thank you. As we said, we're looking into the possibility that Higgins's death may be political. As with the deaths of Svetlana Rostova and her brother.'

'Political?' asked Bidlow. 'What on earth has politics got to do with any of this?'

'Politics has a way of intruding in places where we least expect it,' said Coburg. 'And you are a member of the government.'

'A very junior member. A back-bencher with no influence,' said Bidlow. 'Now, if you'll excuse me, I do have urgent business to attend to.'

'Of course,' said Coburg, and he made for the door. Just before he left, he stopped and asked, 'Pardon me for asking, Mr Bidlow, but does your wife have mobility problems?'

'Mobility problems?' repeated Bidlow, puzzled.

'I noticed she had a black eye. She told us she stumbled into a door.'

'Ah, yes,' said Bidlow. 'Sometimes my wife can be unsteady on her feet.'

'Is she seeing a doctor for it?'

'No, my wife is very self-determined. She prefers to deal with it in her own way.'

Interfering scum, thought Bidlow angrily as he shut the door after him. Then he allowed himself a smile. *Higgins shot dead. Thank God for Danny Bell.*

* * *

'We're starting to get more spectators turning up,' said Eve Bradley, pleased. 'The word's spreading about the team.'

'Yes, about the fact we haven't won yet,' said Lampson doubtfully. 'They turn up waiting to see if we get beaten.'

'Don't be so negative,' said Eve. 'You need to be positive with the boys, keep their spirits up. If you give them the impression you think they're bad and going to lose, they will.' She jerked her head towards where the team were sitting on the ground, lacing their boots. 'Go on, go and tell them how much you believe in them. It's what they need.' She gave him a little secret smile as she added in a whisper, 'Everyone feels better when we've had what we need.'

Lampson did his best not to respond. There were too many people he knew around, people with sharp ears and eyes. As he set off towards the team, he became aware that something was wrong; Terry was squaring up to their inside left, Joe Edgar.

'Say that again,' Terry challenged the taller boy, his face suffused with anger.

'I overheard my mum telling my aunt Dolly she saw Miss Bradley climbing over the back wall of your house and into the back lane at just gone six this morning.'

Terry glared at him. 'Rubbish! I was round our

house at that time, coming home from my grandad's. Dad was on his own.'

'That's cos Miss Bradley had sneaked out. My mum reckons she must have been there in your house with your dad all night.' He gave Terry a leer and added, 'And we can all guess what they were doing! Your dad's a dirty dog, and so is Miss Bradley.'

Terry stared at his tormenter, and suddenly punched him in the face. Edgar stumbled back, then fell to the grass, his hands to his face with blood leaking out through his fingers.

'Terry Lampson hit me!' he shrieked. 'He's broke my nose!'

When Coburg called at the address Bidlow had given him, the door was opened by a short blonde woman in her mid-thirties.

'Good afternoon,' said Coburg. 'Am I speaking to Mrs Pauline Higgins?'

'Yes,' said the woman, but suspiciously. 'Who are you?'

Coburg produced his warrant card and showed it to her. 'DCI Coburg from Scotland Yard,' he said. 'May I come in?'

'Why?' she asked, still suspicious.

'I need to talk to you about your husband, Martin.'

'He's not here at the moment,' she said. Then she looked at him, worried. 'Is he in some kind of trouble?'

'Could we talk inside?' asked Coburg gently.

She nodded and let him in, then led him to a small front room.

'Why do you want to know about Martin?' she asked.

'I'm very sorry to have to tell you, Mrs Higgins, that your husband was killed this morning.'

She stared at him, disbelieving. 'No!' she said. 'How?'

'He was shot outside the former Down Street Underground station.'

'Shot?' She stared at him, even more uncomprehending.

'Yes. His body's been taken to University College Hospital. I'm afraid I'm going to have to ask you to formally identify him. At the moment we only have the word of someone at Down Street that the dead man is Martin Higgins, but that's because that's who the man said he was. But no one at Down Street had seen him before.'

'So it may not be my husband?' she said, hope springing into her face.

'Which is why we need an identification by someone who knows your husband. Do you know where he was going today?'

She shook her head. 'He just said he had some business to sort out.'

'Business?'

'He worked for an MP, Henry Bidlow.' Her face darkened as she said, 'If anything has happened to Martin, that's who'll be behind it.'

'Why do you say that?' asked Coburg.

She shook her head. 'I'm saying nothing more until I've taken a look at this man.' With a look of anguish at Coburg, she said, 'It can't be Martin. It can't be!'

Joe Edgar had been taken off to have his nose inspected and his face cleaned up. As Edgar's replacement, Pete Young, was lacing up his boots, Lampson took his son by the shoulders and looked angrily into his eyes.

'What was all that about?' he demanded. 'Why'd you hit Joe?'

'Cos of what he said.'

'What did he say?'

'He said his mum said she saw Miss Bradley climbing over our back wall just after six this morning. She said she must have been in our house with you all night. I told him he was a liar and to take it back, and when he wouldn't, I hit him.' He looked with a painful expression at his father as he said, 'It was a lie, wasn't it, Dad?'

Bugger! thought Lampson, his heart sinking at the realisation of what Terry had just told him. He and Eve were in big trouble. He forced a smile and then lied, 'Of course it was.'

CHAPTER TWENTY-SIX

Saturday 4th January 1941

Once Pauline Higgins had seen her dead husband's body in the morgue at University College Hospital and said, 'It's him,' the emotions that she had been holding back broke out, and she collapsed in tears onto a chair once Coburg had helped her out of the morgue.

'I'm very sorry,' said Coburg.

'Why?' she appealed to him.

'That's what we're hoping you might be able to help us find out,' said Coburg. 'You mentioned that Henry Bidlow, his MP employer, was behind it. Why?'

She shook her head as she wiped her tear-stained face with her handkerchief. 'I can't talk now,' she said. 'I need to go home.'

Coburg escorted her up the stairs to street level and to his police car. They drove to her house in silence, broken only by occasional bursts of weeping from her. Inside the house, Coburg led her to the small kitchen at the rear of the house, where he put the kettle on to make tea.

'Is there anyone you can call to come and be with you?' he asked.

'My brother's wife, Louise,' she said. 'I'll phone her once you've gone.'

'I'll be as brief as I can,' Coburg promised her. 'But we do need to get as much information as we can, and as quickly as we can. You said that Henry Bidlow was to blame.'

She nodded, her tone angry and bitter. 'Martin had something on Bidlow. Something he'd found out. Something Bidlow didn't want known. Martin said he was going to get a great deal of money out of him for it.'

'Blackmail?' asked Coburg.

'No, not blackmail!' said Mrs Higgins angrily. 'Bidlow owed Martin for all the work he did for him. But getting money out of that horrible man was like getting blood out of a stone. Martin didn't stand up for himself, that's the trouble. But this time he did.'

'Martin found something out about Mr Bidlow and he wanted money to keep silent about it?' asked Coburg gently.

'Yes, but it wasn't blackmail. It was just Martin getting what he was owed.'

'Do you know what it was that Martin had found out?'

She shook her head. 'No, Martin was playing it close to his chest. I don't think he wanted to involve me. But you ask him. You ask Henry Bidlow what he was paying Martin to stay silent about.'

* * *

Danny Bell had summoned Duffy Powell to the Merrie Tumbler and fixed him with a look of very deep annoyance.

'Duffy, I'm displeased,' said Bell. 'This Martin Higgins I asked you to deal with. I said to do it discreetly. Instead, what do we get? A bullet in the back of the head, with all manner of clues being left. The bullet itself, for one thing. I wanted something that looked more like an accident, like falling under a Tube train.'

'And that's what I was planning, boss,' said Powell. 'And then someone topped him.'

Bell eyed Powell suspiciously. 'You mean it wasn't you who shot him?'

'No, boss. Like I said, I had other things in mind; I was just weighing up the best way. My own thought was to bash him over the head and dump him in a bomb crater so people would think he was a victim of the bombing.'

'Yeah, that's good thinking,' said Bell approvingly. 'So who did it? Who topped him?'

'No idea, boss. Do you want me to ask questions? Find out who it might have been?'

'Yeah, but discreetly,' said Bell. 'It's always worth knowing who the opposition is.'

The match had ended with a 2–1 victory for Somers Town Boys, Terry having partly redeemed himself for his assault on Joe Edgar by scoring one of the goals. Lampson left the boys celebrating their first victory and wandered over to where Eve was moving away from Lampson's parents.

'Your mum and dad are pleased,' she said.

'A result at last,' said Lampson.

'A double result,' whispered Eve, with a secret smile.

'Except Mrs Edgar saw you climbing over the back wall when you left.'

Eve stared at him, aghast. 'What?'

'That was what the fight was about between Terry and Joe Edgar. Edgar told him what his mum had seen, and Terry called him a liar, and when Joe wouldn't take it back, Terry hit him.'

'What are we going to do?' she asked, shocked.

'We deny it,' said Lampson.

'We can't if she saw me,' said Eve.

'We deny anything happened,' said Lampson. 'We tell them that after fire-watching you were too tired to go home, so you spent the night on my settee. When my dad came home with Terry early, we didn't want them to get the wrong idea, so you went out the back and over the wall.'

'You think they'll believe us?'

'They'll have to, or I'll go round some people's houses and punch them in the face,' said Lampson firmly.

'I could get in trouble with the school board,' said Eve, worried. 'They're very strong on the whole morals thing.'

'We'll just tell them they've got wicked minds,' said Lampson.

CHAPTER TWENTY-SEVEN

Saturday 4th January 1941

Bella Wilson arrived outside the Coburgs' small block of flats in Piccadilly. In the pocket of the long coat she wore, she felt the weight of the pistol Sam had lent her. She stood in the street, watching the entrance to the block, waiting and wishing for Rosa to appear. When there had been no sight of her, or Coburg, after ten minutes she realised her hanging around like this was suspicious. She went to the door and pushed it open, and found herself on the ground floor by the flights of stairs. Just as she had when she'd left the doll impaled on their flat door, she mounted the stairs to the top floor. There were two flats on this floor. The doors to both were closed.

She cursed herself for not having asked Sam if he had any lockpicks; she was sure he must have, knowing the criminal circles he moved in. She took the pistol from her pocket and pointed it at the flat door, then rang the doorbell. Whichever of them opened the door would get it, then she'd shoot the other one.

There was no answer to her first ring, so she pressed

the doorbell again. She waited, but there was still no sound from inside the flat. The sound of the door of the flat behind her opening made her thrust the pistol into her pocket.

'If you're looking for the Saxe-Coburgs, I believe they've gone out,' said a woman's voice.

Wilson turned and looked at the woman, slightly built but elegantly dressed in expensive clothes.

'Do you know when they'll be back?' she asked.

'I'm sorry, they just said they were going out overnight. I assume that means they'll be back some time tomorrow, but they didn't say when. I'll tell them you called.'

'No, that's alright,' said Wilson. 'I'll catch up with them some other time.'

With that, she made for the stairs.

Daylight was fading as Coburg and Rosa neared Dawlish Hall.

'At least we'll get there before the air raids start,' said Coburg.

'I can't imagine there being an air raid on Dawlish,' said Rosa. 'It's hardly a major military target. A small village and a manor house surrounded by fields for miles.'

'Yes, but small villages in Kent are being bombed,' pointed out Coburg.

'That's because they're in Kent with all those

airfields. It's hardly the same here in rural Buckinghamshire.'

As they drove through the gates of Dawlish Hall and along the long drive towards the manor house at the end, they saw the front door of the house open and Magnus and Malcolm emerge to greet them.

'Being selfish, I'm delighted that we will be having the pleasure of your company once again, Rosa.' Magnus beamed.

'Just for tonight and tomorrow,' said Rosa. 'I'm not going to let this madwoman dictate my life. We both return tomorrow so we're at work on Monday morning.'

'There's been no sighting of this lunatic?' Malcolm asked.

Coburg shook his head. 'I'm afraid not. I'll say one thing about her, she's cunning. The way she managed to escape from Holloway took brains and nerve.'

'I got the impression she was an alcoholic,' said Magnus.

'I got the same impression, but it seems she can operate whether under the influence or not.'

'The main thing is you're here, safe and sound,' said Magnus. 'And Mrs Hilton has prepared a meal for us, so I hope you're hungry.'

'Starved,' said Rosa. She looked at Malcolm and said with mock severity, 'And this time, Malcolm, I hope you'll sit at the table with us instead of disappearing to the kitchen to eat alone. I love your company, and I feel distinctly uncomfortable knowing that we are eating and chatting together and you're on your lonesome ownsome. And don't say it's your place, because it isn't. There's a war on and your place is with friends and family, and that's us.'

Malcolm did his best to put on an affronted look, but both Rosa and Coburg could tell he felt secretly pleased.

'Very well,' he said stiffly, 'but it's against my better judgement.'

'I'm so relieved,' said Rosa, slipping her arm through Malcolm's and leading the way into the house.

Coburg and Magnus followed them. 'It's only because she told him,' whispered Magnus. 'I've been trying to get him to join me for meals for ages, but he's so pig-headed and old-fashioned. Sometimes he's positively feudal.'

'He listens to Rosa,' Coburg whispered back.

'He adores her,' said Magnus. 'He couldn't bear to upset her.'

It was nine o'clock at night, just after they'd finished dinner. When the telephone rang. As always, it was Malcolm who answered it. He listened briefly, then returned to the table.

'That was Mrs Prewitt, the post mistress. There's been an air raid, the Germans using those fire bombs.

The parish hall is on fire. She's phoned the fire brigade, but the regular fire engine has to come from Great Missenden, so they've got Old Bessie going to try and get it under control until it arrives.'

'We'd better go and help them,' said Magnus, getting up and hurrying to the front door.

'Who's Old Bessie?' Rosa asked Coburg as they followed Magnus and Malcolm.

'It's an ancient sort of fire engine, basically a tank of water on a cart. It works with men at each side pushing the pumping handles up and down. It's hard work.'

Malcolm got the Bentley going as they piled in, then they were racing along the country lane. In the near distance they could see the red and orange of a fire.

'The roof is thatch,' said Coburg. 'It'll go up like a bonfire.'

When they got to the parish hall a large crowd was already there. Men using long-handled rakes were pulling the burning thatch off the roof to the ground, with men, women and boys dashing buckets of water over each new fresh pile of burning thatch.

The fire engine, Old Bessie, was a large metal box on a cart and men standing at either side of it pushed and pulled the long handles that sent jets of water through the long hosepipes attached to it, dousing the flames momentarily, before they sprang up again.

Magnus, Malcolm, Coburg and Rosa ran forward

to each take the place of the exhausted men who were working the pump handles, while others came forward to take their turn holding the hoses and directing the water to where it was most needed.

The combination of water and fire resulted in thick smoke, and Coburg and Rosa followed Magnus and Malcolm in stopping momentarily to tie large handkerchiefs around their faces to protect their noses and mouths.

It was a struggle, but they were slowly winning the battle with the fire. Although everyone's face wore an expression of relief as they heard the sound of the fire engine's bell getting louder as it raced towards them.

The large red fire engine screeched to a halt beside the still burning parish hall. The flames had definitely receded. The firemen leapt out and began pouring water from their larger and more powerful hoses on the blaze. Soon the wooden building was in a state of partial destruction, but the fire was out.

The distraught figure of the postmistress, Mrs Prewitt, approached Magnus, tears leaving streaks in the black smoke that covered her face.

'Why, my Lord?' she asked plaintively. 'Why do the Germans want to destroy our parish hall? It's over three hundred years old.'

'Who knows, Mrs Prewitt?' replied Magnus. 'No reason at all.'

CHAPTER TWENTY-EIGHT

Sunday 5th January 1941

Lampson and Terry were just finishing their Sunday breakfast when there was a knock on their door. Lampson went to open it and found his father on the doorstep, his body language and his expression showing a depth of intense indignation.

'I need to talk to you,' said Mr Lampson.

'Come in,' said Lampson.

'In private,' said his father. 'What I've got to say isn't for Terry's ears.'

'Alright,' said Lampson. He took his jacket down from its peg and called out, 'Terry, I've just got to go and look at something with your grandad. I won't be a minute.'

As they walked away from Lampson's terraced house, Mr Lampson said, 'I've heard.'

'Heard what?'

'You know what! About Miss Bradley sneaking out over the back wall after having spent the night with you here. She was seen.'

'She did not spend the night here with me, not in

that way. She spent the night on the sofa. She was tired after the fire-watching so she decided to kip down and go home later. Bombs were still coming down, remember.'

'Come off it!' snapped Mr Lampson. 'Don't you come the old acid with me.'

'It's true!' protested Lampson.

'Whether it is or not, that's not what people are saying. Her reputation's ruined. There's talk she'll have to leave the school.'

'Why?'

'You know why. A teacher having an affair with the father of one of the kids in her class.'

'We are not having an affair. Like I said, she dossed down on my sofa because she was tired and the bombing was dangerous.'

'So why did she climb over the wall into the back lane and sneak off?'

'For the precise reason you just said, to stop people getting the wrong idea. In a way it's your fault, turning up at six o'clock. If you and Terry had seen her, you would have started asking questions. And Terry might have got the wrong impression.'

'So you're saying it's my fault!' said Mr Lampson, outraged.

'Yes,' said Lampson. 'She wouldn't have had to climb over into the back lane if you hadn't turned up so early.'

'And that's what you're going to say when the school sack her, is it?'

'I'll tell them the truth and challenge it.'

Mr Lampson shook his head. 'That'll only make it worse.' He hesitated, then stated flatly, 'You'll have to marry her.'

'Marry her? Because she spent the night on my sofa?'

'No one will believe that. It's up to you to do the decent thing. And your mum agrees with me.'

With that, Mr Lampson turned on his heel and marched off.

There was one major topic of conversation over breakfast at Dawlish Hall: why had the Germans decided to bomb the parish hall?

'I don't believe they did,' said Coburg. 'There are more and more reports of the Germans dumping the remainder of their bomb load before they return home. I think that's what happened here.'

'Three hundred and fifty years that parish hall has stood,' said the angry Magnus.

'We'll rebuild it,' said Malcolm. 'There are enough good people who'd volunteer their efforts.'

'And to think we came here to be safe from the bombing,' sighed Rosa ruefully.

'Not just the bombing. We also left to get away from that madwoman Bella Wilson,' Coburg reminded her.

'It might be better if you stayed here,' suggested Magnus.

'No,' said Rosa firmly. 'I will not be driven out of my own home by her. I'm not going to let her control my life.'

'I don't like to think of you at risk,' put in Malcolm, concerned.

'I won't be,' Rosa assured him. 'Edgar can take me to the ambulance station on his way to work. I'm well protected by Doris and Mr Warren and the others while I'm there. And Edgar can pick me up at the ambulance station and run me home. It'll be a pain, but it's only till she can be found.' She looked fondly at her husband. 'And I have the greatest faith that Edgar will find her.'

CHAPTER TWENTY-NINE

Monday 6th January 1941

'Where to, guv? The Yard?' Lampson asked Coburg as the chief inspector vacated the driver's place and moved across to the passenger seat, letting his sergeant get behind the steering wheel.

'No, the Houses of Parliament,' replied Coburg.

As they drove, he filled in Lampson on his meeting with Pauline Higgins on Saturday afternoon, and her accusations that Bidlow was behind her husband's murder.

'She's hinted that Higgins was blackmailing Bidlow over something, which is why he killed him. Or had him killed. I must admit, I can't see Bidlow having the guts or the skill to come up behind Higgins unnoticed and put a bullet in his head. So we're going to put that to Mr Bidlow and see how he reacts.'

'I can tell you how he's going to react,' snorted Lampson. 'He'll threaten to sue you.'

'I'm pretty sure he will, but it'll be good to rattle his cage. How did the football go on Saturday?' asked Coburg.

'We won,' said Lampson.

'Excellent!' said Coburg. Something in his sergeant's voice made him give him a concerned look. 'You don't sound exactly overjoyed,' he said.

'Yeh, well, there's a complication,' said Lampson reluctantly.

'What sort of complication?'

Lampson hesitated before replying in an awkward and despondent tone. 'After the fire-watching on Friday, it was so late that Eve decided to stay at my place.'

'Oh?' said Coburg guardedly. He, too, hesitated before saying, 'It sounds to me like a good step forward.'

'It was. Is,' said Lampson. 'But then my dad turned up at six o'clock the next morning bringing Terry home, before she'd had time to get away. So, to avoid embarrassment, she nipped out the back door into the yard and over the wall into the back lane.'

'Good move,' commented Coburg. 'Unless someone saw her.'

'Which they did. A real old gossip called Mrs Edgar. Of course, she told someone, and the next minute everyone knows.'

'Oh dear,' sympathised Coburg.

'The trouble is the board at the school is very strong on moral conduct. A teacher spending the night at the house of the father of one of the children in her class is big trouble.'

'You could always tell them nothing happened. That she slept on the sofa because it was late and too dangerous for her to make her way home with the bombing.'

'I did,' groaned Lampson. 'No one believed me. And Terry got into a fight with Mrs Edgar's son after he made jokes about me and his teacher.'

'Worse and worse,' said Coburg. 'What are you going to do?'

'I don't know,' said Lampson helplessly. 'My dad came round and had a go at me for ruining Eve's reputation. He reckons I ought to marry her.'

'Do you want to marry her?' asked Coburg.

'I have to admit, I wouldn't mind,' said Lampson. 'But I'm not sure if she feels the same way.'

'The fact she stayed the night suggests she might not be averse to the idea.'

'Yeah, but if we did, we'd be getting married for the wrong reason. Because we were forced into it.'

'Frankly, Ted, I think your dad's being more than a bit old-fashioned. Downright Victorian. Rosa and I were together for some time before we decided to get married.'

'Yes, but you upper-class people can get away with it,' said Lampson. 'There's no one more Victorian towards men and women in their attitudes than the English working class. Although if she wasn't a teacher at Terry's school, I doubt if anyone would be bothered.' He sighed heavily. 'The trouble is, I'm worried she might lose her job over it.'

When they got to the Houses of Parliament, they found Henry Bidlow in his office, going through letters from his constituents that had come in at the weekend.

'I thought we'd finished our business.' Bidlow scowled when they entered his office. 'I've told you everything I know.'

'You have, but some new information has been brought to our attention,' said Coburg. 'Was Martin Higgins blackmailing you?'

Bidlow stared at the two detectives, shocked.

'How dare you?' he said indignantly. 'What on earth makes you ask that?'

'Martin Higgins had told someone he expected a large sum of money from you in exchange for his silence on a certain topic.'

Coburg saw the alarm in Bidlow's eyes.

'A certain topic! What certain topic?' he blustered. 'I say again, how dare you!'

'In a murder enquiry, we have a duty to follow up every lead,' said Coburg.

'Well, you can ignore that outrageous slander,' said Bidlow stiffly. 'I was not being blackmailed by Martin Higgins, or anyone else. I have done nothing that would give anyone cause to attempt to blackmail me.'

'What do you think?' asked Coburg as he and

Lampson walked down the corridor away from Bidlow's office.

'I think he's guilty as sin,' said Lampson darkly.

Inside in his office, Bidlow was making a telephone call to the Merrie Tumbler.

'Is Danny Bell there?' he asked.

'Not right now,' said the voice at the other end. 'He don't usually come in till after ten. Who wants him?'

'Would you tell him that Henry Bidlow, the MP, wishes to see him. I'd be grateful if he could telephone me and we could arrange to meet.' Bidlow gave the man the telephone number of the Houses of Parliament where he could be contacted and hung up.

Damn Martin Higgins! he thought angrily. *This was supposed to be finished. And now there was another dangerous obstacle to be removed.*

Coburg and Lampson had barely arrived back in their office at Scotland Yard when the telephone rang.

'DCI Coburg,' said Coburg.

'This is Group Captain Crombie, Chief Inspector,' came the group captain's clipped tones. 'We met when you came to Biggin Hill.'

'Yes indeed. What can I do for you, Group Captain?'

'It's not so much me as for young Colin Upton. You remember you met him when you came to ask about that Russian woman?'

302

'I do indeed.'

'It seems he's been arrested. I've just had a telephone call from a police station in Soho. It seems he threatened a woman with a knife. He claims she stole his wallet. I'm sorry to bother you with this, but we'd be grateful if you could make contact with them, tell them you know Colin and what sort of chap he is. Decent.'

'I'll certainly do that, Group Captain. Did you get the name of the officer who contacted you?'

'It was a Sergeant Reg Dancy.'

Coburg hung up the phone and proceeded to pull on his outdoor coat.

'That was the group captain at Biggin Hill,' he told Lampson. 'Colin Upton's been arrested for threatening a woman with a knife. He claims she stole his wallet. He's at Soho police station. Our old friend there, Reg Dancy, made contact with Biggin Hill to let them know.'

'So it could be that simple after all,' mused Lampson. 'It was Upton who did for Svetlana?'

'I'm reserving judgement,' said Coburg. 'But it's definitely a possibility. But why would he kill her brother?' He looked at Lampson, who still hadn't moved from his desk. 'Soho?' he asked.

Lampson looked at him awkwardly. 'Guv, would you mind if I took some time off? I need to sort out this business of Eve, and do it before it gets worse for

303

her. All Somers Town will have been talking about it over the weekend, and she's in there today facing the kids and the staff. I need to stand by her. Sort it out.'

'Can you?' asked Coburg.

'I can at least try,' said Lampson. 'If you'll let me.'

Coburg nodded. 'You can take the car, after you've dropped me off in Soho.'

'Thanks, guv,' said Lampson.

Lampson braced himself to be confronted with accusing and hostile glares when he arrived at the school, but there was no one around in the corridors. All the pupils were in their classrooms with their teachers. Lampson made his way to the office of the headmaster, Jerrold Barnes, and knocked.

'Come in!' called Barnes.

Lampson entered and noticed the very wary look Barnes gave him. *He knows*, he thought.

'Yes, Mr Lampson?' said Barnes.

'Mr Barnes, I need to talk to you. Urgently.'

Barnes continued to regard him warily.

'If it's about what I think it is, I agree.' He gestured at the empty chair on the opposite side of his desk. Lampson sat.

'What have you heard, Mr Barnes?' he asked.

'I've been told that Miss Bradley spent the night at your house, and was seen early the following morning climbing over your back wall and moving off in – and

I use the word as it was said to me – in a secretive fashion down the back lane.' He looked sternly at Lampson. 'Do you have anything to say to that?'

'I do,' said Lampson. 'Yes, it's true that Miss Bradley stayed the night at my house, but not in the way that's been suggested. We were fire-watching the previous night, Friday. At midnight our fire-watching shift ended and my father and Andy White took over. The bombs were still falling and at that time of night the buses have stopped, and you can't get a taxi for love nor money. So I suggested to Miss Bradley that she stayed at my house and slept on the sofa and left for her home in the morning when it would be safer. After she'd considered it, she agreed. But she said she'd have to be up early because my son, Terry, was staying with my parents and they'd be bringing him back, and she didn't want them to get the wrong impression about our relationship.

'Unfortunately, my father brought Terry back earlier than I expected. So it was my suggestion that, to avoid them seeing her there, she go out the back way, over the wall and into the back lane. And that's what she did. But unfortunately, Mrs Edgar saw her and started telling stories about me and Miss Bradley, the wrong stories.

'Now I've been told that because of them she might lose her job. As a policeman I've always been taught that people are innocent until it's proved otherwise.

That doesn't seem to be the case here. Miss Bradley is being found guilty of something she didn't do by a group of people who are acting like vigilantes, without her being given the chance to tell her side of the story.' He looked at Barnes. 'That's what I've come here to say.'

'Thank you, Mr Lampson. I will admit I've heard the story being told. I was accosted by a group of mothers expressing their outrage at what they believed had happened and calling for Miss Bradley's dismissal. I haven't had the chance to talk to Miss Bradley about it; I was planning to do that during lunch break. But I will bear in mind what you have told me.' He looked intently at Lampson and asked, 'Do you swear that's what happened?'

'I do,' said Lampson.

'Very well,' said Barnes. 'Then I shall let you go about your duties, and I shall go about mine.'

Lampson rose, then asked, 'Would it be possible for me to have a brief word with Miss Bradley? I just want to reassure her, because she must be very worried at these accusations about her going round.'

Barnes thought it over, then said, 'Ordinarily, I would say no, because I'd rather hear Miss Bradley's version of events first. But, on this occasion, I will allow you to talk to her briefly.' He stood up. 'I will take charge of her class while you talk to her to ensure the children maintain good order.'

'Miss Bradley is very good at keeping discipline amongst the children,' said Lampson as they walked along the corridor.

'She is,' agreed Barnes. 'That's one reason I'd hate to lose her.'

Barnes knocked at the classroom door and entered. As he did so, the children in the class automatically stood to attention. As Barnes had agreed, Eve had trained her class well in matters of disciplines.

Barnes took charge of the class, and Eve came out to join Lampson in the corridor, pulling the door shut. She looked at Lampson and the sergeant could see the worry on her face.

'I needed to tell you I've squared it with Mr Barnes,' Lampson told her. 'I've told him you spent the night on the sofa, and that nothing happened between us.'

'He believed you?'

'He did. So, bear that in mind when he asks you about the stories. Because he's going to. A party of outraged mothers went to see him this morning, including, I guess that gossiping old cow, Mrs Edgar.' He looked at the door of the classroom. 'We'd better not spend too much time talking. Mr Barnes asked me to keep it brief.'

She nodded. 'Thank you,' she said.

She was about to open the door and walk back into her class when Lampson stopped her.

'There was another alternative my dad suggested,'

he said. 'He told me I ought to make an honest woman of you.'

She looked at him, surprised. 'Us get married?'

'My guv'nor, DCI Coburg, suggested that as well.'

She stared at him, wondering what to make of this. Then she said, slightly sarcastically, 'But you went for this option instead?'

'I'd be just as happy with us getting married,' said Lampson. 'Happier.'

She looked at him, then suddenly laughed. 'That's the worst proposal of marriage I've ever heard.'

'Yeah, well, it's an option,' said Lampson.

'I'll think about it,' she said. And, to his relief, she gave him a warm smile, before rearranging her features into those of a stern schoolmistress, and went back into her classroom.

She'll think about it, thought Lampson happily as he made for the exit.

Henry Bidlow walked into the Merrie Tumbler and found Danny Bell waiting for him, but today there was no welcoming smile on Bell's face, just curiosity tinged, it seemed to Bidlow, with a slight annoyance. This was reinforced by the fact that when Bidlow settled himself into the empty chair at the table where Bell was sitting, there was no offer of a drink for him. There was a definite air of wariness on the part of Bell.

'Thank you for seeing me, Mr Bell.' Bidlow smiled,

hoping to reintroduce the warmth he'd felt from Bell last time they'd met.

'Jerry said you told him it was urgent,' said Bell, still keeping up the formality.

'Yes,' said Bidlow. 'That man I told you about who was causing me trouble.'

Bell gave a curt nod. 'Dealt with.'

'Yes, so I understand, and I am hugely grateful. The problem is that someone else appears to have got involved and is making things difficult for me.'

'Who is he?'

'It's a policeman. A DCI Saxe-Coburg from Scotland Yard.'

Bell held up a hand to silence Bidlow and said in low and definitely menacing tones, 'I hope you're not asking me to arrange the demise of a senior Scotland Yard detective. Trust me, if anything of that nature befell someone of the stature of DCI Saxe-Coburg, the whole machinery of the police force would spring into action, and there is a serious risk that anyone undertaking such an act would be caught and hanged. Only a fool or someone with nothing to lose would even consider it.' He paused, then added, 'And a person with nothing to lose – for example, someone who's already dying – would want to receive a very large sum of money to ensure his family were OK. A *very* large sum of money. Many thousands.'

Bidlow gulped. 'No, I'm not asking for him to

be . . . er . . . killed. I was just wondering if there was a way the – er – situation could be handled.'

'If you're talking of a bribe, you can forget it,' said Bell. 'DCI Coburg doesn't take backhanders. I'd go so far as to say he's the straightest copper in the Met. Or any other police force.' He shook his head. 'I've already done you one favour, gratis.'

'Yes I know—' began Bidlow, but he was cut off with a sharp glance from Bell.

'I don't think we need to meet again,' he said curtly. 'Unless I need to renew our acquaintance in order for you to repay me for the assistance I gave you in dealing with your previous problem. Until that day, Mr Bidlow, please don't contact me. Or I shall have to take steps to discourage you.'

Bidlow gave a nervous nod to show he understood. Then he rose to his feet and walked out into the street with as much dignity as he could muster, fully aware he'd just been chastised and sent away.

Once Bidlow had left the pub, Bell summoned Duffy Powell, who joined him at the table.

'The man who's just left is an MP called Henry Bidlow,' said Bell.

Powell nodded.

'I want you to do some nosing around.'

'What sort of nosing, boss?'

'I want you to find out what Bidlow's hiding. What he's so scared of that he'd consider asking me to bump off a senior Scotland Yard detective for him.'

'No!' said Powell, shocked. 'Is that what he had the nerve to ask?'

'In a roundabout way,' said Bell. He smiled. 'Which means that whatever his secret is, it's going to be worth quite a bit to whoever finds out what it is. So what I need you to do is have a word with Mr Bidlow and get him to tell it to you. I suggest a visit to his house. People like that always feel more vulnerable in their own home.'

CHAPTER THIRTY

Monday 6th January 1941

Coburg arrived at the Soho police station and walked up to the reception desk where Sergeant Reg Dancy was in charge.

'Good day, Chief Inspector,' said Dancy. He looked past Coburg and asked, 'Sergeant Lampson not with you today?'

'He's looking into something else,' said Coburg. 'He might be along later. We heard you had Wing Commander Upton in custody here.'

Dancy shook his head in surprise. 'Wing commander? He's hardly out of his teens.'

'They get promoted quickly with this war,' said Coburg. 'How is he?'

'Better than he was when they brought him in,' said Dancy. 'When he was first brought in, he was completely out of it. Kept demanding to see someone called Miranda. "I must see Miranda!" he moaned. "Miranda!"'

'Was that the name of the girl he attacked?'

'No, her name's Sophia. We've got her statement if you want to see it.'

'After I've had a word with Upton.'

Dancy picked up the bunch of keys to the holding cells. 'Follow me,' he said.

He let Coburg into the cell where Colin Upton was lying on a bunk. The young man was asleep and in a sorry state. He was dressed in civilian clothes, which were crumpled and stained with a mixture of alcohol and vomit. Upton's face had a bruise on one side, either inflicted by the woman he'd attacked or the result of his falling over.

'Wing Commander Upton,' said Coburg. When there was no response, Coburg raised his voice and barked out in parade-ground fashion: 'Officer Upton! Wake up!'

There was a stirring from the sleeping young man, then he opened his eyes one at a time and finally seemed to focus. Moving awkwardly, he forced himself to sit up on the bunk and leant back against the brick wall of the cell.

'You're the policeman who came to talk to me at Biggin Hill,' he said.

'Detective Chief Inspector Saxe-Coburg,' said Coburg. 'You know why you're here?'

'They say I attacked a woman, but I didn't.'

'The accusation is that you attacked her with a knife.'

Upton shook his head. 'I would never attack a woman with a knife.'

'She says you did.'

'No, that's back to front,' said Upton. 'I went up to town to have a bit of fun. Met this woman. A tart, obviously. She took me back to her place, and when I went to pay her I found my wallet had gone. She'd obviously taken it. I told her to give it back, but she denied anything to do with it. She said I must have lost it.'

'It does seem unlikely she would have taken it before you'd paid her,' Coburg pointed out.

'Well, yes, I see that now, but last night I was a bit befuddled. I'd had quite a lot to drink.'

'She said you threatened her with a knife.'

'I didn't really threaten her. I was just trying to make her give me back my wallet.'

'But you had a knife.'

'It wasn't mine, it was hers. When I demanded my wallet, she pulled this knife out and threatened me with it. I took it off her. That was all.'

'Who's Miranda?' asked Coburg.

Upton looked at him, doing his best to put on an air of bewilderment, but Coburg spotted the alarm in his eyes.

'I've no idea,' said Upton.

'You were demanding to see her when you were brought in.'

'I was drunk. I didn't know what I was saying.'

'Where did you go during the three hours you were away from the base on Christmas Day?' asked Coburg.

Upton stared at him, bewildered. 'What's that got to do with this?'

'This woman says you attacked her with a knife. Svetlana Rostova was stabbed to death with a knife on Christmas Day. I'm sure you can see the connection.'

'There is no connection! I didn't even see Svetlana that day.'

'So what did you do when you left the base?'

'I told you before, I drove around just to have a bit of time to myself.'

'You had time to get to Down Street, kill Svetlana and make it back to Biggin Hill,' said Coburg, watching Upton's face.

By now, Upton was fully awake. 'I may have had time, but I didn't do it. I didn't go to London at any time that day.'

Duffy Powell rang the bell of the expensive-looking address he'd been given for Henry Bidlow MP. The door was opened by a middle-aged woman who looked out at him nervously. Powell was struck by the fact that she sported a black eye.

'Yes?' she asked.

'Is Mr Bidlow at home?' asked Powell.

'He is, but he's very busy at the moment.'

Powell nodded sympathetically. 'I understand, but I have an important message from Danny Bell. Would you tell him that, please?'

'I'll tell him,' Eleanor Bidlow said. 'If you'll just wait here.'

She shut the door and Powell stood patiently on the doorstep. After a few moments, the figure of Henry Bidlow opened the door and looked out anxiously at Powell.

'You've got a message for me from Danny Bell?' he asked.

'I have,' said Powell.

'You'd better come in,' said Bidlow.

He led Powell through the house to his study, where he gestured for Powell to take a chair while he settled himself behind his desk.

'I thought Mr Bell said our business was complete,' said Bidlow suspiciously.

'It isn't until Mr Bell decides it is,' said Powell. 'Mr Bell has been thinking over your recent request regarding DCI Coburg.'

Bidlow eyed Powell warily. Had Bell changed his mind? Was he prepared to dispose of Coburg? If so, at what price? Bell's heart sank; he knew whatever the price was, it was unaffordable.

'Mr Bell is curious as to what it is that you don't want to be known about.'

'That is my business,' said Bidlow sharply.

'No, ever since you received his help in getting rid of Martin Higgins, everything you do is his business.'

Bidlow looked nervously at Powell. 'Martin Higgins? That was you?'

Powell didn't reply, just looked blandly at Bidlow. 'Mr Bell wants to know what this very serious thing is that you wish to keep secret.'

Bidlow gave a scornful laugh. 'It would hardly be a secret if I said what it was. And who's to say there *is* a secret? There is no secret. Mr Bell has got it wrong.'

Powell looked thoughtfully at Bidlow, then said carefully, 'If someone wants two men eliminated, one of them a top Scotland Yard detective, then it's to cover up something. That's what Mr Bell thinks. Mr Bell has an intuition about these things, and he's never wrong. So, what are you concealing that you don't want found out?'

Bidlow shook his head. 'This is nonsense. I refuse to be browbeaten. I am a member of parliament.'

Powell studied Bidlow thoughtfully, then reached into his inside holster and produced a pistol, which he pointed at the shocked Bidlow. 'I'm not here to browbeat you. I'm here to shoot you unless you tell me. And don't think I won't. It's what I do.'

'You can't!' blustered Bidlow. 'My wife is here. She'll be able to identify you. She knows you came from Danny Bell. She'll tell the police. You'll hang.'

'Then it will make sense to shoot her as well. The

way I see it, I shoot you, then her, then leave the gun by your hand. It'll look like you killed your wife, then yourself.'

'Why would I do that?'

'Because of this secret of yours. There'll be a note left, so the police will start digging into your affairs to find out what it was.' He looked at Bidlow. 'So, the choice is yours. You tell me and live. Or you don't and you die, and it comes out anyway once the police start looking into things.'

Bidlow shuddered as he looked at the gun pointing at him.

'How . . . how . . . how do I know you won't shoot me after I've told you?' he stammered.

'Because you're worth more to Mr Bell alive than dead,' said Powell. 'To me, it makes no difference. I get paid either way. But hurry up and make up your mind. I ain't got all day.'

Bidlow gulped, then said, 'It's nothing really bad. Years ago, after the First War, I was on a committee to watch over the restitution of Germany, in particular if they started to develop weapons.' He fell silent, struggling with what he was saying.

'Go on,' said Powell.

'I took my job seriously, seriously enough to get involved with one of their weapons companies.'

'Which one?' asked Powell.

'Krupp,' said Bidlow.

Powell nodded. 'Go on,' he said.

'Everything was fine at first, but after Hitler came to power, Germany started to build weapons again. Making newer ones.'

'I thought you said you were on this committee that was set up to make sure it didn't happen.'

'I was, but gradually the committee sort of . . . lapsed. I think the government had other things to worry about.'

'But you didn't lapse?' asked Powell.

Bidlow shook his head.

'No,' he said awkwardly. 'I stayed with the company. For one thing, I had quite a large shareholding in them. And also they'd given me a role of consultant to their board.'

Powell nodded. 'You were earning good money off them.' He gestured at the expensive decor of the room. 'More than you'd make as an MP.'

'Possibly,' admitted Bidlow. Desperately, he tried his appeal: 'I intended to sever my links with them, but somehow the time never seemed right.'

'So instead you kept pocketing their money. From the company making weapons for our enemy.'

'I was going to stop it,' pleaded Bidlow.

'I can see why you were keen for this not to get out,' said Powell. 'You see, to me, and I'm sure to the authorities, this would count as treason, you being in the pay of this country's enemy, Germany.'

'It wasn't Germany!' protested Bidlow. 'Krupp are a private company.'

Powell shook his head. 'That won't be how the authorities see it.' He shrugged. 'But then, that's nothing to do with me.' He slipped the gun back into his shoulder holster. 'Thank you, Mr Bidlow. You've done what I asked. My business here is done.'

With that, he rose to his feet, nodded at Bidlow, and made for the door.

CHAPTER THIRTY-ONE

Monday 6th January 1941

When Coburg returned to Scotland Yard, he found Lampson waiting for him.

'How did you get on in Soho?' asked Lampson.

'I'll tell you on the way,' said Coburg. 'We're going back to Biggin Hill. Fancy doing the driving?'

As Lampson drove them southwards towards Bromley, Coburg filled him in about his interview with Upton.

'So you think he might be the one who did Svetlana Rostova after all?' asked Lampson.

'He's certainly back in the frame,' said Coburg. 'How did it go at the school?'

'I think it went alright.'

'In what way?'

'I told the headmaster she slept on the sofa at my place and nothing happened between us.' He fell silent before adding in a rueful and embarrassed tone, 'In short, I lied.'

'Yes, but you did it for a good reason,' said Coburg. 'To save her job.'

'Yeah, but in all the time I've been a policeman I've never told a lie.'

'But you weren't at the school as a policeman, you were there as a concerned parent,' Coburg pointed out.

'That's just splitting hairs,' objected Lampson.

'Which might keep your friend Eve Bradley in a job,' persisted Coburg.

'Yes, I suppose you're right,' Lampson agreed reluctantly. 'I'm still not sure it's right. A lie's a lie.'

'True, but some things are more important. Which is why they invented the white lie.'

'This isn't just a white lie, this is a big one,' protested Lampson.

'Then it's up to you which is more important,' said Coburg.

On their arrival at Biggin Hill, they were shown to the office of Group Captain Crombie, who asked them, 'Have you seen Wing Commander Upton?'

'I've just come back from seeing him at Soho police station,' said Coburg.

'How was he?'

'Recovering from a serious bout of heavy drinking,' said Coburg.

'Has he been released?'

'Not yet. There are still more questions to be asked about the earlier incident with the Russian fortune-teller.'

'I thought that was cleared up as far as young Upton was concerned,' said Crombie.

'So did we,' said Coburg, 'until this incident involving a young woman and Upton threatening her with a knife came up. Do you know anyone called Miranda?'

The group captain looked at them, bewildered. 'Yes,' he said. 'My wife? Why?'

'Nothing of importance,' said Coburg. 'It was just something Upton was supposed to have said when he was arrested.'

'He mentioned my wife's name?'

'We don't know if that's what he did. It could be another Miranda, someone he'd met.'

'The woman he was accused of threatening?'

'No, her name was Sophia. Does Colin Upton know your wife?'

'Not well. She occasionally comes to see me here at the base. Why?'

'I'm sure it's another Miranda he meant, but would you mind if we talked to your wife, just to eliminate her and save us asking questions where none need to be asked.'

'Of course.'

'If you could give us your address?'

'Certainly.' Crombie took a piece of paper and scribbled an address on it, which he handed to Coburg. 'Here. I've added our telephone number if you'd prefer to speak to her over the phone.'

'Thank you,' said Coburg. 'Was your wife at home on Christmas Day?'

'Except for a couple of hours in the late afternoon when she went to deliver presents to her sister and her family.' Crombie looked at his watch, then said apologetically, 'I'm sorry but I've got a busy schedule today. I'm going to be tied up here at the base for the rest of the day. Perhaps we can talk tomorrow?'

'We'll let you know,' said Coburg. 'It depends on what's awaiting us when we return to London.'

Coburg and Lampson left Crombie's office and made their way to their car.

'He's going to be tied up at the base for the rest of the day,' mused Coburg. 'So now seems a good time to call on Mrs Miranda Crombie.'

The cottage the Crombies occupied was just two miles from the air base. Miranda Crombie was a smart, attractive woman in her mid-forties and she looked enquiringly at the two men on her doorstep. They showed her their warrant cards and introduced themselves.

'Scotland Yard?' she said, surprised.

'Indeed,' said Coburg. 'We are making enquiries into a pilot at Biggin Hill air base, a Wing Commander Colin Upton. Do you know him?'

'No,' she said, too quickly, Coburg felt.

324

'He's a suspect in the murder of a young woman that happened in London on Christmas Day. He's currently being held at a police station in London.'

'No,' said Miranda Crombie again. 'That's impossible.'

'I thought you said you didn't know him,' said Coburg.

'I don't, but I know the kind of men who fly for my husband, and put their lives on the line for this country, and none of them would be capable of such a thing.'

'Unfortunately, evidence has emerged that points towards him. He's currently in the police cell because he attacked a young woman in London with a knife. The young woman who was murdered in London on Christmas Day was stabbed to death. I'm sure you can see the connection.'

'What I can't see is why you are questioning me,' she demanded. 'I can't see that this is anything to do with me.'

'When Colin Upton was arrested in London yesterday he was heard to call out "I want Miranda." Not just once, but he repeated it. We have been unable to find any woman in his life called Miranda except for you.'

'I've told you, I don't know him.'

'He told us that on Christmas Day he signed out from Biggin Hill and drove around the local area, on his own. We've checked the logbook at Biggin Hill and he left the airbase at 4 p.m. and returned at 7 p.m. That would have given him time to get to London and murder the young woman.'

'Why do you think it was him?'

'In the light of the recent attack by him on a young woman while armed with a knife,' said Coburg. 'However, if someone could provide him with an alibi for the hours he was away from the air base, between 4 p.m. and 7 p.m., that would prove his innocence. We understand you were at you sister's at that time?'

'Er . . . Yes,' she said.

'Was there any chance that you met Colin Upton while you were on your way there, or on your way back?'

She hesitated, then said, 'No. That didn't happen.'

'That's a pity,' said Coburg. 'Because if, for example, you had happened to see his car on the road while you were driving, that would lend weight to his story that he was just driving around.' He paused then said, 'Otherwise, it looks as if he'll stand trial for the murder. And, with no real alibi, certainly no one to support his story, it's likely he'll be found guilty. In which case, he'll hang.'

He kept his gaze on her, watching her weighing things up. When she said nothing, Coburg said, in gentle tones, 'The danger is that if he goes to trial, his barrister will be bound to make something of the fact that he called for "Miranda" when he was arrested for attacking this other woman with a knife. We haven't been able to find any other women of his acquaintance called Miranda. It may raise difficult questions at his trial for you.'

'Why should it?'

'You know what the press are like for speculating. However, if he was never charged then there'd be no trial, no possibility for such speculation.'

Miranda Crombie thought this over, then looked at Coburg defiantly. 'I take great offence at what you are suggesting, Chief Inspector.'

'I'm suggesting nothing, Mrs Crombie . . .'

'Yes you are. And I will not be a party to it. I did not see Wing Commander Upton at all on Christmas Day, not in a personal way, nor in passing, and that is the end of it. Now, if you'll excuse me, I have things to do.' She was about to close the door on them, when she stopped. 'Does my husband know you are coming to see me?'

'Yes,' said Coburg. 'But not to check on your movements. Merely because it was he who told us his wife's name was Miranda when we told him what Colin Upton had been heard to call out when arrested.'

'There must be many women called Miranda,' she said stiffly.

'I'm sure there are,' said Coburg.

She closed the door on them and they walked to their car.

'I think there's something going on there,' said Lampson.

'I think you're right, but she's more concerned with protecting her good name than she is in preventing Upton from being charged with murder. Which suggests whatever's going on between them, it's stronger on his side than on hers.'

'So what's next?'

'We talk to young Upton and see if he sticks to his story about what he did on Christmas Day.'

Colin Upton had cleaned himself up when they returned to the Soho police station. His shirt and jacket were still stained and crumpled, but he'd washed his face. As Coburg and Lampson entered his cell, he promptly rose to his feet from the bunk where he'd been sitting and stood to attention. Military discipline resulting in an automatic reaction to figures in authority, Coburg thought, remembering his own time in uniform.

Coburg gestured for him to sit down on the bunk again.

'We're glad to see you looking better,' he said.

'Can I return to Biggin Hill?' Upton asked.

'Not until we've talked a little longer,' said Coburg. 'There's just one or two things we need to clarify. On Christmas Day you signed out from Biggin Hill at 4 p.m. and returned at 7 p.m. Where did you go?'

'I told you before, I just drove around.'

'Did you see anyone who can confirm that?'

'No.'

'So you saw no one who can confirm your alibi for those three hours.'

'What do you mean, alibi? Alibi for what?'

'For when Svetlana Rostova was killed.'

'I didn't do that. I've already told you.'

'Yes, you did. But it would help your case if someone could confirm, say, that they spent some of that time with you.'

'No one did.'

'Perhaps Miranda Crombie, the wife of your group captain?'

Upton looked at them and they saw a mixture of fear and anxiety in his face.

'What do you mean?' he demanded with barely concealed anger.

'When you were brought in you called for Miranda,' said Coburg.

'So? There must be hundreds of women called Miranda.'

'But which one of them were you referring to?'

'I don't know. I must have heard the name somewhere. Someone from my past, perhaps.'

Coburg paused, watching the young man intently. 'Let me put a hypothetical situation to you. You left the base and drove somewhere to see Miranda Crombie.'

'No!' snapped Upton.

'Her husband was on duty at the base and she was home alone. She told us that she went to visit her sister between four o'clock and seven o'clock.'

'You've talked to her?' said Upton, horrified.

'We have.'

'You had no right to do that!'

'This is a murder investigation; we have every right.'

'Does the group captain know you questioned her?'

'He knows we were going to call on her,' said Coburg.

Upton looked at the two detectives, concerned. 'What did she say?'

'The statements of other witnesses are confidential,' said Coburg.

Upton hesitated, thinking this over, then said awkwardly, 'I'd rather you didn't say anything about this to the group captain.'

'Why?'

'Because this is nothing to do with Mrs Crombie.'

'Do you deny that you saw her on Christmas Day?'

'Absolutely I deny it.'

Coburg paused, then said, 'Effectively you are telling us you have no alibi for those hours on Christmas Day. Which, as I've said before, makes you a suspect in the murder.'

'I didn't do it!'

'It would help your case if you had someone who could say you were with them.'

'I can't, because I wasn't with anyone.'

'You weren't with Miranda Crombie?'

'I was not.'

As they got back into the car for their drive back to London, Lampson asked, 'Why didn't you tell him she said she didn't see him on Christmas Day?'

'Because I want him to be worried about that. I want to see if he makes contact with her.'

'My bet is he'll stay away from calling on her.'

'Yes, but he might telephone her when he knows her husband isn't at home.'

'You're going to put a tap on her phone?'

'I am, and let's hope he says something we can use.'

'That'll mean letting him out of jail.'

'I know,' said Coburg. 'I'm planning to grant him bail. A minimal amount, to make sure he leaves, and on condition he's to make himself available if charges are brought against him.'

'You don't think he killed Svetlana?'

'No, I don't, but the young fool is so anxious to protect Miranda Crombie he'd rather go on trial for murder. The trouble is we can't officially eliminate him from our enquiries at this moment, after he attacked that woman.' He gave a sigh. 'Time to turn our attention back to some more likely suspects.'

'Henry Bidlow MP?'

'And Sean Kennedy,' said Coburg.

'We haven't got much against Kennedy,' Lampson pointed out.

'No we haven't,' agreed Coburg. 'Which is why I think it's time to give him a bit of a nudge.'

'Why do you think it might be him?'

'Because his sister drinks and talks,' said Coburg. 'Out of all the people who Svetlana had sessions with, the two that stick out for me are Eleanor Bidlow and Lady Pitstone. Both women who know a secret about the men close to them, a dangerous secret that both men are determined to keep hidden, but that – in my opinion – both men feel that their woman may well have blabbed to Svetlana. And that Svetlana in turn may have passed on to her brother.'

CHAPTER THIRTY-TWO

Monday 6th January 1941

As Coburg and Lampson walked into the main reception area of Scotland Yard, Lampson nudged the chief inspector with his elbow.

'Over there, on the long bench,' he muttered. 'Danny Bell. With a couple of his lieutenants.'

Bell had obviously been waiting for them, because he stood up, at the same time gesturing for the two men with him to remain seated, then walked towards Coburg and Lampson.

'Mr Coburg,' he said. 'Could we have a word?'

'What about?' asked Coburg.

Bell looked around the reception hall, then lowered his voice and said, 'I've got some information about someone you've been talking to recently.'

'Who?' asked Coburg.

'Can we talk in private?' asked Bell.

'I'll go and sort some things out,' said Lampson.

'No need, Sergeant,' said Bell. 'I've got no secrets from you. And whatever I tell your guv'nor, he's going to tell you. After all, you're his number two. I meant, can we talk somewhere else. Your office?'

Coburg nodded. 'Follow me.'

The three men climbed the wide marble staircase to the first floor, and made their way to Coburg's office, where they settled themselves down.

'I must admit I'm intrigued why one of London's top gangsters should want to call on me here at Scotland Yard,' said Coburg.

'*Businessman*, please, Mr Coburg. I've come because I've got some information.'

'Let me guess, you want to trade it for something.'

Bell shook his head. 'Not at all. This is gratis, absolutely free, with no strings. I've come to see you because you've always been straight with me, and with Dennis when he was alive. You were on the other side, but you were fair. You never tried to fit us up, like some.'

Coburg sat and watched Bell warily, wondering what was going on.

'There's an MP called Henry Bidlow,' said Bell.

'Yes, I know him,' said Coburg.

'He had an assistant called Martin Higgins, who I believe was killed recently.'

Coburg's eyes narrowed as he looked at Bell quizzically.

'You *believe*?' he said, letting the irony of the statement show.

'Nothing to do with me, Mr Coburg, nor any

of mine. But it brought me into the picture, out of curiosity, you might say. It seems that Mr Bidlow has a secret that he doesn't want found out.'

'Go on,' said Coburg.

'It seems he's got shares in a firm called Krupp. They make weapons.'

'Yes, I know who Krupp are.'

'As well as having shares, it seems Krupp pay him as a consultant.' He paused, then said, 'Why would they do that, Mr Coburg? A German arms firm pay money to a British MP, a member of the government?'

'I assume you have a theory,' said Coburg.

Bell smiled and nodded. 'As I'm sure you'll have when you think about it. What kind of information would a German arms company be willing to pay for? Obviously they'd want to know what sort of weapons we've got, and what kind of weapons we might be developing to use against them, so they can develop their own to counter them. You see what I'm getting it?'

'Yes,' said Coburg grimly. 'You're suggesting that a member of our government is committing treason and betraying weapons secrets for money. How sure are you of this?'

'Sure enough,' said Bell. 'The thing is, Mr Coburg, you and I may be thought of as being on opposite sides of the fence in our particular businesses. But I'm a patriot. A very strong patriot. I'd never sell my country for money, and I despise anyone who would.'

'Have you got any evidence of what you've told me?' asked Coburg. 'Paperwork? Statements from witnesses?'

'No, just what I've heard on the street.'

'Which street?' asked Coburg.

Bell chuckled. 'Very amusing,' he said. He stood up. 'I leave it with you, Mr Coburg, for you to act on, or not. I've got no evidence, and no way of getting any. But you, you're in with the authorities. You know who to talk to. Because, if what I'm telling you is true – and I'm sure it is – then I think you'll agree this scumbag needs stopping.'

Lampson escorted Bell down the stairs to the reception area and watched as Bell's two lieutenants got to their feet and then walked with their boss out to the street. *What a nerve*, he thought. One of London's top gangster bosses actually walking into Scotland Yard, as cool as a cucumber.

When Lampson got back to the office, Coburg asked him what he thought of what Bell had told them.

'Sounds like treason going on to me, guv,' said Lampson. 'What are you going to do?'

'At the moment there's not much I can do. The allegation has been made against an MP, a member of the government, by a known gangster with no evidence to support it. I need more, and from a reliable source, before I can suggest an investigation by the intelligence services.' He picked up the telephone and asked the switchboard operator to connect him to Dawlish Hall. 'I'm hoping that my brother Magnus might be able to put me in touch with a reliable source.'

It was Malcolm who answered the phone.

'Mr Edgar,' he said, and Coburg could hear the smile of welcome in his voice.

'Is my brother there, Malcolm?'

'If you'll hold on one moment, I'll get him.'

There was a short delay and then Magnus was on the phone. 'Edgar, what can I do for you?'

'I'm hoping you might be able to help me with some information.'

'What sort of information?'

'Do you know Henry Bidlow, the MP?'

'I know of him and met him a few times. It's not a relationship I care to expand on in any way.'

'Having met him, I'm in agreement with you. The thing is, I've had some information to suggest he may be linked with Krupp.'

'The weapons firm?'

'Yes. If what this man told me is true it could point to Bidlow being guilty of treason, passing information to the enemy about our weapons. The allegation is that he's on Krupp's payroll.'

'If that's true it'd be very serious. What evidence have you got?'

'None.'

'What about your informant?'

'He says he's got none, just words he's picked up.'

'Is he reliable?'

Coburg thought it over. 'I've known him for some time and he always seems . . .' He hesitated, before saying 'straight.'

'You seem doubtful,' said Magnus.

'Let's just say he's not the sort of person who the authorities would listen to, especially with allegations against an MP. I wondered if you knew anyone with more respectability who might know something. You do seem to have important links.'

There was a pause, and Coburg could picture his brother nodding thoughtfully, before Magnus said, 'Leave it with me. I'll ask around. If the allegations have a basis in fact, I think I might know the person to ask.'

Coburg hung up and told Lampson, 'Right, that's Henry Bidlow being looked into. Now to nudge Sean Kennedy.'

He picked up the telephone again and asked to be connected to the Irish High Commission in London. Once through, he asked to speak to Sean Kennedy.

'Mr Kennedy,' he said. 'DCI Saxe-Coburg. I'd like to take you up on your offer to talk to your sister, in your presence, as you suggested. When would be convenient?'

CHAPTER THIRTY-THREE

Tuesday 7th January 1941

Coburg had decided to go alone to visit Lady Pitstone and her brother, leaving Lampson in the office in case any calls or information came through about Henry Bidlow.

This time when Coburg arrived at the house, he noticed that Kennedy seemed to have interceded about his sister's drinking. Instead of bottles of spirits, a jug of coffee was the only liquid in evidence in the living room. Lady Pitstone was noticeably not inebriated this time, but her need for a drink showed itself in her hand shaking as she poured Coburg a cup of coffee from the jug.

'Thank you for seeing me, Lady Pitstone,' said Coburg. 'Unfortunately, we're not much nearer to finding out who killed Lady Za Za, but our investigations have suggested a motive. Can I ask if you discussed Irish politics with Lady Za Za?'

Pitstone stared at Coburg, bewildered. 'Irish politics? Why on earth would I talk about that to her? Or to anyone?'

'The sad truth is, Lady Pitstone, that Svetlana was

murdered, and we believe there is a possibility that one of her clients may have let slip something to her that others may not have wanted to be known.'

'What sort of thing?'

'That's what we're trying to find out. Some of her clients have quite important associations. Close relatives of important politicians. You, yourself, your brother is a member of the Irish High Commission and privy to important information.'

'I'm sorry, Chief Inspector, but I cannot see the point of this line of enquiry,' interrupted Kennedy sharply. 'My sister is not involved in Irish politics in any way.'

'But you are, and it's possible you may have mentioned something to her that she might have passed on. And in times of war, information is a valuable commodity.'

'I would never do such a thing,' Kennedy said stiffly. 'And anyway, there is nothing that I could pass on that could in any way be threatening to anyone. The Irish Free State's position on this war is clear: Ireland is and will remain neutral. Officially we support neither side.'

'But there are some in Ireland who wish for a united Ireland and believe that a German victory might assist that ambition,' said Coburg.

Kennedy glared tight-lipped at Coburg, then said in firm tones, 'I resent the implication that I or my family might be involved in some way in what you are suggesting.'

Coburg turned to Lady Pitstone. 'How about you, Lady Pitstone? How do you stand on the subject of a united Ireland?'

Lady Pitstone looked at Coburg in bewilderment, then at her brother, then back at Coburg again. 'I'm sorry,' she said, puzzled.

'Did you ever discuss the matter with Lady Za Za?' pressed Coburg.

Kennedy rose to his feet. 'I must ask you to desist from this line of questioning,' he said. 'It is not relevant and it is distressing my sister. Deirdre does not get involved in politics, not British politics nor Irish, and certainly not German.'

'It is a valid question, Mr Kennedy, in view of the fact that we are investigating a murder.'

'It is not for the reasons I stated. And I must advise you, Chief Inspector, that if you persist in this line of questioning, I shall have to raise it with my superior, Mr Dulanty, and I have no doubt that he in turn will raise it with his counterpart in the British government. There are diplomatic channels for this kind of discussion, not for the involvement of the British police.' He stood up. 'This meeting is at an end.'

In the office, Lampson answered the ringing telephone and found himself listening to the posh tones of Magnus, Earl of Dawlish.

'Good morning, Sergeant,' said Magnus. 'Is my brother there?'

'I'm afraid he's out at the moment, Your Earlship. Can I take a message for him?'

'If you would. Please let him know that I called and ask him if he can telephone me. I think I may have some information he was after.'

'I'll let him know as soon as he returns,' said Lampson.

Lampson had barely hung up the receiver when the door opened and Coburg entered.

'That was quick,' said Lampson. 'I didn't think you'd be back for ages.'

'I got thrown out,' said Coburg. 'Not literally, but certainly I was asked to leave. Anything happening here?'

'Yes. Your brother phoned. He's got some information you were after.'

'Excellent.' Coburg smiled. 'Let's see what he's got.'

Coburg put through a call to Dawlish Hall, and a moment later was speaking to Magnus.

'That Bidlow chap you were asking about,' said Magnus. 'I had a chat with an old friend of mine who knows quite a bit about war machinery production.'

'Oh? Who?'

'Max Aitken, better known to you as the First Baron Beaverbrook.'

'The minister of aircraft production in Churchill's War Cabinet?'

'Ah, so you do keep up with what's happening politically.'

'With Beaverbrook as prominent a figure as he is, I would imagine most people would know about him. At least, those with an interest in who's who in government. How do you know him? I can't imagine you and he were war comrades. He never served, did he?'

'He did his bit for the Canadians, mainly in administration.'

'Oh yes, of course. He's Canadian, isn't he.'

'He is, but I think he sees himself more as a citizen of the world. I know him through the House.'

Of course, thought Coburg. *The House of Lords.* 'Did he have anything to impart about Bidlow?'

'Yes, something quite interesting. As someone who's been heavily involved in armaments and weapons manufacturing, Beaverbrook has made many contacts in that world. Not just British manufacturers but also those on the continent. And in the period after the First World War, he was part of the group that kept on eye on German armaments to make sure they kept within the terms of the Versailles agreement.'

'But they didn't.'

'Not once Hitler came to power. Anyway, without going into the convoluted history of German armaments, it seems that soon after the First War, Bidlow took on an ambassadorial role for Krupp.'

'So my man was right?'

'Very possibly. Bidlow's reasoning behind it was that as a shareholder in the company and also an ambassador, he was perfectly placed to keep an eye on their activities and make sure they stuck to the rules governing German rearmament.'

'Which was a ban on it and a demobilisation of their army, navy and air force.'

'Yes, but Krupp was allowed to manufacture weapons equipment for other countries. Mainly, it was claimed, defensive equipment. The Allies accepted this because it was reasoned that Germany needed to recover economically, and Krupp was a major engineering company and a huge employer.'

'I would imagine that Bidlow got his shares in the company for a rock-bottom price at that time.'

'Correct. But the company became wealthier when Hitler came to power.'

'Surely Bidlow would have been aware that Germany was becoming more belligerent and there was a serious threat of another war. Let's face it, it's all the talk has been about for some years now. Surely he would have deemed it wise to have sold his shares in what could be a company supplying weapons to an enemy.'

'Yes, that's what anyone patriotic would have done.'

'But he didn't?'

'I don't know. To dig into his business matters, shareholdings, his ambassadorship for Krupp, that sort of thing, is out of my sphere of knowledge.'

'What about Beaverbrook? Can he find out?'

'At the moment he's got a lot on his plate looking after aircraft production for our side. Now you've got that much, I'm sure you know the right people to contact to start digging.'

'I do indeed,' said Coburg. 'Thank you for this, Magnus. I'll let you know what happens.'

He hung up, then said to Lampson, 'Magnus has confirmed what we were told by Danny Bell about Henry Bidlow being paid by Krupp.'

'So, treason?'

'It sounds a strong possibility. We need to pass this on to the people who are better placed to look into it.'

'Inspector Hibbert at MI5?'

'That's my thinking.'

'How did it go with Lady Pitstone and her brother? What made him throw you out?'

'When I raised the prospect of a German victory being an advantage to those who want a united Ireland, he called the meeting to an end and told me to leave.'

'So he's a suspect?'

'He is in my book. He claims his sister is apolitical and insisted he would never discuss politics with her, but her reaction was different. More befuddled.'

'Drink?'

'Not this morning. I got the impression she was a bit panicky. Kennedy intervened to stop her saying anything. I think she may well be a political innocent, as Kennedy suggested, but I still think he could have shared his views about Irish unity with her. Or she may have picked it up in overhearing conversations he might have had with his fellow Irish republicans.'

'Would he have talked about the importance to that end of a German victory in front of her?'

'He might have, if he didn't think she'd take notice.'

'So, what are we going to do?'

'Well, it is a difficult situation. As he pointed out, there's a diplomatic issue at stake. The Irish High Commission may be in London but it's the territory of a separate sovereign state, which means we have to let it alone. And that goes for its officials, like Kennedy.'

'Do you think Kennedy is capable of committing the murders?' asked Lampson. 'Isn't it more likely he got one of his mates to do the actual killings?'

'Yes,' agreed Coburg. 'But finding out who could be tricky. When we go to see Inspector Hibbert about Bidlow, we'll also mention Kennedy and see what he has to offer about him.'

Gerrard Halloran was the boss of a large and successful firm of builders, Halloran Estates, based in

South London. Not that there was much in the way of building new homes at this moment; most of Halloran's men were employed in carrying out repairs to bombed properties, mostly government buildings. Halloran had a good relationship with the government, at least as far as business was concerned. They liked the work he did for them, always carried out to the timetable and completed to perfection. Gerrard Halloran's high standards had established him as vital to the Ministry of Works. When this war was over there'd be a whole heap of work in rebuilding, regardless of who won. If the British won then his contracts would increase. If the Germans were successful then they would be reminded of the vital work Halloran had done for them in his role as part of the IRA Operational Division in England.

Halloran had been an IRA man for as long as he could remember, first with the Irish Brotherhood in his home county of Cork, then as part of Michael Collins's brigade during the Easter Rising in 1916. It had been after the victory for independence in 1921 that in 1922 he came to England, after Collins had been assassinated during the Civil War. He still felt angry about the Civil War. De Valera against Collins, the pro-Treatyites pitched against the anti-Treatyites. The fact that more Irish were killed during the Civil War than had died during the War for Independence from Britain was sheer insanity.

Independence, he thought bitterly. Not while Ulster was still part of Britain. An independent, self-governed Ireland meant just that, *all* of Ireland, which they'd been promised by the Germans if the Germans were victorious. At least, that's what Sean Kennedy had told Halloran.

Halloran didn't like Kennedy, but then any campaign was composed of many people with different agendas, different backgrounds, different attitudes, but with a common cause.

In Halloran's eyes, Sean Kennedy – despite his name – was a Brit in every respect: public school, Oxford University, with the resulting upper-class British accent, his sister married to a British lord, now deceased. But Kennedy was a believer and would do anything to achieve their mutual aim. And Kennedy, with his connections, had access to the political routes that the IRA needed to travel if they were to succeed in their ambition.

Halloran had chosen the Embankment for this meeting with Kennedy. Halloran distrusted places like pubs and clubs; they were full of informers and spies. Here, in the open air, two men sitting talking casually on a bench, old friends, by the look of it, the contents of their conversation were safe. Well, as safe as any such conversation could be.

'Gerrard.' Halloran's thoughts were interrupted by the annoying cut-glass accent of Sean Kennedy.

Halloran looked up and smiled, moving along the wooden bench to allow Kennedy to settle himself down beside him.

'I got your message,' said Halloran. 'Something very important, you said.'

'I had a visit from Detective Chief Inspector Saxe-Coburg of Scotland Yard.'

'Saxe-Coburg?' snorted Halloran. 'Another bloody aristocrat. What did he want?'

'He wanted to talk to my sister. I made sure I was there with her when he called.' He paused, then said, 'He knows.'

'You're sure?'

'He virtually said as much. It needs to be dealt with.'

Halloran fell into a thoughtful silence; then he said, 'Your sister is becoming a liability, Sean.'

'No,' said Kennedy firmly. 'No action against her. She gets out of control when she drinks, says everything to everyone.'

'Well, if she's not going to stop drinking – and we both know that's not going to happen – then she has to be stopped another way. Her loose tongue will cost us dear.'

'She knows nothing of current actions.'

'But she knows your stance on the war from before: a German victory giving us what we want.'

'I don't care. She's my sister, for God's sake. I'll take care of her.'

349

'How?'

'I'll persuade her to go to Ireland, just for a short break from the bombing. But once she's there we'll keep her there.'

'Think you can do that?'

'I can, I'm sure of it. But that doesn't solve the problem of this Scotland Yard inspector. He knows, and he'll make enquiries, and possibly charges.'

'You're an Irish national, a member of the Irish Commission. You've got diplomatic immunity.'

'That won't be much help when they've got me in a soundproof cellar and they're beating the details out of me,' said Kennedy bitterly. 'Names. Contacts.'

Halloran nodded. 'Yes, he needs to be put out of the picture. Along with his wife, I suggest.'

'His wife?' asked Kennedy.

'Pillow talk,' said Halloran. 'DCI Coburg is married to the former Rosa Weeks, jazz pianist and singer supreme. A major talent.' He gave a sad sigh. 'We can't take the chance he's told her what he suspects.'

'What he *knows*,' Kennedy corrected him.

'What he knows,' repeated Halloran with a nod. He gave another sigh. 'A pity. I used to listen to her on the wireless. As I said, what a talent!' He sighed again. 'But others have died for the cause.'

'You can arrange it?' asked Kennedy.

'Of course I can bloody arrange it,' said Halloran, annoyed. 'I arranged the last three, didn't I? And made sure a gun was used for the third one, so it would be seen as different from the modus operandi of the first two. Though I still have my doubts as to why he had to go.'

'Because he was working for the British government, according to the letter he showed, and asking question about Lady Za Za and her brother and people Za Za spoke to.'

'It may not mean anything,' said Halloran.

'Can we take that chance?' asked Kennedy. He groaned. 'Anyway, I don't think Coburg was fooled.'

'Very well, leave it to me. Once I've got things sorted—'

Kennedy held up his hand. 'No,' he said quickly. 'As before, don't tell me the details. If I don't know anything, I can't say anything.'

'You know me,' Halloran pointed out.

'I'd never give them you,' said Kennedy firmly. 'You know that.'

'I know that's what you say,' said Halloran. 'But, as you said yourself just a moment ago, things might change if you're in a soundproofed cellar having your bollocks beaten to a pulp. Let's make sure that doesn't happen.'

'That's why I'm telling you this,' said Kennedy. 'Make Coburg go away and things'll be fine.'

CHAPTER THIRTY-FOUR

Tuesday 7th January 1941

Inspector Hibbert looked at Coburg and Lampson with weary resignation as they entered his office.

'I'm seeing more of you two lately than ever,' he complained.

'We wouldn't call if it wasn't absolutely essential,' said Coburg.

'Let me guess, this is still about this Russian fortune-teller woman.'

'Lady Za Za, real name Svetlana Rostova.' Coburg nodded. 'We've got two names in the frame as potential suspects in her killing and that of her brother, Grigor. One is Henry Bidlow MP. The other is Sean Kennedy who works at the Irish High Commission in London. Both have close family members who consulted Svetlana as a fortune-teller: in Bidlow's case, his wife, Eleanor; and in Kennedy's case, his sister, Lady Pitstone. It's possible that both women may have mentioned something that could harm their careers, or possibly even their lives. In Bidlow's case we've discovered that he was – and possibly still is – a paid ambassador for Krupp.'

Hibbert frowned. 'If he's still being paid by them, we need to know what he's doing for the money. There's a scent of treason there.'

'Exactly,' said Coburg. 'Kennedy is in the frame because his sister drinks and talks, and she may have passed on her brother's views about who he supports in this war. You told me before that Sean Kennedy is on your watch list.'

'Did I?' asked Hibbert. 'It sounds a bit loose-mouthed for me.'

'Let's say for argument's sake he is,' said Coburg patiently. 'Do you have the names of any of his associates in London who are sympathetic to his cause?'

'We might have,' said Hibbert guardedly.

'We're looking for someone who might do the dirty work for the group,' said Coburg. 'Someone who might stab people to death.'

'You think that's what happened to that Russian pair? They were silenced because of what Svetlana had learnt?'

'All we have at the moment is a hunch. We could be barking completely up the wrong tree. But it would be useful to look into Kennedy's group.'

'For someone ruthless enough to kill people,' mused Hibbert.

'And who uses a long, thin-bladed knife,' said Coburg.

Hibbert regarded Coburg doubtfully. 'That doesn't sound very Irish,' he said. 'Pistols and bombs are more them, along with a cosh. Long thin-bladed knives sound more Italian.'

'Any Irish-Italians in his group?' asked Coburg.

Hibbert grinned. 'I'll do some digging around and get back to you,' he said. He looked quizzically at Coburg and asked, 'You're sure about Bidlow and his link to Krupp?'

'He was certainly linked to them. Whether he still is might be a case for investigation. And you're better at that kind of digging than we are. You've got the resources and the people who know where to look.'

Bella Wilson hurried through the streets of central London, working her way through the maze of streets that backed onto Piccadilly. The streets were mainly empty of people and traffic; the air raid had started, although so far there hadn't been many bombs falling in this area. From the flames and explosions in the far distance, it looked as if the East End was bearing the brunt of the attack. The docks as usual, Wilson supposed.

As she turned in to Piccadilly, she was approached by a man wearing an ARP helmet.

'What are you doing out?' he demanded. 'You should be in a shelter.'

'That's where I'm on my way to,' she said. 'A friend

who lives in a flat along here said I could use theirs.'

'Well, hurry up and get to it,' said the warden.

Wilson did as he commanded. She entered the block of flats where Coburg and Rosa lived. She'd checked it out when she'd been here before and discovered the air raid shelter in the basement. She guessed that's where Coburg and Rosa were at this moment, taking refuge from the bombs. Not just the bombs, the incendiary devices the Germans were dropping, which blew up and threw flames out. Fire-starters, some called them.

She hurried up the stairs to the top floor. After the fiasco of her previous attempts, she was leaving nothing to chance this time. She'd persuaded Sam Rodney to lend her a lockpick. He'd been worried over what she was planning.

'First a gun, now a lockpick?' he'd said. 'What are you up to, Bella?'

'It's personal,' she said. 'Don't worry, you won't get in any trouble.'

'I will be if you shoot someone and they find it was me who provided it.'

'I'm not going to shoot anyone,' Wilson had lied. 'The lockpick is because I need to get some information that will keep me out of prison. I know where I can get proof I've been fitted up.'

Whether Sam had believed her or not, he'd given her the lockpick and shown her how to use it. He knew if he didn't, he'd feel the rough edge of her temper, and he didn't fancy getting on the wrong side of that again.

Wilson pulled the pistol from her pocket and aimed it at the door as she rang the bell. There was always the chance that the Coburgs were in, rather than in the shelter. When there was no answer she rang it again, and when there was still no answer and nor did the door of the flat opposite open, she used the lockpick and let herself into their flat. She positioned herself in the room closest to the door of the flat and directly opposite. She settled herself down on a small chair and aimed the pistol through the gap in the door at the front door just a few feet away from her. She couldn't miss from this distance. The first one through the door would get the first shot; the following one would be hit by the second.

She'd chosen this method because the blackout meant there were no lights on anywhere in the flats, so it would be difficult to identify her victims in the dark. Whoever opened the door to the flat had a key, so it would be either Coburg or Rosa. The other would be close behind.

She'd decided that Coburg had to die as well because once she'd killed Rosa, Coburg would do everything in his power to hunt her down. By killing both of them, it would slow down the search for her.

All she had to do now was wait for them to appear.

In the windowless room in the basement of MI5, Henry Bidlow sat at a bare wooden table on a hard wooden chair. On either side of him stood a muscular hard-faced man to add to the menace of his situation. On the other side of the table sat Inspector Hibbert, who patted the pile of papers on the table close by him and looked at the haggard face of Henry Bidlow.

'I've got everything we need to make the charges stick,' he said confidently. 'Your associates have been very helpful. But then they would be when they realised they could also be charged with aiding and abetting acts of treason.'

'There were no acts of treason!' burst out Bidlow in a desperate voice.

'What were Krupp paying you for?' asked Hibbert.

'It was an old contract from before the war. I told you, I hadn't got round to cancelling it.'

'There have been regular payments into your bank account every month, right up to and including this month. What were they paying you for?'

'It was just a regular fee as an adviser. It's old. There's nothing suspicious about it.'

'There is when we look at the statement from your stockbroker. He says that as well as your regular share dividends you received from the company, the adviser role was separate. According to him it was for you to supply information to Krupp about weapons that Britain were developing.'

'He's lying!' said Bidlow desperately.

'Really?' said Hibbert. 'Fortunately for us, we have

contacts among the German business community and one of them has told us of seeing reports from you detailing some of the new weaponry and aircraft being made here.'

'I only told them what they already knew!' Bidlow appealed. 'There was no treason, no betrayal. I checked with what knowledge they already had.'

'And confirmed the information?'

'No! It's not how it looks.'

'It looks like you were getting paid to supply Messrs Krupp, part of the German war machine, with details of Britain's new and developing weapons systems.' Again, he patted the pile of papers. 'That's the story I get from all this documentary evidence, and the statements from your associates. Separately, I agree, it could be interpreted as just an unfortunate lapse in memory, you forgetting to cancel your association with Krupp. But when taken with the recent payments from Krupp to you and the reports we've had from our contacts in Germany, something more incriminating emerges.' He looked enquiringly at the member of parliament. 'Is that what prompted you to have Svetlana Rostova killed? Because you suspected your wife had told her about this Krupp business.'

'I had nothing to do with that Russian woman's death!' burst out Bidlow.

'Well, I'm sure Chief Inspector Coburg will have something to say about that,' said Hibbert. 'But that's for another place and another time. Right now, Henry Bidlow, I am charging you with acts of treason against this country for the benefit of an enemy.' He smiled. 'If you're expecting the usual caution that you do not have to say anything, but anything you do say will be taken down, and all that sort of thing, forget it. We're MI5. We have our own rules. And many of them are difficult to uncover. As you are about to find out.'

Bella Wilson heard the lock of the front door click, and then the door swung open. They were here! She couldn't see clearly in the darkness, but her eyes had got used to the lack of light enough for her to make out the shape of a man as he entered, a man who fitted the size and shape of Coburg. She pulled the trigger and the pistol spat flame. The man staggered a step back, and then collapsed face forward into the flat.

Wilson stayed perched on the chair, her finger on the trigger, waiting for Rosa to appear. But there was no one else. Did that mean that Coburg had come up from the basement shelter on his own, leaving Rosa down there?

Nervously, Wilson got up and moved to the body. She took a cigarette lighter from her pocket and flicked it into life, holding the flame near the man's face.

It wasn't Coburg. It was a man she'd never seen before.

She began to panic. Who was he, and what was he

doing here? Was he some protection for Coburg and Rosa, sent up to the flat to check everything was safe? In which case, when he never returned, other men would be coming.

She looked and saw the pistol lying on the carpet beside the dead man. He'd been armed, so the other men who'd be arriving would have guns, too.

In a panic, she ran for the stairs and hurled herself down them. She had to get out, and fast.

Outside in the street, the air raid was still happening, and now she saw that small incendiary devices were landing in Piccadilly, smashing into the pavement and bursting into intense white flames. She dodged one, but then another struck the pavement right beside her, and before she could react the white flames had caught on her long coat, the flames travelling up it at terrifying speed. Desperately, she tried to unbutton the coat to tear it off, but the flames were already at her sleeves, licking at her fingers. She tried to pat them out, but now her whole coat was on fire and her head erupted in burning pain as her hair caught alight. She screamed, both from the pain and in panic, desperate for help, but as another incendiary device struck the ground beside her, she knew that there'd be no help coming. It was all over.

CHAPTER THIRTY-FIVE

Wednesday 8th January 1941

It was 9.30 a.m. when Lampson arrived at the Coburgs' flat.

'Sorry it took me so long,' he apologised. 'I got your message alright to come here, but the buses were a nightmare. A bomb left a big hole in Tottenham Court Road so it was all about detours.' He looked around the entrance to the flat and noticed the chalk outline of a body just inside the door. He looked enquiringly at Coburg and Rosa. 'Someone died?'

'Shot dead,' said Coburg. 'We found him lying there when we came up from the shelter in the basement at six o'clock.'

'Who was he?'

'According to an ID card he was carrying, his name's Steven Sullivan. The body's been taken to Scotland Yard. I've asked them to check his fingerprints and phone me here if there are any results.'

'Would you like a coffee, Sergeant?' asked Rosa.

'Yes please, Mrs Coburg,' said Lampson.

Rosa made for the kitchen.

'Who shot him?' asked Lampson.

'The implication is that he was shot by a woman who was found burnt to death outside the street door of our block of flats. She'd apparently been hit by an incendiary device.'

'In which case identifying her will be difficult.'

'Yes, but I can make a pretty good guess as to who she is. Bella Wilson.'

'Bella Wilson? The mad jazz singer?'

'The same. When I looked at the dead woman's body, she had rings on her fingers that looked like the ones Wilson was wearing when we had her in for questioning. Also, there was a bit of only half-burnt flesh with a fragment of a tattoo that Wilson had on one side of her face. The other interesting thing is that both Wilson and the dead man in our flat had lockpicks on them. And the dead woman had a pistol in her pocket, from which one bullet had been fired. I've asked ballistics to check the gun against the bullet found in the dead man.'

Rosa returned with three cups of coffee on a tray, which she put down on the table, and then joined the two men. Lampson looked at her.

'If the dead woman is Bella Wilson, that's a blessing for you,' he said. 'But why would she want to shoot this bloke?'

'I don't think she did,' said Coburg. 'The way I envisage it is this: Bella Wilson comes here to kill Rosa and me. I've already heard from Mrs Jameson, who lives opposite, that a woman answering Wilson's description called at our flat on Saturday. Mrs Jameson told her we wouldn't be back till Sunday. So yesterday she tries again, only this time she lets herself into our flat and hides herself somewhere, planning to shoot us when we come in. Only someone else turns up with the same intention, this guy Sullivan. He's also got a lockpick. He lets himself in, gun at the ready. It's dark, there are no lights. Wilson sees him in silhouette and thinks it's me. Bang. She shoots. She checks the man and realises it's not me. She panics. She runs outside into the street, intending to get away, just as a hail of incendiary devices come down around her. That's the end for her.'

Lampson nodded. 'It makes sense, even if it's a bit weird. But why would this Sullivan want to kill you?'

'Because we nudged Sean Kennedy to see what he'd do. Remember, we had two suspects for the killing of Svetlana and her brother: Kennedy and Bidlow. We let them both know we were on to them to see what would happen. I believe that Bidlow went to see Danny Bell to arrange for me to be bumped off. Unfortunately for Bidlow, Danny Bell is a sincere patriot. And instead he comes to tip us off about Bidlow.

'That leaves Kennedy. It wouldn't surprise me to find a connection between Kennedy and this man Sullivan. An Irish Republican connection. I've sent uniforms to find Kennedy and pick him up. They're to try his flat, his sister's house and the Irish High Commission.'

He was interrupted by the phone ringing and picked it up. He listened, then said, 'Put out an alert for him at all airports and ferry services.'

He hung up and told them, 'Kennedy's flown the coop. Either he's gone to ground, or he's made for Dublin.'

'We'll have trouble getting him back,' pointed out Lampson. 'Diplomatic immunity, the Republic of Ireland being neutral, all that sort of thing.'

Coburg nodded. Then he said, 'I don't think there's more we can do here. I suppose we'd better get to the Yard and see how things are going there with their checks into Steven Sullivan.' He looked at Rosa. 'Can we give you a lift to Paddington? At least you should be safe from Wilson now.'

Rosa shuddered. 'That was a terrible way for her to die.'

'I find it hard to feel sympathy for her,' said Coburg. 'She came here to kill us.'

'I know,' said Rosa. 'But it's still a horrible way to die.'

By the time Coburg and Lampson had dropped Rosa off at the ambulance station and then proceeded to Scotland Yard, information had begun to accumulate. The bullet that had killed Steven Sullivan was confirmed as coming from the pistol in the dead woman's pocket. The rings and fragments that had survived the savage burning were confirmed as belonging to Bella Wilson.

As to Steven Sullivan himself, it was learnt that he was a plasterer employed by Halloran Estates, one of the largest firms of builders in London. There was also a note to say that he was on a watch list at MI5 for suspected Irish Republican sympathies, although nothing illegal had ever been proved against him. This led to Coburg and Lampson making yet another visit to Inspector Hibbert.

'We're interested in one Steven Sullivan,' Coburg told him.

'The dead geezer in your flat,' said Hibbert.

'You're well informed,' said Coburg.

'It's our job to be,' said Hibbert.

'He's said to be on a watch list,' said Coburg. 'Along with Sean Kennedy.'

'Who's disappeared, so I'm told,' said Hibbert.

'Your network moves fast,' said Coburg admiringly.

'Not fast enough or he'd be in custody,' grumbled Hibbert.

'What do you know about Steven Sullivan?'

'Nothing.'

'He's on your Irish watch list.'

'Half of the Irish living in this country are on that watch list,' said Hibbert. 'Every time there's another outrage, an assassination, a bank raid claimed by the IRA, we get swamped with calls from members of the public naming even more.'

'So you've actually got nothing concrete on Sullivan?'

'No.'

'What about Halloran Estates?'

'Run by Gerrard Halloran, highly successful. One of the biggest builders in the country. Do a lot of government work. Predominantly Irish workforce, which is not surprising as Halloran emigrated from Ireland to here about twenty years ago and is said to prefer having people working for him he can trust.'

'Is he on your watch list?'

Hibbert shook his head. 'No hint of anything political about him, just making money.'

'It still might be worth having a word with him.'

'It might,' said Hibbert. 'But if he is involved in any way with the IRA, he does a very good job of hiding it.'

Rosa and Doris were sitting in the rest room at the ambulance station drinking tea, Doris listening almost open-mouthed in shock as Rosa related the events of the previous night.

'A man came to kill you?' she said, stunned.

'Into our flat.' Rosa nodded. 'The lucky thing was that woman who tried to kill me before, Bella Wilson, she was already hiding in our flat waiting to shoot us. Instead, in the darkness, when this man entered our flat she thought he was Edgar and she shot him. Edgar thinks that when she realised she'd shot the wrong man she panicked and ran out of the flats to get away, just as a load of incendiary devices were being dropped in Piccadilly. Edgar thinks she must have got hit by one because they found her dead body there on the pavement, burnt almost beyond recognition.'

'But it was her?' asked Doris.

Rosa nodded. 'There was enough to identify her.'

'Thank God for that!' said Doris. 'At least she won't be coming after you again.'

There was a knock at the door, then it opened and Chesney Warren looked in.

'There's a telephone call for you, Rosa,' he said. 'That BBC man, John Fawcett.'

'Oh God,' groaned Rosa. 'I'm so sorry, Chesney. I tried tactfully to tell him that any future phone calls should be made to me at home.'

'I expect he tried there first,' said Warren. 'Anyway, he's on the phone now.'

Rosa hurried from the rest room to Warren's office and picked up the receiver.

'Rosa Coburg,' she said.

'Ah, Rosa,' came Fawcett's smooth, cultured voice. 'I'm sorry to trouble you at work. I tried your flat but when there was no answer I took a chance on catching you here. Ordinarily I would have left it and tried you later at your flat, but the powers-that-be here at the BBC are eager for an answer today.'

'An answer?' asked Rosa, puzzled.

'Yes, they're keen on you doing a one-off show, a pilot we call it, *Rosa Weeks Presents*. If it's successful, they'd like to try a series.'

'A series?' repeated Rosa, stunned.

'The format would be you doing a couple of numbers on your own, then a guest would do a number, then you and the guest would duet. It would be a half-hour show so we were thinking of two guests a show. If the first one meets with approval, of course. We'd be making the pilot show here at Maida Vale. How do you feel about it?'

'Well . . . I'm enormously flattered. Thank you, Mr Fawcett.'

'Please, call me John. If this succeeds we'll be working together. So I can tell the powers-that-be that you'll do it?'

'Yes, indeed. I'd be delighted.'

'Excellent. I'll get on to Contracts and they'll be in touch, and I'll find out when the theatre at Maida Vale has spare dates. We'll be doing it with a studio audience. Thank you, Mrs Coburg.'

'Rosa, please,' said Rosa. 'If I'm to call you John it's only fair.'

She hung up and turned to Chesney Warren, who was hovering, curious.

'News?' he asked.

'They want me to do a show called *Rosa Weeks Presents*, doing a few numbers then having guest artistes. If it works, they hope to make it a series.'

'My God, you're going to be famous!' Warren beamed. Then hastily, he added, 'Not that you're not famous already. But a series on the wireless is something else.'

'We'll see,' said Rosa. 'Let's see how this pilot show goes first. But, I promise you, it won't stop me driving ambulances here.'

Coburg had been anticipating meeting with obstruction when he and Lampson went to the reception desk at the offices of Halloran Estates and asked to see Mr Gerrard Halloran. Coburg fully expected to be told that Mr Halloran was unavailable, or that he only saw people who had an appointment. Instead, he was surprised to be told the receptionist would check with Mr Halloran, and, when she did, to be told he invited them to be taken up to his office.

'He's not scared about talking to us,' commented Lampson as they caught the lift up to the fifth floor. 'What do you reckon? A man with nothing to hide, or a man who's confident we can't pin anything on him?'

'If my hunch is right, it's the latter,' said Coburg. 'But we rattled Sean Kennedy. Let's see if we can rattle Mr Halloran.'

Gerrard Halloran was a tall man who had retained his muscular build. He came from behind his desk and walked towards the two detectives, hand held out in greeting.

'Welcome, Chief Inspector; welcome, Sergeant.' He smiled, shaking their hands. 'Always pleased to talk to the police.' He gestured for them to sit in the two chairs opposite his desk, then asked, 'What can I do for you?'

'A man who works for you called Steven Sullivan has been found shot dead,' said Coburg.

'Steven?' said Halloran, with a look of surprise. He shook his head. 'Some dispute, do you think? Gambling, maybe? Steven was always too keen to get involved in a game of cards, in my opinion.'

'We don't think so,' said Coburg. 'The woman who shot him was called Bella Wilson, a sometime jazz singer. Does the name ring any bells?'

Halloran thought it over, muttering the name, 'Wilson. Bella Wilson', before shaking his head and saying, 'Sorry I've never heard of her. You're saying she shot Steven?'

'It looks that way. A gun was found in her pocket, which matched with the bullet in Mr Sullivan.'

'What does she say about it? Why did she shoot him?'

'We can only guess. It appears she died soon after shooting him. She was killed when an incendiary bomb fell beside her and burnt her to death.'

'Incredible,' said Halloran. 'Where was Steven's body found?'

'In my flat in Piccadilly.'

Halloran stared at him. '*Your* flat?'

'Yes.'

'What was he doing in your flat?'

'The circumstantial evidence points to the fact that he went there to kill me, but instead he encountered Bella Wilson, who shot him.'

'Protecting you?'

Coburg shook his head. 'We think she also went to our flat to kill me, and possibly my wife. The way we see it, she got into my flat and lay in wait for me to come home. Because of the blackout, when Sullivan entered the flat, Wilson thought he was me and she shot him. When she realised her mistake, she panicked and ran out into the street, where she got hit by an incendiary device.'

Halloran shook his head, a look of astonishment on his face. 'Two people come to your flat to kill you, neither of who knows the other. What makes you so unpopular?'

'Being a detective getting too close to a murderer,' said Coburg. 'How well did you know Steven Sullivan?'

'Outside of work, hardly at all. I have the occasional drink with my men, to let them know at heart I'm one of the lads, but I don't really socialise with them. They work for me. Providing they do their work, that's all I ask of them.'

'We've heard gossip that Sullivan was involved with Republican circles.'

Halloran chuckled. 'You'll hear that about nearly every Irishman in England, Chief Inspector. I wouldn't be surprised if you hear it about me. It's usually spread by jealous English builders who resent this Paddy from the bogs getting so much work in government contracts. I do a lot of work for the government, Chief Inspector. Public buildings, railway stations, that sort of thing. I hardly think the British government would be so free with their contracts if they thought I was an enemy working against them.'

'A good point.' Coburg nodded. 'But, going back to Steven Sullivan, did you ever have any suspicions about him and his Republican activities?'

'To the best of my knowledge, there were no Republican activities, as you call it. He was a good worker.'

'What sort of work did he do for you?'

'A plasterer, and an excellent one at that. A wall plastered by Steven Sullivan was like a work of art.'

'Do you know a man called Sean Kennedy?'

Halloran chuckled. 'I'm Irish, Chief Inspector. I know about seven men called Sean Kennedy. It's a common name for the Irish, a bit like Smith for the English.'

'This Sean Kennedy works for the Irish High Commission in London.'

'Ah, the posh one! Indeed I do. Not that we socialise much; he's out of my class, an aristocrat, public school and all that. But he's got useful contacts.'

'In the British government?'

'And the Irish. My men go where the work is, and if there's Irish government work going in Dublin or Cork, for example, I won't say no to it. I'm from Cork so for me it'd be like going home.'

'Have you seen him recently?'

Halloran thought it over. 'Actually, I did. Maybe a week ago, I think. I was sitting in the Embankment

Gardens, just taking the air, when he suddenly appears and sits down on the bench I'm on and starts talking.'

'What about?'

'Buildings. He wanted to know about our contracts with the British government. I told him, with all the bombing that's going on, the contracts for rebuilding will come later, once this damned war's over. Right now we're building with repair jobs.'

'Why was he so interested in your government contracts?'

Halloran shrugged. 'He never said and I never asked. But it always does to keep friendly with potential clients.'

After Coburg and Lampson had taken their leave of him, Halloran waited a few moments before picking up his telephone and calling an internal number.

'Patrick,' he said. 'I need your assistance.'

A few moments later, the short wiry figure of Patrick McClary entered the office.

'What can I do for you, Gerry?' he asked, his face showing a mixture of wariness and concern.

Halloran gave a heavy sigh. 'It seems there's a loose end needs tying up, Patrick. I'd like you to make the arrangements.'

CHAPTER THIRTY-SIX

Wednesday 8th January 1941

In Dublin, darkness was falling. Sean Kennedy walked beside the River Liffey, lost in worried thought. He still didn't know what was going on. He could tell something had gone wrong when the phone call woke him while he was still in bed in the early hours of the morning at his flat. One simple word, in Irish: '*Gluais*.' In English: run. Move. Shift. Travel.

He'd reacted immediately. He always kept a small suitcase ready to move fast, just in case. There was no one to tell he had to depart in a hurry, no wife, no family, except for his sister, Deirdre.

Using his diplomatic credentials, he managed to get a seat on the first plane to Dublin. As a further precaution, he'd used an alias for the seat holder, in the name of Michael McLiamor. All the time the plane was sitting on the tarmac preparing for take-off, he kept expecting DCI Coburg or someone else to appear and take him off the plane, despite using an alias, but no one did, and the plane took off without a delay.

Once in Dublin, he sought out members of the

group of Republicans who were his contacts in Ireland. The group was small, deliberately so, so that each member knew only two others. His attempts to contact the two known to him came to naught; both men were unavailable.

What had gone wrong? He'd expected one of those two to meet him in Dublin and tell him. The one thing that was obvious was that Coburg hadn't been killed, as planned. Had the assassin been captured? Was he even now in a basement in Scotland Yard or MI5's HQ with names being forced out of him? The names of Gerrard Halloran and Sean Kennedy? It must be that the assassin had been able to hold out, otherwise Kennedy would have been stopped from getting on the plane for sure. Only if the assassin or Halloran were broken under interrogation would they find out about Kennedy's alias of McLiamor. The fact that he'd been able to get on the plane showed that so far the assassin hadn't broken.

He became aware of footsteps approaching from behind, and then two men joined him, one on either side.

'Sean,' whispered a voice.

He turned, expecting to see one of the two men from his group he'd been seeking out. Instead, the men were two he'd never seen before.

Suddenly something heavy came down on the back of his head and he stumbled, then fell to the pavement.

Before he could defend himself, one of the men had grabbed both his arms and forced them painfully up behind his back. Still dazed, he became aware that the other man had pinched his nose tightly, cutting off air. Desperately, he opened his mouth to breathe in, and was aware of a bottle being forced into his mouth and then whiskey cascading down his throat. In vain he tried to move his head to get the bottle out of his mouth; the man who was pouring it into his mouth held his face in a firm grip with his free hand. Already dazed from the blow on his head, and now with the whiskey pervading him, muddling his senses, he was unable to fight the men off. Finally, the bottle was removed from his mouth and the other man let go of his arms. Kennedy tried to push himself up off the pavement, but his strength failed him and he fell face forward to the pavement. There was another blow to his head, then blackness . . .

CHAPTER THIRTY-SEVEN

Thursday 9th January 1941

Coburg and Lampson were in the office, preparing a report for Superintendent Allison on the deaths of Steven Sullivan and Bella Wilson, when there was a knock on the door. At Coburg's call of 'Come in', it opened and Inspector Hibbert entered.

'Chief Inspector,' said Hibbert, and he smiled.

'You look like you have good news,' commented Coburg.

'Let's just say interesting news,' said Hibbert. 'I thought you might like to know that the body of Sean Kennedy, a member of the Irish High Commission in London, has been found in the River Liffey in Dublin. The suspicion is he fell into the river while under the influence of drink and drowned.' He looked at them quizzically and added, 'Another interesting thing – there were stones in his jacket pockets. What do you think? They're usually indicative of suicide.'

'Unlikely in this case,' said Coburg. 'My guess is that he and his sister were Catholics, judging by some of the ornaments in her house. If so, suicide is a mortal sin.'

'Which means what?' asked Hibbert.

Coburg shrugged. 'Your guess is as good as mine. But, for what it's worth, I'd keep an eye on Gerrard Halloran. I mentioned him before. The man who was found shot dead in my flat worked for him.'

'Are you saying that Halloran's tied in to the murder of the two Russians?'

'I suspect he's linked to the IRA or some equivalent organisation in some way. I just think it's worth you adding him to your list and keeping an eye on him and his workers.'

The ringing of the telephone interrupted them.

'DCI Coburg's office,' said Lampson.

'Is the chief inspector there?' asked the familiar voice of Group Captain Crombie.

Lampson held out the receiver towards Coburg.

'It's for you,' he said. 'Group Captain Crombie.'

'In that case I'll leave you,' said Hibbert, making for the door. 'I'm sure we'll be in touch again soon. It seems to be becoming a habit.'

As Hibbert left, Coburg took the receiver.

'Group Captain,' he said. 'What can I do for you?'

'I'm sorry to have to tell you that Colin Upton was killed last night. He went up against a Heinkel and the Germans shot him down. Very tragic. I thought you'd like to know.'

Coburg gave a heavy sigh, then said, 'As you say, very tragic. He was a brave young man.'

'He was indeed,' said Crombie. 'I hope his memory won't be tarnished because of that unfortunate recent incident with that young woman?'

'No,' Coburg assured him. 'All mention of that will be stricken from the records. There was no crime committed. Thank you for informing me of his death. Do please pass on my condolences to his friends.'

Coburg hung up.

'Upton's dead?' asked Lampson.

Coburg nodded. 'Killed last night in a fight with the Luftwaffe.' He gave a heavy sigh as he asked, 'Do you think it was us who caused it? The way we left things in the air with him about the young woman, and Miranda Crombie, preying on his mind when he should have been concentrating on the air battle?'

Lampson shook his head. 'He was a troubled young man. Brave, but troubled. Whatever complications were going on in his life were no fault of ours.'

Coburg nodded, but he didn't look convinced. He looked down at the report he'd just compiled.

'Svetlana Rostova and her brother Grigor murdered. Also Martin Higgins. Suspected culprit: Steven Sullivan acting on instructions from Gerrard Halloran at the request of Sean Kennedy. Sean Kennedy dead. Again, my suspicion is on the orders of Halloran to ensure silence about any IRA connection. Bella Wilson dead. And now Colin Upton dead. Not one arrest.'

'That's not quite right, guv. Henry Bidlow's been

arrested on a charge of treason.'

'But there have been no arrests as far as the murders are concerned.'

'Bidlow had nothing to do with the murders; he was just a traitor for money. The man who killed Svetlana and her brother and Martin Higgins was this Steven Sullivan, and he's dead. Sean Kennedy's death is a job for the Irish police. As for Halloran . . .?' Lampson shrugged. 'Yes, he was behind the killings, but the only real witnesses against him, Sullivan and Kennedy, are dead. But you've tipped off the secret services about him. They'll keep an eye on him and root around for evidence against him. That's all we can do.'

'Yes, I suppose you're right. So, can we call this a success?'

'In as much as you and Rosa didn't get killed, and that scum Bidlow is under lock and key, it is,' said Lampson. 'Yes, I think we earnt our wages with this one.'

Coburg nodded thoughtfully, then he smiled. 'By the way, I forgot to tell you: Rosa's been offered her own show on the wireless. *Rosa Weeks Presents*. If the pilot show is successful, they want her to turn it into a series.'

Lampson gave a broad smile. 'That is brilliant! Now that's what I call a success!' He looked at the clock. 'Twelve o'clock, guv. I think all of this calls for a celebratory pint. I'm buying!'

ACKNOWLEDGEMENTS

This is the fifth book to feature DCI Edgar Saxe-Coburg, his jazz-artiste wife Rosa, and his sergeant Ted Lampson. It is also the second in this new series set in disused London underground stations. These stations are haunted by ghosts and memories, not always benign, especially when they were also used as shelters to protect London's population from the devastating air raids by the Luftwaffe. For me, this series, as with the Hotel Mysteries books, is an opportunity to explore and share with readers what Londoners experienced during this time. Although I wasn't born until what's known as The Baby Blitz (the massive and highly destructive V1 and V2 rocket attacks on central London in 1944 and early 1945), I saw, at first hand, the effect of The Blitz of 1940/1941 on my elder sister, who was just five years old when war broke out in 1939 and who endured the attacks on London for the next six years. For my father, who was a volunteer fireman during the Blitz, it must have been desperate, never knowing if he would be alive the next day, and for my mother, who was terrified for her two young children, it is truly unimaginable. I cannot see the effects of the brutal Russian attacks on the cities and towns in Ukraine without recalling my life post-World War II in the Kings Cross/ Euston area of London, growing up amidst street after street of ruined buildings.

Because of this I have to offer my thanks to the wonderful team at Allison & Busby: Susie Dunlop, Lesley Crooks, my brilliant editors Fiona and Becca, and also Christina Griffiths for her superb artwork. They have given me the opportunity to show the readers what it was like at this time. I hope that you, as that reader, if you like these books, will pass on your experience of them to others.

JIM ELDRIDGE was born in central London towards the end of World War II, and survived attacks by V2 rockets on the Kings Cross area where he lived. In 1971 he sold his first sitcom to the BBC and had his first book commissioned. Since then he has had more than one hundred books published, with sales of over three million copies. He lives in Kent with his wife.

jimeldridge.com